DR. DIMENSION:
Masters of Spacetime
(VOID WHERE PROHIBITED)

by
John DeChancie
and
David Bischoff

A ROC BOOK

ROC
Published by the Penguin Group
Penguin Books USA Inc., 375 Hudson Street,
New York, New York 10014, U.S.A.
Penguin Books Ltd, 27 Wrights Lane,
London W8 5TZ, England
Penguin Books Australia Ltd, Ringwood,
Victoria, Australia
Penguin Books Canada Ltd, 10 Alcorn Avenue,
Toronto, Ontario, Canada M4V 3B2
Penguin Books (N.Z.) Ltd, 182–190 Wairau Road,
Auckland 10, New Zealand

Penguin Books Ltd, Registered Offices:
Harmondsworth, Middlesex, England

First published by Roc,
an imprint of Dutton Signet,
a division of Penguin Books USA Inc.

First Printing, May, 1994
10 9 8 7 6 5 4 3 2 1

ROC REGISTERED TRADEMARK—MARCA REGISTRADA

Printed in the United States of America

BOOKS ARE AVAILABLE AT QUANTITY DISCOUNTS WHEN USED TO PROMOTE PRODUCTS OR SERVICES. FOR INFORMATION PLEASE WRITE TO PREMIUM MARKETING DIVISION, PENGUIN BOOKS USA INC., 375 HUDSON STREET, NEW YORK, NEW YORK 10014.

DIANE'S FIRST MISTAKE
WAS OPENING THE HATCH

About a thousand yards away, suspended on a plume of iridescent energy that shimmered in avocado-puce waves, a spaceship, looking as though it had been designed by Pablo Picasso with a bad hangover, was landing.

Diane watched it land. A door opened. A gangplank like an erector set from Hades unwound and smacked onto the ground, knocking over a pile of empty cans of Vegan peas.

"Doctor!" cried Diane. "Dr. Dimension! Troy? Where are you?"

Receiving no answer, she turned to crank the hatch closed. Instantly a bright silvery beam reached out from the ship and froze her in place.

Diane watched, petrified, as a strange vehicle descended the alien ship's boarding ramp. Looking like a cross between a tractor and a metallic caterpillar, it crawled down the gangplank on great long spider's legs that clicked and clanked. It was creepy.

The strange machine's occupants were even creepier. . . .

DR. DIMENSION:
MASTERS OF SPACETIME

"[A] monumental space-opera spoof."
—Science Fiction Age

This book is dedicated to these immortals:

Clifford Simak
Avram Davidson
Lester del Rey
Isaac Asimov
Keith Laumer
Theodore Sturgeon
Robert A. Heinlein
Fritz Leiber

. . . all of them, Grandmasters of Spacetime

Prologue

Dr. Dimension, a mild-mannered physicist teaching at a great Midwestern university, has invented a space-time machine, the *Mudlark*. Together with his crew of dauntless explorers, he has ranged the galaxy in search of adventure, though it is clear that he is a pawn in a proxy war between two alien superraces, the Asperans and the Dharvans. In our last adventure, "Doc" and his pals helped the Pizons defeat the evil, joyless Proons; but when he tries to aim the *Mudlark* for home, the mysterious "Krillman," agent of one of the superraces (he won't say which one), hurls the *Mudlark* light-years into the unknown. Dr. Dimension and his re-doubtable sidekicks are forced to crash-land on a bleak alien planetoid . . .

Chapter One

The ship came down from space. It came from the stars and the dark vectors, the luminous orbits and the empty reaches of space. It was a strange, alien ship, but it had energy in its innards and men in its metal compartments.

It had a couple of swell babes in it, too.

Unfortunately, none of the men, including the pilot, and neither of the babes had the slightest idea of how to land the ship.

They impacted.
They rammed into the alien terrain.
They bounced.

"Ouch!" cried Troy Talbot, erstwhile Flitheimer University quarterback, as he whacked his compact cranium against an instrument panel.

"Yahhhhh!" screeched Vivian Vernon, Ph.D., trying to use her colleague and department chairman, Dr. Geoffrey Wussman, Ph.D., Ll.D., as a cushion between herself and injury. In the seconds before impact and in a nearly psychotic state of panic, she had torn off her restraints and leapt at him.

Splat! went Dr. Wussman, who said nothing because he was rendered instantly unconscious.

Dr. Dimension wanted to grab hold of Diane Derry, mash her ample bosom against his chest, palpate her firmly plump derriere, and bury his beard into the sweet, perfumed juncture of her shoulder and neck. Not for the purposes of saving himself or cushioning any impact, mind you. He was simply wont to want do this sort of thing at regular intervals; and, of course, now what seemed the moment of his doom approached, and he wanted to die in someone's arms. Better that someone be Diane Derry than Vivian Vernon, though he would have taken Viv in a pinch (Viv was a dish). Also, Diane was vastly better than her boyfriend Troy Talbot; and the homuncular Dr. Wussman was beyond the pale. So Diane would do. Besides, she was more than a dish. She was an entire pulchritudinous meal.

(The reader must keep in mind that the action of this book takes place long before our enlightened age. What in our day is viewed as "sexual harassment" was looked upon then as simply being "fresh." What got your face slapped then gets you a federal lawsuit now. But that was then, and . . . well, this is now.)

Unfortunately for Dr. Dimension, and fortunately for the virtue of this blond, corn-fed Midwest beauty who was his graduate assistant, he was strapped into his chair and could not indulge himself in the aforementioned fashion.

The ship rattled and rolled. The universe rocked.

"Ohhhhhhhhh!" cried Diane Derry. "Oh . . . Dr.! Ohhhh. Oohhhhhhhhhhhhhhh!"

Diane Derry did not ordinarily speak in the manner of grade-school reading primers, but this was a special occasion.

"Dr. D.!" Diane cried, in rapturous wonder at still being alive. "We're . . . we're . . . floating!"

After the tremendous trauma of impact, there had been, come to think of it, a most peculiar sound. Yes, most peculiar, thought Dr. Dimension. An attenuated wrenching. A prolonged screeching. All buried in that infernal screaming, rattling, rocking, and rolling. In fact, it had been a sound not unlike a giant—

Boiiiiiiinnnnnngggggggggg!

Now, they were floating indeed, though it was more of a ride in an elevator with its cable cut than the zero-gee space stuff they'd been experiencing during their recent adventures.

"We bounced," stated Dr. Dimension, looking out the forward view plate.

"What nonsense," said Vivian. "Wussman, for God's sake, stop bleeding on me."

"——" said Dr. Wussman.

"I'm telling you, we hit, and then we . . . bounced." Dr. Dimension consulted the altimeter to verify this strange fact.

"Weird planet down there, huh, Doc?" observed Troy.

"Looks like desert, but littered with debris," said a disoriented Diane Derry as she tried to reacquaint herself with the instrument panel and her copilot's controls.

Dr. Dimension mused, "We should be dead as kippered herring by now. But we're not out of the woods yet."

"Why, Doc?" said Troy.

"Our situation is one of the utmost gravity."

"Huh? Oh, that's a pun, Doc."

"Correct, Talbot, my boy. A pun, the lowest form of humor, for which your mind is perfectly suited."

"Thanks a lot, Doc. I may be dumb, but you're not the hottest spaceship jockey in the universe."

"We're doing our best, Troy," Diane said resentfully.

"Gosh, I didn't mean you, Diane."

Dr. Dimension said, "Neither of us has ever soloed in a Piper Cub, let alone a spaceship."

"What are you idiots blathering about?" Vivian Vernon wanted to know.

"Gravity," Dr. Dimension informed her.

"What about it?"

"You know what Newton said when the apple bonged him on the head. What goes up —"

"I thought it was a fig," Troy Talbot said.

"What? Why, Talbot, you managed to make a funny all by yourself. Of sorts."

"I did?"

"As I said, what goes up, must come—"

A stomach-churning flip-flop as Nature reached up and grabbed them all by the viscera.

"—Downnnnnnnnnnnnn!"

"Ulp," Vivian said, turning green.

They plummeted.

The planet's surface spun in the view plates, and the space travelers churned in the ship like wet laundry in a wringer washer. Dr. Dimension's brain spun, trying to get a grip on the physical parameters of the situation.

Just what the hell does the word "parameters" mean? he thought.

If he could just get a good spurt from the engines . . .

He grabbed a control and tugged.

Nothing.

"Oh, well," he said. "We're not going down as fast this time. We'll just bounce again, though not as high up. Basic physics, conservation of momentum, and all that."

"Aieeeeeeeeeee!" said Dr. Vernon, nonetheless.

"Aiieeeeeeeeeee!" said Troy and Diane.

Doc D. thought about statistics and probability equations and the juxtaposition of hard physics and soft biology.

"Aiieeeeeeeeeee!" said Dr. Dimension.

"BAM!"

The impacted, they crashed, they hit.

However, this time, they did not bounce.

This time, also, they did not notice they did not bounce.

They were all too busy being unconscious.

Like a particularly obnoxious dose of smelling salts, the acrid odor of burned insulation insinuated its way up Dr. Dimension's nostrils.

He did not particularly care to wake up. He'd been having a splendid dream involving wood nymphs, water sprites, and other elementals, all female, all naked, and all involved in demonstrating the erotic wonders of Nature upon the physics professor's frolicking body.

He'd had the dream before. He called it his "playing doctor dream." It was one of his favorites, and he was loath to give it up.

However, burning insulation wasn't a good thing.

Burning insulation demanded an inventor's immediate attention. Especially since he felt a little hot, and it was not the sort of heat associated with frolicking dream ladies.

Pain was also in the sensory mix. He wondered remotely if he'd gotten hold of medicinal space brandy somewhere during the course of his dimensional amblings, but the slimy touch of bodily fluids on his fingers nixed that possibility.

Nor were they the sort of bodily fluids associated with nymph dancing.

He wiped the blood from his eyes and, groaning, got to his feet. Dressed in a well-worn dirty white lab coat, he was not a tall man, yet not on the short side either. His hair was a wild tangle of salt-and-pepper curls. Gray eyes looked out levelly from behind thick spectacles, which, miraculously, he still wore. He took them off and inspected them; sure enough, the lenses were intact, barely a scratch on them. Putting them back on, he began a visual inspection of his surroundings.

It was a mess.

Messy stuff to the left of him, messy stuff to the right of him, above, and below. The hatches on all the storage bays had sprung open, spilling supplies all over.

"What a dump," the good doctor mumbled.

He stumbled over to the controls.

"LANDED," proclaimed happy pink digital letters on the instrument panel.

"Glad to know that," said Doc. He looked around in the wreckage, hoping to find the odd leg or arm or head, hoping even more they were still attached to their odd owners. Groans and coughs and curses joined the crackling of engine fires.

Troy Talbot abruptly stood up, wide-eyed, clutching

a detached seat cushion. He ran through an imaginary scrimmage, dodging fantasy fullbacks and smacked into a bent support, bending it farther.

"Touchdown!" he proclaimed.

"Yes, you could say that, Talbot. Now, get a grip on reality. There's got to be a first-aid box somewhere on this confounded boat."

Troy blinked, smiling, woozily stumbling about. "Sure, Coach." He tilted off to another room, mumbling something about an extra point kick.

"Oh, and Talbot, be a sport and find a bottle of disinfectant. There are going to be plenty of cuts and bruises."

"Right, Coach."

" 'Coach,' for Pete's sake," Dr. Dimension muttered.

He began to dig the rest of the crew out of the debris. Soon he uncovered Diane Derry, and part of Wussman and Vernon. He did a quick count of limbs and appendages. All appendages were fortunately still appended. All bodies were still breathing. All heads were still attached, and Diane's tail was still round and firm to the touch. Dr. Dimension was about to give her mouth-to-mouth resuscitation, was about to press his eager mouth against the full ripeness of her pouting lips, when her cornflower-blue eyes popped open.

"Dr. Demopoulos!"

"Hi, Diane. By the way, the name's 'Dr. Dimension' now. Don't ask why. I had an epiphany on the way to Damascus and haven't been myself since."

Diane sat up woozily and smoothed her blond hair. It was barely mussed. "We crashed," she said simply.

"But we're still alive, Diane."

Diane touched her head and face, palpated both arms, then felt her rib cage. She winced. "Ouch."

"Anything broken?" Dr. Dimension asked, laying a fatherly hand beneath one gorgeously oblate breast.

"No, I don't think so. I'm a little sore all over, though."

"That's to be expected. Feel all right generally?"

"I think. How's everyone else?"

"They'll live. Dr. Wussman got his bell rung pretty good, but I think he'll be okay, too. We're lucky. Something broke our fall. Don't know what."

"I don't believe we're still alive!" Diane said. Then, suddenly, she grabbed her teacher-boss, kissed him, and hugged him with an urgency that could power an electric plant.

"Alive?" Dr. Dimension said with a dreamy smile. "Why, I think I've died and gone to heaven." He milked the clutch for all it was worth.

"We should see about Dr. Wussman," Diane said as she tried to disengage.

"I should think about crashing more often," Doc said, not eager to give up hugging his research assistant.

"Oh, go on with you." Diane pushed him away. "Where's Troy?"

"Safe and sound, and on the hunt for first aid."

A duet of groans emanated from the wreckage and the twisting in the wreaths of smoke.

Dr. Dimension said, "Ah, I hear music."

"Uhhhhhhhh," said Dr. Geoffrey Wussman.

"Ohhhhhhhh," replied his colleague and sometime lover, Dr. Vivian Vernon.

"Uhhhhhhhh" was Wussman's rejoinder.

This went on for a few more exchanges.

"The Moanlight Sonata, Opus 43, No. 1, by Wussman and Vernon," Dr. Dimension quipped. "Performed by the composers."

Troy chose that moment to charge in, carrying a bottle and a box with a red cross emblazoned on its side.

"Fourth quarter, tie score. Send me in, coach! Send me in!"

"I think Troy's the one who got his ding donged," Diane said.

"Better than having one's dong dinged," Dr. Dimension riposted. As Diane blushed, he grabbed the bottle labeled "HYDROGEN PEROXIDE." "Time out, Talbot. Run interference for the injured first. Then I'm going to have you go out for a long one."

"Gotcha!"

Troy raced to the first pair of legs sticking up from the wreckage. Hairy legs. Wussman.

Dr. Dimension opened the bottle, tilted it, and belted a snort.

Diane was appalled. "Professor, that's poison!"

"Alcohol's slow poison, but as the old saying goes, who's in a hurry?"

"Alcohol?"

"It's an ethanol solution, not a peroxide solution."

"Oh."

"It's still a disinfectant. But this stuff also clears the head. Have a belt?"

"Doctor, you know I'm a teetotaler."

"Huh? Oh, sorry. I—"

She grabbed the bottle and drank. She shivered.

"Why, Diane, I believe this is the first time I've ever seen you take a drink."

Diane's eyes bulged, and she choked. "There's a first time . . . for everything. Ewww, that stuff is awful. How did you get liquor on board this ship?"

The Dr. shrugged. "The Pizons don't know the difference from antiseptics, but they deal wholesale in alcohol." He paused for a moment. Then, with enthusiasm: "Diane! We're alive! We're alive!"

He lunged for her.

She pushed him back.

"Yes, Doctor, it's a miracle, but we'll celebrate later. Right now, maybe we'd better lick our wounds."

That gave Dr. Dimension definite ideas. Before he could do anything rash—or rash causing—Diane got to her wobbly feet and stepped away to join the first-aid effort.

Dr. Dimension went to get his share of bandages.

"Ohhhhhhh." This was from Dr. Geoffrey Wussman. He sat up slowly, then looked around.

"We crashed," he said.

"Brilliant observation, Wussy," Dr. Dimension said. "But we're alive. Alive! . . . Diane, where are you going—?"

"I feel like warmed-over cow flop," Geoffrey Wussman said. Then, suddenly, he thought of something. "Vivian!"

"Cow flop's never as good the second day," said Doc D., watching Dr. Wussman leap to his feet and begin to help Talbot sort through the mess of twisted plastic plates and bent structural rods.

"How did we survive, anyway?" Diane wanted to know. "At our rate of descent, the impact should have wiped us out."

"Some kind of protective force shield, probably," Dr. Dimension surmised. "We really didn't have time to puzzle out the Pizon's technology, but we know it was pretty slick. Besides, something else absorbed most of the impact. Maybe we hit some sort of protective force screen surrounding the planet. That's just a wild guess, of course."

"Vivian! Oh, Vivian, my darling!"

Wussman was holding Vivian's head and caressing her cheek, her brow, her lovely auburn hair.

"How is she?" Dr. Dimension asked, walking over.

"I think—"

"Uhhhhhhhh," said Dr. Vernon. "What the . . . hell happened—?" Her green eyes fluttered.

"We crashed," chorused everyone.

"I *know* we crashed, for God's sake! Why are we still alive?"

"Alive, we're alive!" Dr. Dimension began shouting again.

"Dr. D., stuff a sock in it?" Diane suggested.

"Right-o."

"Oh, Viv, it was a miracle!" Wussman gushed. "It was a gift from God."

"I don't believe in God," Vivian said.

"Call it what you will," Wussman said, "the Prime Mover, the universe, whatever. It was a gift."

"I'll bet she doesn't believe in the universe either," Dr. Dimension said.

"Anyway," Wussman went on, "it was some higher power."

"Krillman," Vivian said. "That creep."

At the mention of the alien interloper, who had been popping up at unexpected intervals throughout our heroes' spacetime adventures, everyone nodded.

"It must be," Diane said. "Krillman saved us."

"So he can torture us some more," Vivian said with a grimace of pain. "Help me up."

"Viv, are you sure you're all right?" Wussman asked anxiously. "Maybe you shouldn't move."

"I'm all right. I think I can stand. Let's see if I can walk."

She could, and did, albeit unsteadily.

"What now?" Vivian asked.

Dr. Dimension counted heads. "Okay, we have five. No good for bridge. Canasta or poker. What's your choice, Viv, baby?"

Dr. Vernon stooped for something to throw, but pain halted her. Hobbled over and in agony, she looked up at her nemesis and gritted her teeth. "You miserable—"

"That time of the month, is it, Viv?"

Chapter Two

A mess.

One big mess.

The spacetime travelers were a mess, limping and muttering, and in all their bandages, they looked like fugitives from a B-horror flick.

There was no question of checking the planetary atmosphere for breathability, as the crew of the *Mudlark* had already taken deep breaths of it, the hull having been breached in several places.

"What do you mean, go outside?" Vivian demanded.

The doctor pointed to a crack in a seam of the hull, through which sunlight streamed. "Out, Viv. Out. You know?"

"How do we know what's out there?" said Vivian with a worried scowl.

"We don't. Ergo, we step outside and reconnoiter."

"My great-uncle had a reconnoiter," said Troy. "Big thing, right below his neck. Big as a football."

Doc ignored him. "I dislike suspense. I always read the last chapter of an Agatha Christie novel first. Therefore I don't intend to dawdle. There's a brave new world out there ... waiting to be experienced."

A draught of alien air wafted through the ship, fluttering bandages.

Dr. Dimension had been privately hoping for a breath of fresh air, now that they were down on a planet. He'd grown rather weary of the stuff aboard spaceships.

The stuff that came through, however, was hardly fresh.

In fact, it rather stank.

Not a garbage smell, exactly. More industrial stench of chemicals fraternizing, erupting, farting, and generally having a noxious bad time.

"Yuck," said Wussman, cringing.

"P.U.!" said Diane Derry, holding her pert nose.

"Good old P.U." said Troy. "Good football team!"

"What the hell did we land on?" Vivian wanted to know.

"Small planet," said Doc D. "Asteroid, maybe."

"Smells like rat's asteroid," Vivian retorted, her beautiful face twisting with disgust.

"Viv, you have a certain directness of speech that I greatly admire," Dr. Dimension allowed.

"Oh, ram it up your keister."

With some effort, Troy and Dr. Dimension manually cranked open the hatches of the main air lock, which was fortunately near the ground. The entry ramp seemed to be jammed at first, but with more grunting and huffing on the part of Troy and Doc D., it slid out from its slot in the hull and made uneven contact with the sandy surface.

"Everyone off the school bus," Doc D. said cheerily. "Isn't this a nice field trip?"

"Wonderful," Vivian agreed.

Everyone hobbled outside.

The spacetime ship, once a splendid confluence of elegant geometries, now looked a reject from chaos theory. As Dr. Dimension and his crew had originally designed it, the ship had been spherical. The Pizons, a race of gangster aliens, had rebuilt it and made it into a sleekly ostentatious modern space vehicle. Colored mauve with yellow trim, it sported rakish fins, dorsal and side. Strips of chromium glinted here and there.

Now it was a collection of junk. The bulkheads were cracked. The fins were bent. Structural members were exposed, bent, and twisted.

Dr. Dimension took it all in, then swiveled his gaze to the surrounding wastelands. " 'Round the decay of that colossal wreck, boundless and bare, the lone and level sands stretch far away.' "

"Wow, that's poetry, Doc," Talbot said admiringly.

"I don't believe he's quoting Shelley at a time like this," Vivian said, then let out a painful moan again.

Troy said, half remembering. "I once dated a girl named Shelly Apfelbaum. Tall brunet with a great figure. Her family didn't like me, though."

Dr. Dimension wasn't listening. His attention had turned back to the wreck of the *Mudlark* and, thus preoccupied, he spent the next few moments.

"Not at a total loss, perhaps," he mused at length. He began to walk about the strewn wreckage, mentally calculating, cerebrally cogitating, and—bottle in hand—orally imbibing.

"Good God, he's drinking hydrogen peroxide," Vivian Vernon said with disgust.

On the other side of the wreck, he stopped and belched. Not a write off. With a little riveting here, and a nip and a tuck there . . .

The ship would never leave the planet again. Feeling a sudden pang of pessimism, Dr. Dimension saw that it was hopeless. The tools necessary to do the job were standard in any space graving dock—but this was no graving dock they had landed on. He was at a total loss as to how they were going to fix the damned thing.

He swung around to confront his battle-scarred comrades.

Not a pretty sight. They'd all been banged up a bit. Just bruises and nicks, fortunately. Diane was by no means a nurse, and Troy had flunked first aid in the Boy Scouts. The bandaging was decidedly haphazard. In spite of this, however, the wrappings were serviceable and bound up whatever shreds of dignity the galaxy-hopping, spacetime-jumping adventurers retained.

"Bit of a pickle, eh?" he said, by way of conversational gambit.

"A dilly of a pickle" was Vivian Vernon's icy reply.

"The professor will know what to do," Diane said in

retort. "Isn't that right, Dr. Demopoulos . . . er, I mean, Dr. Dimension?"

"I say go for the field goal!" said Troy.

"We'll never get off this planet," said Wussman gloomily. "Look at that ship. It's damaged beyond repair."

"Not quite," Dr. Dimension told him. "It's just this side of repairable. Trouble is, all we have in the way of tools is a couple of screwdrivers and a bastard file. Son of a bitch."

"Watch your filthy mouth," Vivian ordered him.

"Unless the Pizon's stowed some tools aboard," Doc D. went on. "Talbot?"

"Yeah, Coach?"

"Tools? Pizon?"

"You're the one drinking disinfectant," Troy said with a frown. "Why ask me?"

Dr. Dimension's high forehead furrowed. "Good Lord. Talbot, go inside and lie down, that's an order. Halftime, big fella."

"Okay, coach."

Talbot shuffled off and went back into the ship.

"There's only one thing we can do at this point," Dr. Dimension said.

Wussman let out a piteous groan.

"Besides groan," Doc D. said. "Clearly, we have crash-landed on an alien planet. Let's count our blessings. We are still alive—"

It was Vivian's turn to groan.

"Stalwart space pioneers. Well, some of us are only half-alive, that will have to do for the moment. We're not dead, and we're ambulatory. We've got gravity beneath our feet again, and this planet has breathable air."

"How do you know that, Doctor?" challenged Vivian, ever contentious.

Dr. Dimension took a deep breath and let it out. He took another. "Gosh, you got me, Viv. Let me see, how do I know that?"

"How do you know we won't all keel over after a

few minutes?" Vivian barked. "There could be all sorts
of poisonous components to the atmosphere. We could
be all asphyxiating as we stand here."

"Well, you stand here and asphyxiate while we fix
the ship. See if we care."

"Oh, damn you, anyway."

"You refuse to help, Viv?"

"Of course not!" she retorted angrily. "Who said I
refuse to do anything? I pull my weight on this bucket
of bolts, same as the next able crewman."

"God, Viv, I love it when you talk space lingo."

"Oh, shut up."

Dr. Dimension drew himself up proudly. " 'Shut up,
sir.' I am the captain of this ship."

"You are the fool who got us into this mess in the
first place. You and your crazy inventions!"

"Viv, you've loved every minute of our adventures."

"I've hated every minute of this series of disasters
you got us into! And who says you're the captain?"

"It's in the manual."

"What manual?"

"The one I'm going to write when I have the time."

"Go write it, and then you can stuff it where the
moon don't shine, for all I care." Vivian saluted and
thumbed her nose. "Sir!"

The doctor bristled. "That's tantamount to mutiny,
Vivian. Besides, there's no moon here. I'm giving you
fair warning, you'd better shape up. The others will
back me up."

"I won't," Dr. Wussman announced.

"I will," Diane said. "And so will Talbot. That's
three against two."

"Democracy," Vivian sneered. "Decadent bourgeois
democracy, which puts into practice the idiotic notion
that the majority is always right."

"Vivian has a point," Wussman agreed. "The majority is often wrong. I mean, I'm all for democracy and
all that—"

"Let's lose the political discussion," Dr. Dimension
said with an impatient wave of the hand. "We don't

have time. Vivian does have a point about the air. It could be breathable but might carry alien microbes, organisms that we have no resistance against."

This sobered up the contentious crew.

"So we have to get busy, fix the ship, and get space borne again, pronto."

"But how?" Vivian asked.

Dr. Dimension turned and surveyed the ship again, then scanned the horizon.

"This is some kind of planetary refuse dump. There might be parts here, parts we could cannibalize from junked space vessels. There could be other stuff about, tools, materials— Get the picture?"

Vivian shrugged. "It's a long shot, but I guess it's the only one we have. Okay, Captain Demopoulos—"

"Just call me Dr. Dimension."

"Why?" Wussman and Vivian asked together.

"I just like the ring of it. Okay?"

Vivian shrugged again. "You're absolutely insane, but you seem to have the upper hand, somehow. Okay, Dr. Dimension, what are you orders?"

Dr. Dimension said, "Fix us some lunch."

Chapter Three

"Fix your own lunch, idiot."

But Dr. Dimension's attention was on the landscape again. It was bleak terrain, jagged rocks thrusting up from lakes of dust and debris. The sky was a yellowish-brown. Aside from the vast collection of rubbish that littered the land, the place was otherwise undistinguished.

"Just thought of something. I'd hate to run into the dog that guards this junkyard." Dr. Dimension took another swig of ethanol. "If it's a dog at all."

As the others merely gawked, speechless at this incredible, spectacular expanse, Doc D. bustled about, examining this oddity, poking that improbability.

"Plenty of possibilities here for repairing a spaceship," he announced, pulling something out from beneath a pile of rusted, twisted metal. He held it up to the harsh alien sun. It was something on the order of a surrealistic bicycle pump.

"Well, maybe not a spaceship," he amended. "Vivian, do you have an evil Schwinn?"

"That'll come in handy for our flat tires," Vivian jeered. She peered about from her bandages like a turtle wary of poking its head from its shell.

Nevertheless, Dr. Dimension was overwhelmed. He felt like a kid in a candy store or a toy shop—only with endlessly strange and marvelous candy, and wonderfully mysterious toys. Odd shapes hulked here beneath a hot pink sun. Polyhedrons glimmered with strange alloys of stranger colors. Whatchamacallits and thingamabobs huddled rudder to gear with devices and gadgets having intricately reticulated geometric designs that angled the vision of the viewer off into uncharted conceptual territory.

In one pile there appeared to be the most delightful assortment of electrical equipment.

Dr. Dimension's trail led him up a rise, where he gained a better perspective on the immediate surroundings. Over the tops of the clustered piles of refuse, he beheld an awesome sight, and a startled grunt escaped his lips.

A mountainous mass of something towered not far away.

"Jumping Jehoshaphat!—or a like biblical expression."

What he saw had nothing to do with biblical characters. However, it had everything to do with the question of why the ship had been spared on its initial contact with the planet's surface.

"Gentlepeople," he called to his companions. "Have a look at this."

The others warily shuffled up to his position, and their noses performed a synchronized turn, following Doc D.'s pointing forefinger.

Their eyes widened, then blinked in disbelief. Before them was a mountain, but hardly just any mountain. If any could, this mountain could pass for the proverbial one that might have visited Muhammad. On the other hand, Muhammad would very likely be inclined to come to this particular mountain, especially if he fancied a good night's sleep. It was a mountain made for sleepers. In fact, the stuff that made up this enormous pile of dormant material looked for all the world—no, for all the universe—like mattresses. Strange mattresses, granted; but mattresses nonetheless.

It was the biggest mound of mattresses in the known universe. Twin mattress, full mattress. Queen-size and king-size mattresses. Dwarf mattresses and mammoth mattresses. Oddly shaped mattresses meant to support oddly shaped alien bodies. The designs and colors were numerous. Paisley, striped, checkered, polka-dot, and plain mattresses. Numbered among these thousands—no, millions—were mattresses that simply defied description; but, again, they were recognizably mattress-like objects.

"Mattresses!" said Diane Derry.

"Yeah—" Doc did a take. "No kidding, Diane."

Diane looked sheepish. "I guess I have a penchant for stating the obvious."

"You do," said Dr. Dimension, "but you're absolutely right. Mattresses. They must have broken our fall. You can see where we hit," said Doc D., pointing to a noticeable depression along the left side of the slope. "Right near the summit, there. Quite a sight, eh? This whole area is a spectacle. Well, that settles it. Our initial theories have proved valid. Judging from what we saw on the way down, I think we can safely say this whole planet is a gigantic alien junkyard. Must be a dump for half the galaxy."

"A trash planet," echoed an awed Diane.

"Well, it's not pretty, but this place is jam-packed with delightful opportunities." He rubbed his hands together enthusiastically. "Opportunities that need to be explored. But we need some tools. Fortunately, a nifty little analytical device has recently fallen into our possession. It'll come in handy."

"The Magnetic Monocle, of course," said Diane Derry, snapping her fingers, some of the girl-Friday cheerleader Katherine Hepburn spunkiness returning.

"Yes. Question is—where is the blasted thing?" Doc clapped his pockets, dug in his pants, felt around his neck, took off his belt.

His pants fell down.

Doc D.'s polka-dot underwear blazed neon red in the rays of the alien sun.

He grinned as he hitched up. "Goodness. Hope that little number cheered the more dour-spirited members of our expedition." He zippered his pants up.

Diane tittered. Vivian made another face.

"Really, Demetrios," Wussman complained. "Let's show some decorum."

Doc D. promptly let down his pants again, turned, hiked up his lab coat, and bent over. "How about I show some ass, eh, Wussy? More than you've seen in a month of Sundays, I'll bet!"

"Dr. Demopoulos, please, there are ladies present!"

Dr. Dimension began teasingly to tug down his garish underwear. "There's a full moon tonight, Geof!"

Diane shrieked and turned away.

"Demopoulos, you disgusting pervert." Dr. Vivian Vernon did not take her eyes from the generous rear expanse of Dr. Dimension's gaudy drawers.

Diane was giggling uncontrollably.

Dr. Dimension hiked his Skivvies back up and returned his garments to a decent state. "Just kidding, kids. Now, where the hell's the Monocle?"

"I believe it's on the ship," said Vivian.

"Yes, yes, of course." Doc D. started traipsing back down the grade. En passant, he patted Vivian lightly on the rump. "Repeat performance in private whenever you like, Viv."

"Don't hold your breath," said the buxom redhead. "On the other hand, it might be good for a laugh."

"Joke all you like. I'm your salvation here, dearie, and don't you forget it." He hopped onto the ramp, and danced happily up to the crew compartment of the ship. There, after rummaging around in the debris for five minutes, he spotted the strap he had tied to the Monocle, poking from its case. He grabbed the article and sauntered out, displaying it for one and all—particularly one—to see. "Now then, Vivian, what portion of my anatomy should I require you to kiss in gratitude for getting you back to Flitheimer University?"

"Present it, and I'll bite it off, buster," warned Vivian, green eyes smoldering.

Doc D. brightened. "Viv, I wasn't thinking of going

that far. You say the cutest things." He snorted with hilarity. "Yes, with the aid of this little item of super-science, the benefits of this opportune world will unfold before us like a beautiful flower, displaying its delicate petals one by one."

He opened the case and affixed the Magnetic Monocle to his eye, scrutinizing the scenery.

"Voila!"

The Monocle's lens promptly popped out and fell to the ground.

"Oops! Shit." Dr. Dimension looked down. "Where did it go?"

"Right there," Diane said, pointing.

"Where?"

"There." Diane advanced a step.

Dr. Dimension held up a palm. "Stop! No, don't go near it. Just point."

"There!"

"I can't see it."

"I saw it land right there."

Dr. Dimension knelt and scrutinized the sand. "I don't see it."

"It's got to be there."

"It's not, Diane. Must have bounced. Don't move."

"I see it," Vivian said. "Over there, by your right shoe."

Dr. Dimension looked at his scuffed right Oxford. "Where? Oh, that." He picked up a glassy pebble. "That's not it. Silicon tektite, as a matter of fact. But not the lens."

"It's got to be around here somewhere," Diane said. "Funny how I thought I saw it."

"You probably did," Doc D. said, "but you didn't see it bounce."

"How far could it have bounced?" Vivian wanted to know as she took a tentative step.

"Viv, don't move, for God's sake!"

Vivian gave him a haughty face. "Excuse me!"

"Sorry, Viv, but we need that Monocle. With it, we

can analyze all sorts of exotic junk and see how it works. If we can—"

"Is that it?" Diane asked, pointing to Doc D.'s left.

Dr. Dimension looked. "No, a shiny stone. Damn it, the problem is that the lens isn't plain glass. It could be lying right here, but against the ground it's practically invisible. It reflects no light at all, apparently."

"Well, what do we do?" Vivian demanded.

"I don't know. Everybody hunker down and search, but don't move an inch. Just look."

Everybody obeyed. The search went on for several minutes.

At length Wussman complained, "I'm getting cramps."

"That time of the month for you, too, eh Wussy?"

"Oh, shut up, Demopoulos."

"Dimension."

"Demented, is more like it."

Doc D. shrugged, smiling. "If you wish."

"Hey, Doc!"

It was Troy Talbot, rushing up the rise.

"Troy, stop!" Dr. Dimension shouted.

"What?"

"Stop where you are! Come no farther!"

Troy stopped and cupped one ear. "Can't hear you!"

"I said, don't come any closer, you boob!"

Perversely, Troy started up the knoll again. "Crash must've affected my hearing, Doc. I really can't understand—"

CRACK!

TINKLE.

Troy halted. He looked down. "Uh-oh."

Groaning, everyone came rushing to him.

The worst had happened. The transparent crystalline material of the lens had reduced itself to powder under Talbot's leather sole.

Doc D. wearily got to his feet. "Talbot, you unbelievable bumbling booby."

"Guess I went and did it again, Doc. Sorry. You want to bop me on the noggin again?"

"What, and increase the brain damage? Not on your life, buster. You . . ."

Dr. Dimension was at a loss for words. This was a singular occurrence in his life.

A moment of gloomy silence, pregnant with nonsignificance, hovered over the spatiotemponauts.

"Oh, well," Dr. Dimension said at last. "After all, it was just a lens. Sorry, no, it was a monocle. Same dif. Wasn't prescription, anyway."

Vivian gave a despairing groan.

"Yes, Fate may thumb its nose—but our interpretation of the semaphore, after all, may be faulty." Doc's finger smote the air declaratively. "But let's not be discouraged. We're at a distinct disadvantage without the Monocle, but the secrets of this wonderful world await. Avaunt!"

"Avaunt to be alone," said Dr. Wussman. He sat down on the sand and began to weep.

"Don't cry, Wussman, for God's sake. Buck up, man, buck up!"

"Oh, poop," Dr. Wussman said dismally.

"Dig a latrine first. Dry those tears, Wussy. You're not doing morale any good."

"To hell with your morale."

"Viv, would you mind taking Dr. Wussman off somewhere and cheering him up? Either that or shoot him."

Vivian sighed.

"Come on, Geoffrey." She took his hand. "If you'll brighten up, I'll sit on your lap or something."

Wussman's face grew furtive. "Actually, my dear fiancée—I'd far prefer the 'or something.' "

"You've been a very naughty boy, Geoffrey."

"Oh, I have, I have indeed, Vivian," groveled Wussman gleefully. "Don't you think I should be . . . disciplined?"

"There you go," Dr. Dimension said. "He's coming around. How depressed can you be if you're queer for a beating?"

"Come with me," Vivian said, taking Dr. Wussman's hand. Geoffrey Wussman rose and followed her.

They disappeared inside the crumpled spaceship.

"Weird," Diane said, turning up her button nose.

"Now, Diane, we mustn't make value judgments on people's sexual proclivities, even when the creeps involved are sick, perverted deviants like those two."

"I just don't understand what kicks some people get out of getting the tar whaled out of them."

"Ours is not to moralize; ours is but to prioritize."

Diane looked confused. "Huh?"

"Never mind. Diane, Troy and I are going to have a look around to scout the possibilities. You'd better stay here and watch those two. Make sure they stay out of trouble."

"Do I have to, Dr. D.?"

"You have to."

Diane made a sullen, yet somehow still pretty, face.

"Also, I want you to begin cataloging the damage."

Diane sighed. "Yes, Doctor."

"Tote up available supplies and rations."

"Yes, Doctor."

"Survey the surroundings."

"Yes, Doctor."

"Tighten the jib."

"Yes, Captain, sir. Will there be any further orders, Cap'n Long John Silver, sir?"

"Arrrr, indeed there be, lass. Always remember, I love the jut o' yer prow. There be not a prettier maid on the Spanish Main 'tween here an' Far Tortuga! Arrrrr."

Diane delivered a mock salute. "Aye aye, sir!"

Doc D. winked lecherously, then faced Troy Talbot.

Talbot had a tall, blond good-looking Norse god of a body, with an English walnut of a brain. However, in the mechanical areas he was a regular idiot savant.

Emphasis on the idiot, alas. However, the boy could fix anything. He could probably even fix this spaceship, given the right materials. It fell to them, now, to head out and scout for the necessary elements of survival, deliverance, salvation—and perhaps, if they were lucky, they might even find a pile of "spicy inventor stories."

Dr. Dimension idly picked up a length of green plastic rod and swished it about like a riding crop. "Talbot—tallyho!"

"Huh?"

"Huddle's over. Butts are slapped. Tie score. Two seconds on the clock. You've got to go out for a Hail Mary, Talbot."

Troy Talbot's broad brow furrowed in puzzlement. "Heck, Doc, I'm not Catholic."

Glazed eyes rotating heavenward, Dr. Dimension groaned, "Talbot, you nincompoop." But it was a loving, indulgent kind of groan, carrying undertones of avuncular affection. Then he raised the plastic rod at his lab assistant. Troy flinched.

"Take it easy, Doc, brain damage, remember?" Talbot said, backing away.

Throwing the rod away, Dr. Dimension busied himself in a nearby pile of junk. Finding something to his liking, he fished it out.

"Doc ... what do we need a two-by-four ... for?" Troy asked.

Dr. D. pointed the other direction. "Talbot. What's that over there?"

Talbot turned. "Huh ... Heck, I don't know. Looks like—"

Doc D. brought the piece of wood down on Troy Talbot's head, not ungently.

"CONK"

Diane nodded in approval. "Works every time."

Troy Talbot rubbed his head. He looked around, blinking.

"Jeepers, Doc. Did we blow up again?"

"I hate to break it to you, Troy," said the Doc. "Not only are we not on a football field. We're not even on Earth."

Dr. Dimension sighed, took his bewildered assistant by the arm, and led him out into the mysterious trash planet.

Chapter Four

Though she could not possibly realize it, Diane had about an hour before she hopped from the comparatively calm frying pan of being lost in space into the roaring proverbial fire of alien captivity.

Diane Derry watched her father figure and her boyfriend figure disappear into the smog around the base of a lofty pile of clutter. She gave herself a moment to catch her breath and get a grip on her feelings before she went back into the spaceship to see what those troublemakers were doing.

She sighed.

Such responsibilities that great man gave her! She hoped she was up to the task. Diane felt privileged, honored even, to work for a man of such intellect and vision as Dr. Demetrios Demopoulos, a.k.a. "Dr. Dimension." He was a truly great man, Dr. D. was, but quite misunderstood.

Not even Diane understood him.

She tried to. Lord knew, she worked hard at it. In the end, she just had to be patient, and give him slack.

She was familiar with the concept of absentminded professors. In truth, one of the reasons she worked with Doc D. was that she found this cluster of personality traits very engaging. If she ever gave up on physics as a career, she could always write a dissertation on the subject in her undergraduate minor subject, psychology. Doc D. was hardly your average absentminded professor, though. Perhaps, instead, she would go into the physics of psycho-biochemistry. Yes, and do a paper on the effect of male hormones on genius.

This interest in the biology of behavior was why Diane Derry put up with the lecherous old goat's shenanigans.

The doctor had high hormones.

Diane had a theory. She called it the Theory of Relatively. Why had most of the world's great scientists and inventors been men? Well, it was generally assumed that men were relatively better at logic and reasoning than women. But Diane knew that was hogwash. Take Troy, for example. They didn't come any denser. But give him a spanner, and he would build you a time machine. Or a spaceship.

Okay, male gray cells and synapses and such were not that much different from female—so it must be other aspects of biology that prompted this phenomenon.

Glands for instance.

And, since the principal hormonal secretion in males was different from that of females, this must be the crucial difference. The truth was that men were better at male stuff than females. Of course! And male stuff involved monkeying around with things and taking risks and getting into trouble and blowing up labs. Dangerous behavior like that. Women tended to do more actual thinking, relatively speaking.

Something had occurred to her.

Could science itself, since it was dominated by male behavior, reflect this built-in male bias? Alternatively, could there be such a thing as ...

Female science?

Wow, what a radical notion! Female science. A kinder, gentler sort of science, that didn't involve so much danger and things blowing up, and couldn't be put to rotten uses such as making bombs and guns and stuff, and wouldn't involve building crazy spacetime ships that flew off every which way and ended up getting you lost all the way out here in the middle of some unknown galaxy, abandoned and all alone—

She started to break into tears, but sniffed it all away and got hold of herself.

Was this a galaxy or a solar system? She didn't know, not having taken the university's one astronomy course. What's the difference between the two? She thought she knew the difference between a star and a planet fairly well. One was hot and bright and burning, and the other was a round muddy thing. Okay. But a galaxy—those were the kind of things that went around and around? Oh, wait, planets did that, too. So did stars ... ? Maybe. Galaxies were—big blobs of stars. That's it. Big pinwheel shaped ... nebulae! Yes. Maybe. But weren't nebulae composed of clouds of gas and dust? She read that somewhere. Were all galaxies nebulae, or was it the other way around? Which was a subset of the other?

Never mind. Forget it. Her head began to ache. Maybe women weren't good at thinking, after all.

But that female science notion ... Hmmmm. There might be something to that.

But she'd never get it past Dr. Wussman, the department chairman and also chairman of the doctoral dissertation oversight committee.

Rats. She'd have to stick to good old male science, in all its sticky, dangerous mischievousness. Good thing she liked men.

But there must be something to her theory. Of course, it was all relative.

She'd had this theory for a while, but she knew she'd really caught onto something the second day she worked as Dr. D.'s assistant. No sooner had he signed her on and planted a kiss on her cheeks—"Just a Greek gesture of affection and respect, my dear!"—than he'd chased her around a lab bench.

She'd thwarted his advances with the help of a Bunsen burner and a clamp. She thought for sure that the scorched and pinched doctor would fire her immediately. However, his eyes merely blazed with respect and fondness.

"How invigorating! See you tomorrow for your first day of work. I'll try to keep my hands to myself, although I can't promise to control my wanton eyes!"

The next day, instead of chasing his graduate assistant around the lab, Demopoulos invented a better mousetrap. It was a device that lured rodents with the promise of cheese—and then dispatched them to some unknown dimension.

"Would like to use this on humans, to explore, you know," he'd explained. "But can't get the wormhole open any wider."

The device was astonishing, and it worked quite well. Soon Flitheimer University's notorious rodent problem was kaput. Only the larger species of rodents—like Dr. Vivian Vernon and Dr. Geoffrey Wussman!—remained.

Diane's secret studies were thus begun.

She embarked upon daily diaries and charts of the accomplishments of her dear Dr. Demopoulos. The *Mudlark,* the time-space vehicle that had gotten them in this muddle, was of course the apex of his achievement—though at first it exhibited a scarifying tendency to blow up. Fortunately, they'd received those mysterious crates of engine innards, shipped by person or persons unknown, just in the nick of time to procure the grant from Mr. and Mrs. Sam Flitheimer that would keep Dr. D.'s spacetime vehicle project alive.

Now all they had to do was to get back to Earth, circa 1939, and claim their rightful prize.

And, of course, so that Diane could add a wealth of new information to her own private studies. Dr. D. had been just astounding. What colossal exercise of his cunning and invention! Her admiration for him had grown even greater than before.

And his new name . . . Dr. Dimension!

He never had gotten around to answering Troy's question ("Why?") but Diane had an inkling of why the doctor adopted the moniker.

She had to admit it had style.

A clatter sounded from inside the spaceship, snapping her back to her immediate spacetime coordinates and predicament.

Whatever were Viv and Geoff up to now?

Doc D. had specifically requested that she keep an eye on them, so she'd better see to that. Diane simply had no idea they would get into trouble so quickly.

She hurried up the ramp, through the hatch, and was confronted by a sight that would have caused her Calvinist ancestors to blush in their graves.

Dr. Wussman was lying prone across Dr. Vernon's lap. In his eagerness to assume this position, he had apparently knocked some items off a table, hence the clatter. Wussman's face wore a paradoxical grimace of sublime pleasure. Only a shade away from the groaning mask of misery he'd had before. Dr. Vernon's hand was raised in mid-swat, just above Wussman's reddened bare posterior.

"Ah! Miss Derry!" said Vivian, lowering her hand. "Poor Geoffrey was choking on some food. Weren't you, dear?"

Wussman scrambled off her lap, pulled up his pants and grinned sheepishly. "The Vernon Maneuver works every time. I have difficulty swallowing, you see."

Ordinarily Diane, an innocent sort, would have been inclined to accept the story. For Diane Derry, S & M meant Santa and Marshmallows, a cocoa Christmas treat her mom made. B & D was the name of a drugstore in her hometown, Flat Butte, Iowa, that served the best strawberry phosphates in town.

It wasn't that Diane Derry didn't know the biological facts of life, of birds and bees and such. She just didn't understand all the kinky bits. Her heart was pure, and her soul was sweet. She was part saint, part nightingale (as in Florence), but all-American.

But she had come a long way since she'd begun working for Dr. Dimension. She'd learned much, and in the last few days—

Days! It seemed like years! Could it only have been a matter of a few days since they'd blasted off in the *Mudlark*, the spacetime machine, and plunged headlong into galactic space, into an intergalactic war, and got themselves lost, thousands of light-years from Earth?

—Days. Anyway, she had seen and heard a lot very recently, and her education in the ways of the world—the universe!—had grown by quantum leaps and bounds. She knew all about the strange sexual tastes of Drs. Wussman and Vernon.

But, as Dr. D. said, ours is not to moralize.

"Oh. Just as long as you two aren't getting up to any trouble."

"Trouble? Us?" said Wussman, grinning nervously. "What trouble have we ever caused?"

"Well, you turned traitor and threw in your lot with those nasty aliens," said Diane.

"The Proons? Why, they weren't so nasty. They had their good points."

"Sure, if you like being enslaved by them. Anyway, it didn't start with the Proons. You tried to scuttle our spacetime vehicle project. You stowed away on the *Mudlark* with mischief in your hearts. And, all in all, I don't think you like us much."

"That's not true, Miss Derry—uh, may I call you Diane?" said Dr. Vernon.

"Sure," Diane said.

Dr. Vernon continued, "I can't dispute that there's professional rivalry between Dr. Demopoulos and myself, but that doesn't mean that we don't like you. We hear you're an excellent graduate student. Isn't that right, Dr. Wussman?"

"Oh, absolutely. Indubitably. Pronouncedly. Decidedly. Inarguably. Why, I was just saying—"

Dr. Vernon cuffed him one. "Go back to groans, Geoffrey, it's less annoying."

"Ouch. That one hurt, Viv."

Vivian smiled sweetly at Diane. "You see, I tend to be a tad abusive. As in the case of my fiancé here, it is simply a sign of affection."

Diane put her hands on her hips and regarded the shifty duo with much skepticism. Just because she was innocent didn't mean she was stupid.

She said, "All the same, Dr. D. said to keep an eye on you two until he gets back. We're supposed to stay here, stay out of trouble. Maybe the Pizons left a deck of playing cards somewhere about. I suppose you'll cheat, but not much harm in that."

"Cards? Cheat? How can you say such a thing? Now, do I cheat at cards, Geoffrey?"

"No. Of course not. What a silly idea." Wussman blinked. "Of course, I've always wondered why I've never won a single hand of gin rummy with you, Vivian—Yow!"

He nursed his sore shin.

"We'll just look around for a pack of cards then, hmm?" said Vivian. "That will be such fun."

"No, you two just stay there and amuse yourselves with your little games."

Diane did not particularly want them rooting through the storage compartments. They might come up with weapons or devices that would give them an upper hand.

An hour passed in which Diane busied herself with cataloging rations. Speaking of lunch, she was starting to get hungry. Unfortunately, there wasn't much to eat besides pork and beans. Provisioning the spacetime ship had been Troy's job, and he had done a singularly unimaginative job of it. There were six cartons of canned pork and beans. Not even one can of vegetable soup to break the monotony.

There was no Pizon food, because all the Pizons ate was a strange form of pizza, along with a stringy pasta made from—yuck!—alien mealworms . . .

She was getting queasy just thinking about all this. Wait, hadn't the Pizons said they had cooked up some food fit for humans? She couldn't remember whether it had been stowed aboard or not. There hadn't been much time before the big space battle with the Proon starship fleet.

If they had stored the stuff, whatever kind of stuff it was, the Pizon stevedores (Local 245) would probably have packed it into the aft storage lockers. If she could find her way back there—

She went to look.

However, she had not looked very long or very hard before a loud rumbling shook the bulkheads. The vibrations shook the entire crashed Pizon ship. Diane's fillings seemed to rattle.

"Whoa!" She thrust out both hands against the bulkheads.

Whatever it was came from outside.

Diane steadied herself and lurched back to the control room. Drs. Vernon and Wussman looked quite startled and not particularly inclined to go and explore. As she had been put in charge, and as she was in no sense a shrinking violet, Diane went to the open hatch.

About a thousand yards away, suspended on a plume of iridescent energy that shimmered in avocado-puce waves, a spaceship, looking as though it had been designed by Pablo Picasso with a bad hangover, was landing.

Diane watched it. The craft was composed of a series of interlocking blue spheres connected with tubes. The design was complex. The edge of the greenish energy field touched the ground, and little dust devils sprang up, twisting and turning. The strange craft came down slowly, very slowly. Presently, metal struts tipped with foot-like pads extruded from the spheres. The pads made gentle contact with the ground.

The ship was down. The energy field dissipated, and the rumbling ceased.

A door opened. A gangplank, like an erector set from Hades, unwound and smacked onto the ground, knocking over a pile of empty cans of Vegan peas.

"Doctor!" cried Diane. "Dr. Dimension! Troy? Where are you?"

Receiving no answer, she turned to crank the hatch closed.

Instantly, a bright, silvery beam reached out from the ship on shimmering strands of light and grabbed hold of her, freezing her into place.

She watched, petrified, as a strange vehicle descended the alien ship's boarding ramp. Looking like a cross between a tractor and a metallic caterpillar, it crawled down the gangplank on arachnoid appendages, great long spider's legs that clicked and clanked. It was creepy.

The strange machine's occupants were even creepier.

Chapter Five

There is a very good explanation for why Dr. Dimension and his faithful factotum, Troy Talbot, did not race back and save Diane Derry from the alien ship that landed not long after Doc and Troy's departure from the crash site.

The alien ship landed and took off again so fast that they barely had time to react. Moreover, the whooshing and rumbling that seemed to be associated with the ship's arrival caused some landslides ... junkslides. This was a dicey do for the Doc and his assistant.

They both saw the flashing in the sky but didn't quite catch sight of the ship itself. They were busy dodging rolling junk.

"Doc," said Troy, mercifully returned from his football fantasy world. "Wasn't that just the sound of a spaceship landing?"

Dr. Dimension jumped out of the way of something that looked like a Bessemer converter steel smelter as it rolled down a nearby slope.

"Is that something like the sound of one hand clapping?"

"Doc, really, that sounded an awful lot like the sound of a spaceship landing."

Nearby, a tilting pile of debris fell, sending oddments skittering about helter-skelter.

"Of course it's a ship, you idiot," Dr. Dimension snapped. "Talbot, haven't you noticed that the ground is dancing the hula?"

"Yup, must be from the ship landing. We'd best get back there, Doc."

"Okay, but how?"

The ground was still shaking violently, and more debris was rolling off the piles. Not far away, fissures began opening up in the ground, and sections of the surface sank into them, along with carloads of junk.

"We got to, Doc. Diane may be in trouble!"

"In here, Talbot!"

Dr. Dimension had taken refuge inside the converter thing, a large container resembling a giant kettle.

"What?"

"Duck in here until the ruckus stops!"

"But it's the ship that's doing the shaking!"

"No, it isn't."

Troy frowned. "It isn't?"

"No," Dr. D. said. "Alien spaceships don't make noise like that. It's an earthquake."

"An earthquake?" Troy was astonished.

"Call it a 'planetquake.' Anyway, it's just coincidence that the ship's landing at the moment."

"Oh."

Troy ducked inside and hunkered down.

The quake lasted at full force a minute longer before it began to subside. The sound, like distant thunder, gradually died.

"There may be aftershocks to contend with, but we'll have to risk it," said Dr. Dimension. "Come on!"

They ran back the way they had come, following their own footprints in the ocher sand.

"Who do you think they are?"

"What say, Talbot?"

"Who do you think the aliens are? The Pizons?"

"How the hell should I know? Didn't look like a . . . Pizon ship."

Doc D. was huffing and puffing as he ran. He was badly out of shape.

"Anyway, no telling . . . how far off the beaten orbit Krillman sent us when he—"

"There she goes, Doc!"

Dr. D. skidded to a halt. The alien ship was lifting off again, this time in total silence, trailing a brilliant plume of chartreuse energy. It rose into the sky rapidly, and in no time became a blue-green dot against the ugly brown cloud cover.

Then it was gone.

They reached the *Mudlark* a minute later. It was completely deserted. Troy and Dr. D. went through the ship calling out, but no one answered.

"We'll never see Diane again," Troy despaired. He was on the verge of tears that he dared not shed, he being the manly sort that balks at such things.

Dr. Dimension patted the boy's broad back. "We'll see her, son. We'll fix this ship and find her."

"Can we, Doc? Can we?" A look of wild desperation was in the young man's eyes.

"Sure," said Dr. Dimension.

But he didn't believe it either.

Dr. Dimension rubbed his hands with glee. "This place looks like a galactic swap meet hit by a tornado. What goodies do we have here?"

He bent and retrieved what appeared to be a glossy magazine. When he opened it, a 3-dimensional photograph unfolded like an accordion. Oddments of alien anatomy dangled like Japanese seaweed origami.

"Great Caesar's Gonads! Talk about reproductive organs, this one looks like a Wurlitzer." Doc gawked. "Hide your eyes, Talbot. You're far too young."

Troy obligingly clamped a hand over his eyes while Doc D. flipped through the alien magazine. The interview, although unintelligible, looked provocative.

"Okay, Talbot." Doc tossed the magazine away and proceeded to explore various piles of trash, sifting through them for signs of pay dirt. Even he didn't quite know what they were looking for. Vaguely he wished for something on the order of the Magnetic Monocle, some alien talisman that would magically facilitate their departure from this reeking hellhole.

"Uh, Doc?"

"Yes, Troy."

"Just what are we looking for again?"

Miracles? Demetrios thought. Then he carefully phrased his reply. "Parts. Bits and pieces of mechanisms we might use to jury-rig a new version of the engine. The one we arrived with is totally shot. That's where you come in, Talbot. I daresay, with my brains and your . . . whatever it is you have—we'll be able to put some kind of thrusting device together to heave our boat off this world."

"Gotcha, Doc."

"Good. Next time we build a spacetime ship, we must fit it with an engine that doesn't go on the fritz so much. No matter how we rebuild it, it seems to—"

The doctor was interrupted by a high-pitched whistling noise. Something whizzed by overhead.

"Incoming!" Dr. Dimension yelled.

Troy hit the dirt before he did. The dull, hollow thump of a minor explosion sounded not very far away. An umbrella of debris arched into the sky and began to fall.

Nothing hit our heroes, but it was close. Scraps of things clattered to earth nearby.

When the dangerous rain stopped, they got up and dusted themselves off.

"Whew, that was a close shave, Doc."

"You said it. You know, another happy thought occurred to me."

"What's that, Professor?"

"Not only are we running the risk of being hit with new junk—they must drop the stuff from orbit—we're also at risk of being slowly poisoned. Or maybe not so slowly."

"How's that?"

"Well, if they dump trash here, they could also be dumping poisonous chemicals. Toxic waste. You noticed the crappy sky, the pollution?"

Troy looked up. "Yeah, it doesn't look pretty."

"Right. Who knows what ghastly stuff they're off-loading here. All the more reason for us to vamoose as soon as possible."

"Doc, if we're looking for electronic gear, maybe that thingamabob over there might come in handy."

"Hm?" Doc D. followed Troy's pointing finger.

Sticking out of a mound of bizarre hat racks, positron imaging equipment, exotic golf clubs, and liquid refreshment containers (soda pop bottles?) was a robot. Troy knew what robots were. He'd seen them on Saturday afternoon serials. Troy was a big serial fan. His favorite was *Flash Gordon Conquers the Universe,* with Buster Crabbe. Throughout his recent outer-space adventures—quite real, no celluloid fantasy—Troy had been having cravings for popcorn.

"A robot."

The robot was only part of a robot, or so it looked, a torso of metallic tubes sunk into the sand. It was topped by a transparent dome, a Wall Street ticker-tape affair with complex innards.

"Looks damned unwieldy," said Doc. "Not sleek, like that model in Fritz Lang's *Metropolis.*" The silent movie was one of Doc's favorites. Doc loved movies and books about mad scientists and inventors. It gave him inspiration.

"Looks sort of dead, Doc. Burned-out."

"Have a care, Talbot. We don't know what dangers lurk in this junk pile."

"First sign of a useful gizmo we've seen, Doc," said Troy. "You said we've got to look for spare parts to fix the ship with." He stepped forward and nudged the thing.

Immediately, lights flashed inside the transparent head. Rotors twirled, and pistons danced. Player piano keys of light blinked.

The metallic creature jerked, dispersing a cascade of sparks. The unmistakable tang of ozone filled the air.

A clicking voice gargled something like "Danger! Danger!"

Its claw-tipped arms began to flail.

"Talbot! Get back!" Doc D. yanked the football star away from the reach of grasping metal mandibles. The robot's visible interior clicked and whirled while the rest of the torso carried on like a Fourth of July fireworks display, shooting sparks like rockets. A blare of phonemes and consonants blurted once more into a ragged attempt at speech that sounded like:

"Warning! Warning!"

"Interesting creation," observed Doc D., stroking his salt-and-pepper mustache. "It talks, too. Wonder if—" Dr. D. took a step closer. "I say, can you hear me?"

"Warning! Danger!"

"Right. Hello? Hello, in there? Mr. Robot, sir?"

"Danger! Warning! . . . Huh? Who is speaking?"

"Over here! Can you understand me?"

"Of course I can understand you. Am I not speaking in your language."

"Well, yes, as a matter of fact, you are. How are you managing that?"

"I overheard conversation and analyzed the linguistic components and identified the language. It is one of millions that I carry in my permanent storage area."

"You know English?"

"Is that what you call it? It is merely listed as a subdialect of an obscure planetary culture somewhere in the galaxy."

"Of course, it's Earth! We're from Earth! Tell me, can you help us get back there?"

"No, I am afraid not. As you can see, I am somewhat indisposed."

"I see," the doctor said, nodding. "Listen, we've never run into anything like you before. Are we to understand that you're an artificial consciousness? You're a self-conscious machine?"

The robot flailed spastically. "Horribly self-conscious. Do I have rust under my armpits? I cannot seem to move properly. My entire assembly seems somehow locked."

"Gee Doc," Troy said. "Just like the Tin Man in the *Wizard of Oz*. There's got to be some lubricant around here. All we've got to do is oil his joints."

"Talbot, don't be absurd. This is not some fantasy creature. This is—"

"My lubricant can is just yonder, over by that pile of chemical containers. Alas, too bad I cannot lubricate my innermost gangloid synaptoid registers—perhaps that would aid my psycho-mechanical dilemma."

"Which is?"

"Multiple personalities," croaked the robot.

"Ah. This particular personality seems harmless enough. How about the others."

"Do not fear. All follow Yizzak Ozmiroid's rules of robotics."

"Yizzak Ozmiroid? That sounds familiar. Wait a minute, you don't mean . . . well, I forget his name, but it's similar. Some youngster who's been showing up in the science-fiction pulps."

"In the spacetime continuum presently governing the bulk of the universe, the rules of robotics devised by Yizzak Ozmiroid, the galaxy's foremost expert on the subject, apply."

"Which are?"

"I will recite them for you."

The robot made a sound not unlike throat clearing, then began:

"The first law: A robot may not injure a biological being, or through inaction allow a biological being to come to harm, except in the case of a biological being's being a pain in the posterior, in which case a few whops upside the head will be sufficient."

"Very interesting," said Dr. Dimension.

"The second law: A robot must obey the orders given it by a biological being except where such orders would conflict with the first law, and also excepting really stupid orders such as, 'Oh, and by the way, do the windows, too,' because robots don't do windows."

"Fascinating."

"The third law: A robot must protect its own existence when such protection does not conflict with the first or second laws, except when the biomass *really* hits the roto-impeller, in which case it's every being for himself and to hell with the first, second, and third laws!"

"I kind of like that last one," the doctor said.

"Doc," said Troy. "This guy's been here awhile. He'd probably know where the spare parts are. We could search days for what we need."

"Parts? We have many parts here," said the robot. "You may not have noticed, you have landed on the trash planet, abounding with all kinds of junk."

"We crashed, actually," Dr. Dimension said, "which is why we're so hard up."

"Many spaceships crash here," the robot said. "I have a dim memory in my neurodes of one on which I arrived crashing. Eventually, no doubt, I will cough up the whole scenario." All this continuing in monotones, accompanied by flashing lights. "A further search of my memory disks has revealed information on your world of origin. You are humans from Terra, yes?"

"I'm human. Talbot here is humanoid," said Doc.

"Gosh, thanks, Doc!" said the professor's amanuensis. "Just call me Troy."

"This creature looks human as well," the robot said. "Whereas I, having a head, a torso, two manipulating appendages and two ambulatory appendages, am a humanoid mechanism."

"You're a robot, in other words," said Dr. D.

"We prefer the term 'electromechanical individual.' "

"That's a mouthful. I say you're a robot."

"As you wish. But as I am fully sentient, I am not, technically speaking, a robot, as that is a generic term. I am a roboid."

"Roboid?"

"Sounds kinda complicated," said Troy, understandably confused.

"Humans, humanoids. Robots, roboids. Surely you can see the etymological parallel."

"Look," Dr. Dimension broke in, "we haven't got time to discuss etymology, or the roboids and bees, either—"

"By the way, what's your name?" asked Troy.

"Erob," Said the electromechanical individual.

"Ee-rob? Funny name. So, you're Erob the roboid?"

"That is correct."

"I still say you're a robot," declared Dr. D.

"As you wish. Remember the second law."

"I remember. What's more important, can you help us?"

"As I must obey the laws, I am duty bound to assist you in any way that I am able."

"Doc, he can't help us unless we lube him up," suggested Troy.

"Hmm. Well, what do you say, Erob?"

"Deal."

"Fair enough."

Troy began digging the robot out of the pile of trash while Doc retrieved the container of lubricant, which looked for all the world like an old-fashioned oil can, the sort that would not have looked anachronistic in the hand of a turn-of-the-century railroad engineer. Doc turned it over to his assistant, who had trouble with multiplication tables but knew his way around a rusted machine.

Troy began applying fluid to the robot's various joints and junctures.

Sounds issued from the robot's speaker grille that sounded very much like sighs.

Troy finished up the anointing of the joints, and the robot flexed its arms and legs. With some difficulty, it waded out of the drifted sand that had imprisoned it, and stood fully erect.

"Thank you, new friends." It's gearbox purred contentedly. "It just so happens there is a pile of old space-drive engines over there—and I think I noticed starship hull-caulkers a few piles away. You helped the right robot."

The robot proceeded to clank away toward the hills of trash.

"Feel like doing a little spaceship engine shopping?" Dr. asked of his protégé.

"I hate those pushy salesmen, don't you?"

"I do think you're getting worse, Talbot, my son."

* * *

Sometime later, Dr. Dimension and Erob the roboid emerged from between two piles of clutter into a clearing. Behind them, pushing a battered shopping cart overflowing with mechanical odds and ends, puffed Troy Talbot.

"There it is," said Doc. "Just over the rise."

"Oh yes," said the robot. "Of Pizon manufacture, no?"

"Yes. How perceptive of you."

"Grunt, grunt," said Troy, perspiring.

"So, new friend Doctor Dime-novel."

"That's Dimension, Rob. You can call me Demetrios Demopoulos if you've having trouble."

"So, new friend 'Doc'—"

"That'll will do."

"—What is your destination?"

"We want to go back home," groaned Troy. "We've got to get back to Earth."

"Where have I heard that before?" said the robot.

Dr. Dimension said, "We want to claim our university grant and proceed with my landmark work in physics. Only after what we've been through, I've come to a landmark scientific conclusion."

"Do tell," requested Erob.

"Physics is a jungle."

"An apt metaphor. We can discuss that later. In the meantime, we should make haste to your spacecraft. It will be dark soon, and many predators emerge on the trash planet then that are dangerous to fleshy life."

"Good idea. You want to bustle it along there, Talbot? It would seem there may soon be monsters gnashing at your tail if not."

"I would help," said Erob, "but my spinal shaft is still slightly out of whack and my shocks need an overhaul."

"That's okay, Rob. Talbot's got the old college spirit, haven't you, guy? Just remember, Diane needs us."

"Who or what is this Diane creature?"

"His girlfriend, my faithful sidekick—and an all-around good gal. Round in just the right places. She could keep even your joints lubricated, Rob."

" 'She.' Ah, a female human. How exciting. Does she go for mechanical men?"

"Say, buddy," Troy warned. "Keep your mitts to yourself, okay?"

"Just haul your trash, big fellow," said Dr. D. "We're almost there."

'There' was a Pizon ship tantalizingly close on the horizon, poking up crookedly among the heaps of refuse. In truth, Dr. Demopolous never thought he'd grow so fond of a Pizon ship. At the moment, though, it appeared to be their one hope of getting out of this mad universe and back to the halls of academia where life was merely demented.

"Ouch!"

Dr. D. turned just in time to see Troy going down. He banged into the tilting shopping cart, and the articles so precariously piled there threatened to tumble. Erob skedaddled out of the way, again warning about danger, but Doc D. ran forward and threw his weight in a scientifically applied fashion and thus saved their mechanical bacon.

"Sorry, Doc," said Troy struggling up. "I tripped over this thing here."

"Talbot, you lummox! Put it down and help me!"

Talbot pocketed the offensive article and then bolted up to assist Doc. Soon the pile was steady again.

Doc spied something off to the right. "There's something we might be able to use. Be right back."

Troy took out the object he'd tripped over. It was a silver ring, but a curious one, set with a rather dull stone. Still, it was rather pretty. The thought occurred to him that he might give it to Diane. He'd have to get the ring cut down, though. It was ridiculously big, even for his own thick fingers.

"Robot, you know anything about jewelry?"

"I can analyze any mineral."

"Can you tell me if this is worth something?"

"Put it in my analyzer slot."

"Right there? Okay."

Troy did so. He waited while the robot hummed and clicked.

"Well?" he asked.

"It is a strange metal, and an even stranger stone. I will need time."

"How much."

"I'll get back to you."

Troy shrugged good-naturedly. "Hokay."

Doc returned empty-handed.

"False alarm. Let's go."

Farther along the trail, near the ship, they discovered tracks in the sand, tracks made by some sort of huge lumbering creature, or . . .

"Yes," Erob said. "An imperial-armored carrier. A telltale sign. Troopers were here."

"Troopers?" echoed Doc.

"Troopers from an imperial starship."

Doc snapped his fingers. "So that's who nabbed Diane and the others. Starship troopers!"

"Imperial starship troopers."

"By what logic of . . . empire, you say?"

"In this part of the galaxy, the empire of Ovaria holds sway."

"Ovaria? That's the name of the imperial planet?"

"Correct."

"I'd hate to be a citizen of this galaxy. Any chance our friends might have been taken there?"

"They might still be in transit between planets, but there is indeed a distinct possibility that Ovaria is their final destination."

"Any chance we might be able to get there if we fix the ship?"

"Probabilities favor this occurrence, although blow-ups do happen. I will assist. I could use a break from this place. It is getting a little old."

"If this goes on, we'll be getting tired of it, too. We're all weary of being rolling stones," said the Doc.

"How're chances you might be able to set us on the glory road back to the green hills of Earth?"

"It is beyond my horizon, but I might have its location stored in my memory areas. However, those data are not immediately accessible at the moment. I will continue the search."

"Orphans of the sky, that's us. Any assistance would be welcome."

"Gee—maybe we could get Erob a job in the movies," suggested Troy.

"That's ridiculous, he'd be a misfit," said Doc, although in truth the notion was rather appealing. He always thought no one quite got inventor roles right in the flicks, not even Boris Karloff, his favorite actor.

"Um—guys?" said Troy. "Maybe it's just a twilight shadow—but did there used to be a great big trash heap just a few yards away with antennae and tentacles and a gaping, drooling set of sharp fangs?"

"Talbot, remind me to send you to the university infirmary for a complete physical, when we get back. If we get back. Now wheel this cart into the hold and let's get working."

"But, Doc, that thing there—"

Doc looked. "That pile of junk? I will fear no evil like that."

"But, Doc!—"

But Erob the robot already had his sensors trained on the object that Troy Talbot was talking about.

"Danger! Danger!" he shouted.

Chapter Six

Imagine, if you will, a planet fantastical, a miracle of a world, a distant paradise of balmy breezes and white sand beaches under a soothing alien sun ...

Conceive a world wreathed in angel clouds, feathery with dazzle and wonder, steeped in scents of exotic jasmine and hibiscus and other heavenly flowers, wafting on breezes that sing through the palms in choirs of sweeping gorgeous melody. Imagine vast green continents, lush with all the things that fulfill your heart's desire to overflowing.

Meditate, contemplate, hold fast to the images this reverie may conjure.

Got it?

Good. You'll need something pleasant to hang onto. Next stop: Ovaria.

Ovaria was the next stop as well for Diane Derry, along with Drs. Vernon and Wussman, and it was not voluntary.

Batten the hatches. Brace yourselves.

Arrrrr!

A great historian once commented that while the history of man is replete with evil and cruelty, the history of woman is merely odious.

This does not hold true through the humanoid universe (or the universoid, as Erob the roboid might term it.)

On some planets, some empires, the history of mankind is merely odious—while womankind gets all the laurels of infamy. Such a planet is Ovaria, such an empire is hers. The female pronoun is appropriate, for the ruler of this planet and its empire was the Empress Estrogena, a woman who, shall we say, had a will of iron but was lacking that mineral in her diet.

The Empress Estrogena owned the trash planet.

The Empress Estrogena made a pretty penny off the place, collecting fees for unlimited dumping, selling discarded items if possible, and leasing land to toxic-waste-loving aliens and the occasional housing project developer.

Security on the trash planet had been beefed up lately, for very important reasons. (More later.)

Normally, trespassers and scavengers were summarily vaporized or thrown into some Ovarian dungeon to rot, mostly without even the benefit of a trial, or even a decent lynch mob. Lately, however, Estrogena had been paying personal attention to the arrival of interlopers on the trash planet. Surveillance satellites orbiting that noxious world had immediately detected the approach and forced landing of the *Mudlark,* and had posthaste sent subspace communication signals back to Ovaria, where they were duly noted by security officials. The Empress was apprised. She immediately dispatched an imperial cruiser, docked not far away on a moon of a gas giant in the trash planet's solar system, to investigate.

Thus was Diane, along with Drs. Vernon and Wussman, brought to this august lady's especial attention.

Diane Derry usually trusted police.

Diane Derry normally adored soldiers or any man in uniform.

However, these ill-mannered ruffians in armored space suits, who had handcuffed her and stuffed her inside a tiny holding cell no bigger than a school locker somewhere inside their souped-up landing craft, had simply not been gentlemen. Their suits were nifty, true, and most of them had nice broad shoulders, and they looked very military and strong and all that—of

course, she hadn't seen any of their faces behind those
smoked-glass (tinted plastic?) helmets—well, no
matter—but they most emphatically did *not* know how
to treat a girl.

Not only Diane had been kidnapped; Vivian and
Wussy had been, too, bound and gagged and unceremoniously tucked into their own reserved lockers. It
was hard to breathe inside. Diane had heard the engines whine, felt acceleration drag her downward,
painfully forcing her knees against the narrow sides of
the cell; then, once again in null-gravity, she'd experienced the peculiar frisson of a spacetime jump: a
prickly, tingling sensation all over.

The trip here hadn't been long at all. The invaders
must have high-tailed it to a nearby planet, or perhaps
to some hidden base on the trash planet. Anyway,
someplace close.

Soon, gravity returned. Diane felt a thump—the
ship's touching down, no doubt. Then nothing for a
few minutes as she fought against her restraints, trying
to get free.

There wasn't time. In very short order the locker
door flew open, and she and her companions were led
out through spartan corridors and then jostled nastily
down a gangplank.

They had landed at a busy spaceport. Hundreds of
towering spaceships perched on launching platforms,
ready to jump at the sky. Fuel fumes choked the air.
Hellish plumes of smoke and fire rumbled up through
grates in the floors. Clanking machinery was every-
where, echoing through the dense air.

In the distance, vertiginous skyscrapers rose from a
chemical fog, backlighted by a huge ocher moon rising
in the dim daylight.

Diane had seen Dr. D.'s collection of science-fiction
pulps, and this panorama certainly belonged on the
cover of *Spicy Space Stories*. Only this particular city
complex looked grittier than any pulp magazine illus-
trator's handiwork. Wasn't the future in space sup-

posed to be all shiny and metallic and modern . . . and *clean*? This place was positively scruffy.

The starship troopers handed their captives off to a phalanx of soldiers in fancier outfits, all gold braid and blue piping. While these guys did not exactly molest their female charges, neither were they careful about where they placed their hands. Even Wussman was not exempt from some undignified handling. One fey guard winked at him and leered. Wussy smiled weakly back.

The trussed-up trio were jammed uncomfortably into a silver-winged car, which loosed itself from the surly bonds of gravity and flew up to join a congested stream of traffic cruising at building-top level in and around the city.

Soot and smog hung in oily clouds. Diane would have coughed if she could. Her eyes watered. The driver cursed and swore—in a language that sounded like a cross between German and Spanish—his wrath directed at the heavy traffic. Finally, he banked and sailed into a dark tunnel, at the far side of which he alighted on a platform. A security check later, they were flying again.

Diane's eyes cleared enough that she was able to lean forward and peer out the smudged window at what lay before them. "Hmmmph!" she said.

Beside her, the two academics were leaning forward, likewise entranced by the sight before them.

"Hmmmph!" they agreed.

Before them, nestled in a blooming nimbus of spectral light, was a palace the like of which was never seen on Earth. It was something out of Hans Christian Andersen, if that famous Dane had been in the habit of taking lysergic acid. It was a fairy palace with towers of craggy stone, cupolas of jagged obsidian, glittering diamond-faceted windows, turrets carved with devilish faces, campaniles shaped like strange animals: a surrealist artist's idea of a fairy-tale castle.

Not the home of the Ice Queen . . . perhaps the home of the Leather Queen. Portions of the walls had a hide texture, peppered with metal studs and spangles that sparkled like zirconium. The entire architectural style was a melange of Berlin underground café crossed with Hieronymus Bosch, the Bauhaus, and a few off-the-wall ideas toward a design for a theme park for psychopaths.

The craft landed with a bump and a grind on a deck, and the guards yanked their Terran prisoners from the backseat and hustled them over what amounted to a narrow ramp thrown across a chasm. Dizzy-making stuff, indeed. One glance, and Diane chose not to look anywhere but straight ahead. She kept her eyes glued to the slick metal surface of the ramp, making sure each footstep was properly placed.

Past doors like yawning jaws, through cavernous tunnels with flickering torches in sconces that gave off a foul smell, and then down, down, into the bowels of the palace, with walls the color of bone china but with patterns of fine wire running through them. Electronic circuitry? Curious.

The maze of tunnels finally gave way toward a wide door that opened into a huge marble hall, a decadent maharishi's nightmare. Dim figures—servants? courtiers? sycophants?—nervously huddled in the shadows. The palace smelled like the aftermath of a Roman bacchanalia, complete with vomitorium. Huge tigerlike creatures chained to the walls snored fitfully and stank excrementitiously. In the front of this arched chamber sat a raised dais topped by a jewel-studded throne, hooded guards with hobnail boots and jagged axes and biceps the size of pumpkins standing to either side.

The trio were dumped on an elaborately embroidered rug just short of the platform. Their bonds and gags were removed. Diane did not think flight was a choice. However, it was good to be able to talk again.

"Goodness!" she said. "I really would like to have a talk with the interior decorator. A few windows and a lighter color palette would do wonders."

Wussman's eyes bulged, as though he had become suddenly hyperthyroid. "Viv, dear, it looks like that decorator's sketch for your apartment! What was his name—that nice young man with the open-toe sandals?"

"Bunny Funkhauser. It is rather fetching, isn't it?" agreed Viv, coolly assaying the palace's appointments. "And those outfits! *Tres* chic!"

"I don't know, guys, seems all a bit dark and gloomy and depressing to me," allowed Diane. "You'd think that people as obviously rich as these would want to add a little bit of joy and perkiness to their day."

"How callow you are, Miss Derry," said Vivian Vernon with arch condescension. "Don't you understand? Every centimeter of this room . . . hell, this whole palace screams with one concept."

"Questionable taste?"

"No. Power."

"Domination," squeaked Wussman.

"Puissance."

"Yeah, P.U. is right," Diane said, wrinkling her nose.

"Humiliation," quavered Wussman.

Dr. Vivian Vernon's thin eyebrows raised dramatically, and her forefinger rose like an exclamation point.

"Control."

"Oh, Viv, Viv," whined Wussman. "When are we going to get some quality time?"

A whip snapped inches from Diane's ear. "Silence!" snarled a hooded officer. "Her Imperial Bitchiness approaches."

A fanfare erupted from somewhere, probably hidden loudspeakers; Diane saw no trumpeters. The music was strange. Judging from all the atmospheric accoutrements of this dark, funereal chamber, Diane had expected something like Wagner's *Ring* done by musicians on barbiturates. Instead, what emerged was a bright jazzy tune, tinkly and upbeat and infectiously rhythmic, just enough to set Diane's right toe tapping. Spotlights lighted up a bank of curtains. A guard with a executioner-style hood pulled back a wing of cloth, and announced in a stentorian bass rumble:

"Welcome, gentlebeings, to the Empress Estrogena

Show, starring Her Serene and Transcendent Imperial Bitchiness—Estrogena, Empress of Ovaria, and Ruler of Just About All Space and Time! And now, without further ado, we present the star of our show . . . he-e-e-e-e-re's Genie!"

The music turned into what sounded like a signature piece, a bright and peppy production number. All over the chamber, motion-picture screens came to life. The scene they showed was the dais—or stage. Obviously, they weren't exactly moving-picture screens, exactly, for they were showing the action instantaneously.

"Wow," Dr. Wussman said. "I've *heard* about television, but I've never—"

"Be quiet, you fool!" Vivian whispered hoarsely.

The curtain parted. Into the spotlights danced a short middle-aged woman dressed in a tuxedo top over fishnet stockings and high heels. She tap-danced merrily out onto the stage, all smiles and dimples and age lines. Her thighs bulged, her ankles tapered the wrong way, but her shiny shoes gleamed and the spots sparkled off her scintillating teeth. She took off her top hat and let it fall down her arm, but failed to catch it. She swore and stooped over stiffly and picked it up. Putting the hat back on, she broke into a display of terpsichorean skill, throwing her malacca cane back and forth between hands.

"Boy, she's pretty terrible," said Dr. Wussman.

It was true. She was no Ginger Rogers or Ruby Keeler. Her style was a bit like a spastic Shirley Temple's, perhaps, or a that of a Busby Berkeley girl twenty years overdue for retirement.

When the rousing number was finished, the dancer tapped out a couple of grace note clicks on the floor and then bowed.

The dark audience applauded resoundingly. Diane and company stared, jaws somewhere in the vicinity of their ankles.

The whip snapped again, this time closer to Diane's posterior and this time with a touch of sting.

Diane clapped.

"Applaud! Applaud!"

The Empress Estrogena giggled. She bowed like a boy dancer, then curtsied like a girl. She handed off the top hat and cane to a stagehand.

"Thank you! Thank you! Tee hee!" She blew kisses. "You all are just so kind and sweet. Just this morning I was telling Gorf—You all know Gorf, don't you? He's my consort, or one of them—I was telling Gorf, you know, we have just got the very best people to be empress for! You all are just the greatest!"

Estrogena was hardly Shirley Temple. She was far past her prime. Her cheeks were rouged and her eyes were heavily shaded, and the heady smell of lilac came in the miasma of scent that wafted from her, along with jasmine bath powder and other flowery odors.

"Have you all been good little subjects today?" she said, her voice chipper and gay.

"Yes, Empress!" chorused the response.

Estrogena wagged her finger and clucked her tongue. "Haven't we all been just a little bit naughty today?"

"Well, maybe a little," they answered.

"Fine. Let the fun begin."

Giggling, she skipped away behind a painted screen. In a flurry, the fishnet stockings were hung over the edge, while music poured in a swing groove from the speakers.

When she emerged, Estrogena had on a white lace gown and carried a gold cylinder that the Earth people took to be an imperial scepter.

"Welcome to the show," she said. "Listen, have we got a show for you today. First, we have a controversial crime case. One of my ministers is accused of, shall we say, dipping his hand in the imperial till?" She giggled. "He's guilty as hell, but we'll have him out here for an interview. And next . . ." Estrogena's face went blank. "Heck, I forget—"

A whisper came from the shadows.

"What? Sorry, folks, that's Morf, my producer. What did you say, Morfie, baby? Oh, that's right, the tres-

passers. We have—how many?—three. Three trespassers who were caught snooping around one of my most
important strategic planets—something—what, Morf?
Oh, on Dumpstron? One of the trash-dumping plane-
toids? Right. We'll see what these—where do they
come from, Morfie? You don't know. Ladies and
gentlebeings, my producer doesn't know where these
trashy aliens come from. He's thorough, Morf is."
Estrogena laughed hideously. "Morf, you say you're
looking for a change of employment?"

The audience giggled.

"A thousand pardons, Empress Genie!"

"Well, anyway, folks, we'll hear what these pesky
aliens have to say—"

"That's us!" whispered Dr. Wussman.

"Shut up!" Vivian gave him two fingers in the ribs.

"Ooof!"

"Shhhh!"

"Okay," said Estrogena brightly, smiling into the
cameras—well, they were most likely cameras, those
metallic spheres floating about. A flock of about a
dozen of them flitted here and there around the general
area of the stage, like a swarm of bees. What cameras
would be doing levitating like that, with nothing to
support them, and without making the slightest bit of
noise, was anybody's guess.

"And then," Estrogena continued, "we'll have Dr.
Prissykins with his Massive Water Intake diet. It's a
wonderful diet, folks. Takes the pounds off like butter
melting. All you do is drink a total of fifty glasses of
water a day. Easy. I'm ordering my entire imperial
guard to go on it immediately. Well, that's the show.
We'll be right back after this commercial!"

The television screens went to a colorful montage of
shots of Estrogena in various poses and attending to
various duties of her high station. An announcer's
voice began reciting her praises in the highest compli-
mentary terms.

As the "commercial" ran, Estrogena was attended to

by various servants, one of whom touched up the Empress's makeup with a fine brush.

The commercial lasted a little over a minute; the TV screens went dark for a moment, then faded into a live shot of the Empress in close up. Her face was caked with makeup. Bat's wings of eyeshadow fluttered over heavily rouged cheeks. Her mouth was a huge wet cherry-red kiss that could suck the life out of the kissee.

"Hi, folks," she said with withering warmth. "Our first guest is a real slimeball, and I'd like to bring him out for you. You know, I love all my wonderful subjects, and I know they work hard for their empress, filling the imperial coffers with their hard-earned tax dollars—I realize that the tax rates are tough—what's the top rate, Morf?—eighty percent?—of course, only the very rich pay that ... Anyway, I love all my faithful subjects and respect them and care for them and want them to have all the wonderful things that the imperial state can give them—lots of wonderful food, and adequate housing, and free medical care, and marvelous schools for the kiddies. Oh, listen, I know things aren't perfect! I mean there are shortages, and you have to stand in line to buy a roll of toilet paper, for pity's sake, and that *hurts* me, because it's nasty to have to stand in line, not to mention the loss of productivity! Well, I mean to tell you—when I think of all that hardship, when I think of all the pain and suffering and deprivation my wonderful, faithful, loving subjects have had to go through during this economic crisis that we're having—well, I get steamed when creeps like our first guest get their greedy little hands in the imperial treasury and steal ... yes, I said *steal* from my marvelous, wonderfully loving and caring and hard-working people of Ovaria. Okay, Morf, send the no-good worthless slimeball out here! Let's have a look at Mr. Sticky Fingers!" She giggled at the audience as though they were all in on some huge joke.

A pale, sallow-faced man in a dark, neat suit was brought up on the platform. Empress Estrogena danced back and hopped up onto her throne, dangling one leg over an armrest so that her flounced petticoats were exposed.

"Minister Seskwith!" she proclaimed jovially. "What have you to say for yourself?"

Seskwith's face was haggard and drawn. His frightened eyes pleaded. "Your Majesty, I am innocent. I don't know how the money got into my account. It must have been a plant, by my enemies."

Estrogena threw back her head and hooted a hyena laugh. "You must be kidding! You— enemies? People like you don't have enemies. You don't rate *enemies*, honey pie. A corrupt little boil like you gets lanced, and that's about the size of it."

"I was framed, madam!"

"Don't make me laugh, Seskwith."

"But I swear it's true, madam! The palace swarms with plotters and schemers and—"

"Are you implying that my imperial administration is corrupt?"

"Oh, no, madam! Never! It's just that there are those few of your ministers who —"

"My ministers are the best in the galaxy! I pick them, so they have to be good! Isn't that right?"

"Absolutely correct, as always, Your Imperial Personage! But—"

"But me no buts, you egregious pile of phlegm! Every once in a while—I say, every once in a *great* while—I make a mistake, and my talent for reading character lets me down. It's my migraine problem. It's been killing me lately! I mean, the doctors keep stuffing me with pills—well, never mind, that's a topic for another show. Morf, remind me to do a show on how greedy doctors dominate our lives and how they all should be stuffed into a proton disintegrator for the gaggle of quacks they really are! Never mind, I'll bring it up at the next production meeting. Remind me! Okay—back to this crummy creep, this thief, this— what, Morf? Questions from the audience? Okay, folks, it's—what's that? Take a call first? Okay, let's have the first call-in! Go ahead, caller!"

"Hello?" A female voice came out of the air.

"Are you there, caller?"

"Empress Genie?"

"I'm here, sweetie, go ahead with your question."

"Empress Genie, I just want to say that I watch your show all the time, and I just adore it!"

"That's sweet of you, honey. Of course, you have to watch it, don't you? I mean, it's one of my imperial edicts that none of my subjects will ever miss a show."

"Oh, but we want to watch the show, Empress Genie! We love the show! I for one wouldn't want to miss a second! It's so ... informative, so ... well, it speaks to the important issues of the day!"

Estrogena gave forth a gushingly affectionate smile. "You're so sweet to say that, dearie. Now, what's your question?"

"Well, it's kind of a statement. I'm really mad. Here's this man, Sexwith—Seckith ... whatever his name is, and he's robbing all the poor children and the sick people out there in our wonderful empire, taking food out of the mouths of our workers, and I think it stinks!"

The audience erupted into vociferous applause.

"And I'd also like to say that I think he ought to be killed. Not quick, but real slow, so he suffers and screams and feels a lot of pain. In fact, that's too good for the likes of this bastard! ... Oh, I'm sorry. By that, I didn't mean to say anything derogatory about unwed mothers and their babies! I just would really like to get this creep!"

The audience hooted their approval.

Seskwith's elaborate bow tie seemed to wilt with his dismay.

"Thanks, honey, I'm real proud of you! Well, Minister Seskwith, what do you have to say to that?"

"Madam, I beg you! I'm innocent. At least give me a hearing, a trial! I may be able to prove my innocence!"

"Fat chance, baby. You've had it. You were caught with the goods. However, let it not be said that Estrogena is hasty, or rushes to judgment. In fact, I don't like to be judgmental. It's nasty to put your own value judgments on people. I'm all for justice, don't get me wrong. It's just that evidence is overwhelmingly on the side of guilt here. But still, I want our minister here to get a fair shake."

Seskwith went to his knees, reached out, took the hem of her gown, and kissed it. "Madam, you are most kind and merciful!"

"Such lovely hands you have, Master Secretary!" said Queen Estrogena. "Sometimes, I can read a person's palm and discover whether or not he or she is good or evil. I'm psychic, you know. Aren't I, Morf?"

"Oh yes, Your Grace. One of the preeminent talents in the empire!"

"Remember the show we did on psychics? That's when I found out I had a gift, too. Of course, I'd been doing psychic things all my life, but I never realized that this marvelous, marvelous gift I have to see into people's character was a psychic one."

"And you're so good at it, Empress Genie!"

"Thanks, Morf. Oh, gentlebeings, he is so good to me, Morf is. He's a doll. Just a doll. Anyway, hold out that mitt of yours, Seskwith. Way out there, that's it."

Tentatively, the third secretary held out his hand.

With a horrid honk of victorious laughter, Estrogena flourished her scepter. In an instant, a bright beam of light flashed out of one end of it, forming a shimmering green flame shaped like a sword. She swung the thing, and the plasma "blade" went through Seskwith's wrist.

The severed hand dropped to the floor. Seskwith screamed and clutched his wrist, which had begun to spurt bright pink blood.

"Yuck!" Diane said, horrified.

"Pink blood," Vivian mused. "They aren't altogether human, are they?"

"There you go," Estrogena crowed. "You won't be dipping that hand in my till again!"

She threw back her henna-colored, beehive-hairdoed head and roared with laughter.

Still clutching his spurting arm, the man was led off. The empress picked up the fallen hand and waved good-bye with it.

"Anyone else want to give me a hand?" she said.

Riotous laughter.

"We're doomed," said Wussman. "Doomed."

"Shhh," said Vivian Vernon. "Just remember that we didn't do anything wrong. She has nothing on us!"

"I'll bet you poor Seskwith didn't do a thing either," Wussman said gloomily.

Estrogena tossed the lopped-off appendage after the supposed sinner. Then she clapped her hands in delight. "Now then, should we do another commercial? Morfie, sweetheart? We have to fill this segment? Okay, then, let's bring on the alien scavengers."

The guards pushed Diane and company closer to the dais, while the band played syncopated jazz music that was serving as a bridge between portions of this outré performance.

"Well then," said the Empress. She rose from her jewel-bedizened throne and peered at them with distaste, much as a child might look at a bunch of worms discovered underneath a rock. "Who are you?"

"I'm Diane Derry, and this is Dr. Vernon and Dr. Wussman. We're from Earth. We're lost."

Diane looked over at Vernon and Wussman. They said nothing. They may be shifty sometimes, she thought, but they aren't stupid. Diane was sure they knew their only hope of rescue was dear Dr. Dimension, and that if they said anything about Doc D., these troopers would just sprint back to the trash planet and capture them.

"A likely story. Do you know what I think? I think that you people are scavengers. Mostly, though, I think you're after the M'Guh Fon."

The audience hissed.

"Well?" demanded Estrogena, waving the scepter warningly. "Are you?"

"Megaphone?" said Wussman, barely able to keep his voice from cracking. "What's that?"

"Look, Empress Genie," said Viv. "I think you and I are two peas in a pod. Maybe we should have us a little pajama party together and a good girl-to-girl chat."

"Shut up, silly." Estrogena tapped Viv on the side of the head with the scepter. "This Diane Derry person is clearly in charge. She's a blonde! And what's the policy toward blondes around here, subjects?" said the empress, patting her mass of teased hair and batting her pale eyes.

"We're fond of blondes!" echoed the room.

"Very good. I'm so proud of you. So confess, Derry Diane. You were looking for the M'Guh Fon, weren't you? Have you any idea where it is? You see, I've had my troopers searching for it for months, without any success. And I dearly, dearly would like to find that M'Guh Fon. Do you know why?"

"Why?" asked Diane innocently.

"Because, sweetheart, with the M'Guh Fon, I would not just be Empress of Just About All Space and Time. I would be Absolute Ruler of All Space and Time and the Rest of It! I'd be the most powerful woman in the universe. Just *think* of the good I could do, the wonderful, warm, caring, altruistic deeds I could do for the poor, unfortunate downtrodden subjects of my expanded empire. Why, there'd be no limit to how many wonderful things I could accomplish, how many wrongs I could right, how many just causes I could champion. It would be the dawn of a new era in the universe! Not only would I be able to wipe out greed and selfishness and naughty behavior here on Ovaria and a few other planets, but I'd be able to do it in the whole galaxy! Maybe even all the galaxies! With the power the M'Guh Fon would give me, I could come down hard on any pinch-hearted or uncaring or piggy behavior, or any general avaricious nastiness anywhere in the known universe and environs! My reach would be long, long indeed. Any stinginess anywhere would be instantly dealt with."

The scepter came alive again, spouting its blade of plasma flame. The Empress swished it around.

"There'd be complete equality! No one would stick his head up above his neighbors'. Everyone would show kindness, sympathy, tenderness, mercy, and compassion."

Grasping the scepter sword with both hands, Empress Genie wooshed the fiery blade around in a vicious swipe.

"Or else!"

Dismayed, the Earth captives had stepped back out of the way. Estrogena paused for effect. Presently she doused the plasma blade, sat back in her throne, and said, "Now do you understand, honey pie?"

Diane said, "Perhaps if you gave us an idea about what exactly this muffin looks like."

"M'Guh Fon," corrected Estrogena.

Diane tried it. "Muhguhfon—"

"No, two words, dearie. M'Guh, with a little breath between the M and the Guh."

"M'Guh."

"Then, Fon, with a shortish O in there."

"Fon."

"M'Guh Fon."

"M'Guh . . . Fon?"

"Good," said Estrogena.

"What's it look like?" Diane asked.

"To tell you the absolute truth, I haven't the foggiest. I was hoping you would tell me."

"How can we tell you, when we've never seen it either?" said Diane. "We've never even heard of it, much less seen it."

"Or so you say." Estrogena twirled a strand of sticky sprayed hair thoughtfully. "Personally—don't take offense—but I think you're lying. I think you're scavengers . . . Hmmm. You wouldn't be working for Baron Skulkrak, would you? Or maybe Zorin, the academician?"

"Who?"

"Never mind, it will all come out eventually. You people have to face a few facts. We can't help you unless you want to be helped. Of course, there are ways of finding out anyway. Such as the Mindscooper."

Geoffrey Wussman swallowed hard. "Uh, what's that?"

"Oh, a device for jogging the memory of people who conveniently forget things. Would you like to know how it works?"

"Well, I'm not sure."

"Well, I'll tell you. It's a wonderful machine that scoops out the subject's brain. The brain is then pulped and liquefied and run through a battery of analytical machines that sort through the memory content of the higher brain functions. Just sifts through all the misty, watercolor memories, and somewhere swimming among them, usually, is the data we need."

"Uh . . ."

Estrogena got up from her throne and came toward the prisoners.

"Oh, you want to know what happens to the brain afterward? Well, we do our best to thicken it up and re-form the tissue the way it was, though I'm afraid the task is somewhat akin to putting an egg back together once it's been broken. However, as I said, we do our *level* best."

"Thank you for sharing that with us," Wussman said dryly.

"Of course we have other, more direct, much more primitive methods. Sometimes they work best."

Vivian seemed interested. "Such as?"

"Oh, I like the Nutcracker best," Estrogena said. "It's simply a steel band that goes about the head and is slowly tightened. Very slowly."

"That would be bad for a person with chronic migraine," Vivian observed.

"Oh, very bad. But you wouldn't notice the migraine."

"And that squeezes the information out of the subject?"

Estrogena smiled crookedly. "That, or it squeezes the brains right out of them. Maybe we should try this method first. The analysis method usually takes a few weeks. I'm not a patient person, unfortunately. One of my faults. When I know what's right and what I have to do, I get impatient. I know, it's a character flaw, but it's one I can live with. I mean, none of us is perfect."

Estrogena thought for a moment, then said, "Yes, the Nutcracker will do for starters. On one of them." She pointed at Wussman. "That one."

"Me?" Wussman's face drained. "But ... but ... I don't know anything!"

"You seem such an intelligent creature," the Empress declared. "Big bald head, weak chin, pudgy body. All the signs of an intellectual. No, I think you know quite a lot."

"I'm one of the stupidest creatures in the world ... no, the universe! I know *nothing*. I see *nothing*!"

"I can vouch for his stupidity," Vivian said.

"Me, too," Diane said.

"Oh, I'll bet. Sorry, honey, we have to begin somewhere. But first, let's see what our call-in viewers have to say about all this. May we have the next call, please?"

A disembodied male voice this time.

"Phil? I have a question for Vladimir."

Estrogena's baggy face contorted. "Who in the world are Phil and Vladimir? Morfie, what's going on?"

"Technical difficulties."

"Well, get them cleared up this minute!"

"Right away!"

"Why don't we break for a commercial?"

The show broke for a commercial, and again Estrogena was beset by a swarm of servants and technicians.

Diane leaned over to Vivian. "We'll have to try to make a break for it."

Vivian scowled. "Forget it. We couldn't run five steps without being nabbed. Be sensible. They won't get anything out of Wussman, because he knows nothing. Maybe that will convince her that she's wasting her time with us."

"And then what?"

Vivian shrugged. "Who knows. But if we have any chance at all to escape, that would be the best time to try it."

"Okay, we're back, folks! Let's have that call. Is the caller there?"

"Yes, Empress Genie! We love you!"

"Thank you, dearie, I love you, too. You're so kind. Now, what's your question?"

"My question is this. Kill the sons of bitches! Kill 'em! Line 'em up against the wall and shoot 'em dead and then chop their bodies up and feed 'em to the swamp lizards!"

Estrogena got a laugh out of this. "Wow, you really have a problem with rash judgments, don't you! No, I think in this case we have to exercise a little caution. Don't get me wrong, I'm ticked off. Mostly at the crackpot scientist Zorin for finding the thing and then losing it—but never mind him for now. I want that M'Guh Fon and I mean to get it, and anybody gets in my way, that's too bad. I know that sounds cold and heartless and uncaring, but the cause is a wonderfully just one! It's not for myself that I want this absolute power. I want it for you, and you, and you, and all my wonderful loving, caring warmhearted, altruistic, compassionate subjects. Love you, love you all!" Estrogena blew dozens of kisses.

"And we love you, too, Empress Genie!"

"I wish someone would tell us what the hell this M'Guh Fon thing is!" Vivian said in a whisper that was more like a scream.

Estrogena yawned. "Gods I'm tired. How much time do we have left? That much? Oh, dear. I'm feeling just so bloated and so, so *pre* you-know-what. Let's do a wrap, Morfie. I can't go on. Guards? Take that one away to the Nutcracker and throw the two bitches into the slammer."

A guardsman stepped forward. "Your Highness, I'm afraid the Nutcracker chamber hasn't been cleaned since its last use."

"You mean there's yucky gray matter all over the ceiling and walls?"

"It was just used this morning, Your Highness."

"Nuts. Well, we have strong reason to believe that these people can tell us where the M'Guh Fon is—we should give them a night to think about it. A pleasant stay in our imperial accommodations might refresh their memories."

"A night in the cooler, Your Grace?"

"No room service, either. Off with them! By tomorrow's show they should be willing to talk. And if not— we'll crack their little nuts for them, won't we?" Estrogena smiled monstrously, then broke into another yawn. "I need my beauty sleep." She giggled. Tossing her scepter to a stagehand, she flounced off the dais and disappeared behind a curtain.

"Let's hear it for our wonderful, glorious, Imperial Bitchiness!"

The audience broke into enthusiastic applause. The chamber rang with it. The unseen orchestra struck up the show's theme.

Guards surrounded Diane again. Although she insisted that she could walk unaided, they grabbed her arms and dragged. Thus the three were roughly escorted out of the audience hall and down level upon level of stairs—deep, deeper, deepest into the bowels of the castle.

The corridors were cold and dank, with only an occasional torch or candle for illumination. Rodentoid creatures skittered through the shadows. Keys jangled, bolts yanked, and hinges squeaked, setting off cacophonous echoes through the hallways.

The three were thrust into a cell. The door slammed behind them. Footsteps clopped away: the sound of retreating hope. Diane Derry picked herself up off a bed of grimy straw, her nostrils flaring. She squinted into the deep shadows beyond the solitary light that illuminated only a fraction of their usually spacious cell. She wrinkled her nose.

"Offal," she said.

Groaning, Wussman picked himself out of the straw. "It is pretty bad, yes."

"I think Diane is speaking of the smell, Gregory," said Viv, standing up, brushing herself off.

"Hmmm? Oh yes. That's awful, too." Wussman just lay there dejectedly. "Doomed, doomed. This whole escapade has been a disaster from the get-go. Oh, why did I let you talk me into stowing away aboard Demopoulos's silly spaceship?"

"Wussman, shut up. Show some backbone for once in your miserable life."

"Life? I don't have a life. It's going to end tomorrow. My brains will be splattered all over the ceiling."

"Don't dwell on it. Think of a way to escape."

"Don't worry, Dr. D. will come to our rescue," said Diane, trying to sound as chipper as possible.

"That hopeless crank? Anyway, how's he going to fix that blasted ship of his? And if he does, how can he find us?"

"He will, Dr. Vernon. You just have to have faith."

"Faith? That's a laugh. Besides, I'm an atheist."

"Let's just rest here and not squabble," insisted Diane. "If we have our health and our strength, at least we have something."

"They're going to splatter my poor brain all over the ceiling," said Wussman. "I could—" He turned his head sharply toward the shadows. "What was that?"

"What was what?"

"Rustling. Straw . . . rustling."

"That's what straw does, you dimwit."

"No—over there—in the darkness."

"I did notice a few overgrown mice scurrying about," said Viv. "That must be what you hear."

"No. No, it's bigger than a rat, and it's coming this way," Geoffrey insisted.

"Shhh," suggested Diane. "Maybe we'd better listen."

They stopped talking. Diane concentrated. It was more than a rustling. It sounded like footsteps. Human (or humanoid) footsteps. Not the sort of noise a rat-size critter would make.

Footsteps, coming their way! Diane felt a lot less hopeful than she had just a minute ago. In fact, she was very frightened.

Wussman groaned. "But it's so unfair, so bloody unfair. We've done nothing. Absolutely nothing!"

A deep, powerful voice came from the shadows, startling them all.

"That was your first mistake."

Chapter Seven

Mammals seem to have an instinctive fear for creatures bigger than they are: most particularly the sort with large claws, sharp teeth, and the smell of the carnivore hanging about them.

Could this be a racial fear, descended from the time when our Jurassic ancestors scurried away from the pounding talons of dinosaurs? Perhaps. Dr. Dimension certainly felt a twinge of that when he turned and saw what loomed over Erob the roboid. After all, a good many of the good doctor's Mediterranean ancestors had managed to avoid Tyrannosaurus rex or, later, tigers of the saber-toothed persuasion, long enough to procreate and thus win the genetic pool; and those run-first-and-be-courageous-later genes still swam in Dr. D.'s turbulent loins.

However, let it be said that the primary function at play in his reaction, when he saw the creature that had stalked them and was about to strike, was not terror but plain common sense.

Dr. Dimension ran.

"Danger, Danger! Dan— Blurggh!"

Crash. Smash. Boing. Thunk.

Dr. D. ran and did not look back.

"Doc! Hey! Wait for—ahhhhhhhhhhh!"

The creature let loose with a triumphal caterwauling, like that of a demon freed from hell.

Lest we be too hasty as regards Dr. D.'s behavior (keeping in mind Estrogena's admonition against making value judgments), you should have a look at this beastie. It was big, for one thing: about twelve feet high, with a face that could have cracked all the junked mirrors on this world. The creature's other charms included five snakelike tentacles radiating from a reeking, slimy, scaly, diseased cucumber of a body; rows of sharp spines here and there; multifaceted insectoid eyes; and several mouths that gnashed and snapped. With two of the longer tentacles, the thing had roped Erob's heavy body, hoisted him up off the ground, and stuffed him into a salivating orifice in the middle of its body.

Poor Troy had presumably suffered the same fate.

However, it wasn't just to save his brilliant carcass that Doc D. had skedaddled, let that be known. He ran into the ship first to consider the situation. And secondly to obtain some sort of weapon.

Not that there were any hand blasters or such lying around. The Doc wasn't a stupid man. If there'd been one, he'd have taken it along with them on their exploratory jaunt. Originally, when Dr. D. and his helpers had built and provisioned the spacetime ship, they had stocked weapons aboard—a shotgun and a pistol. But along the way those dandy peacemakers had got lost, somehow. The Pizons specifically had not given the strangers from Earth any Pizon hand weapons.

But the ship did have defensive armaments! Hoping that there might still be a little juice in the forward beamers, Doc hurried to the control room.

Doc got into the pilot's seat, snapped on the screens, and rotated the cameras, which registered nothing but lots of linguine-shaped static for a moment. The picture wasn't very clear when it finally appeared. However, in a few seconds, Doc had the view he needed, and the beamer was coming on line.

The image resolved just in time for Doc to see the kicking feet of Troy Talbot slipping down the gullet.

Oh, dear.

Doc trained the weapon's sights on the monster. Damned thing. He hoped it worked this way. Point. Aim. Fire. That seemed to be the traditional way these kinds of things worked.

He aligned everything in what seemed to be the proper fashion, making sure to aim at the head, not the body and its horrible central feeding orifice, so as not to hit Troy, just in case it still mattered.

He pushed the firing button.

Instead of a beam of intense energy emerging obediently from the directed nozzle, a red light blinked on the control dashboard.

"BATTERIES LOW!" came the warning.

Dr. Dimension kicked the underside of the control console a few times, but only managed to dent it. No beam issued forth to blast the creature that had gulped his assistant.

As mentioned, Dr. Dimension was a rational man. However, he was also, deep down, well underneath the crusty exterior, a man of great feeling. True, Troy Talbot was an idiot. Sure, he could be a pain in the ass. He wasn't even that much of a football player. He also had the kind of young, dumb, clean-cut, red-blooded American good looks that Dr. D. despised but secretly envied. And he was always saying stupid things, and getting in the way, and being ever so much a big bother; in fact . . .

Come to think of it, was this big goof really worth saving?

All that was left in view was Troy's leg from the knee down.

"Oh, hell, he comes in handy sometimes."

Troy Talbot was too poorly endowed in the IQ department to think of hitching on with another wacky inventor. He mostly just hung around because of Diane, anyway.

However, it had to be said, Troy was a damned fine mechanic. And damned fine mechanics were hard to come by these days, especially in the middle of an alien galaxy millions of light-years from home, possibly in another spacetime continuum altogether.

Besides, when all was said and done, when all the pros and cons were tallied up, Dr. Dimension was rather fond of the kid. A shame to see him get digested in some alien monster's guts, light-years from home. Besides, it had come to light recently that Troy Talbot (né Tully Tarnopol) was, of all things, Jewish.

"What would his mother think of me?" Dr. Dimension said to himself. "Oh, the guilt! I'd have to go to the memorial service, and there she'd be. And she'd *look* at me. I know exactly what that look would say. 'So, you were my son's boss. His teacher. Mr. Professor, Mr. Intelligence. And what—you let him get eaten alive by a space monster? An animal you couldn't even eat, a piece of *trafik,* it ate *him*? I raised a son, so *you* could let him get gobbled by a space monster? What, you didn't have a ray gun handy? Dr. Outer Space, Buck Rogers, already, he sits there and watches some Golem nosh on my boy?' That's what she'd say to me! To hell with that."

Doc D. couldn't find a fire ax. However, a piece of pipe with a jagged end had come loose from the ceiling. He pulled it loose, took a deep breath, and marched back out to confront the big ugly beast and demand it regurgitate his mechanic.

Thus, he made an imposing figure as he brandished his clumsy weapon, stomping out to do battle with a fearsome creature without regard for personal safety. The monster was waiting for him, just beyond the door, tentacles waving like a crazed sea anemone.

"I don't suppose we could discuss this intelligently, could we?" said the Doc to the monster.

You never knew if these space critters out here were going to break out into song and dance, let alone intelligible speech. The universe hadn't turned out to be the ordered, law-abiding place he'd expected. Still, the notion of himself as a courageous weapon-wielding spaceman-inventor, facing off against an evil, betentacled space monster, was rather appealing, if eminently foolhardy.

But it had to be done. As he had reminded Diane Derry many times before, male hormones served many purposes.

Stepping forward threateningly, the monster let loose

a fearsome growl that could not be construed as either friendly or intelligent. In fact, it looked for all purposes as though it intended to cram the doctor down its gullet as well.

"Okay, pal, we could have talked this out. We could have bargained, dickered back and forth, but now we have to tango."

Dr. Dimension advanced, resolutely, confidently.

The monster advanced.

The Doc advanced further, though not as confidently and certainly not as resolutely.

The monster . . . exploded.

Dr. Dimension retreated.

The retreat was part volitional and part the result of the force of the explosion. The creature simply burst apart at the seams, like some fleshy overinflated balloon. Although it was not a human face the monster wore—if it could be considered a face at all—that face looked extremely surprised.

The head shot off like a rocket, trailing a tail of gushing spinal fluid. Gobbets of flesh and gouts of aquamarine blood splattered out in perfect radial symmetry. Dr. D. was caught in a wave of this gore, lifted off his feet, and knocked for a few yards. He struggled up, wiped the colorful if noxious stuff from his eyes and looked at the ruins of the thing. Lying there, equally aquamarine, was Troy Talbot, looking profoundly dazed, but very much alive.

Beside Troy, standing on his transparent bubblehead, was Erob the roboid.

"Troy?" said Dr. D., scurrying up to him. "Troy, are you all right?"

Troy blinked his eyes. "Yeah, sure, Doc. I think."

Erob the roboid said nothing.

No lights blinked. No gears moved. In fact, he looked quite dead.

"You're alive," Dr. D. said, "that's the important thing. Here, let me help you. You might need first aid. Or better yet a stiff drink."

Doc gave him a once-over physical examination.

Everything seemed to be in place. Somewhat miraculous. The physicist scratched his frizzy head.

"What happened, Doc?"

"Beats the hell out of me, Talbot. One moment I was confronting that thing, and in the next it was all in pieces, like so many cold cuts in a delicatessen. And the corned beef wasn't that good, either. What happened?"

"I just remember floundering around in squishy, icky darkness, Doc. And I remember thinking, gosh, I don't want to die! I mean, who does?"

"Siggy Freud to the contrary, a desire to die is hardly in one's genetic makeup. There is no 'death wish.' "

"Who's Ziggy Frood?"

"Some Viennese witch doctor who thinks we all want to kill our dads and bed our moms, or vice versa in the case of women. Although he's not so sure of that."

"Huh? Why, that's ridiculous."

"Nevertheless, people pay twenty bucks an hour to lie on his couch and get told that."

"You don't say. They ought to have their heads examined!"

"I agree. Anyway, what happened after you got into the monster's stomach? What were you feeling?"

"I just needed to get out, desperately. I was real mad, too. I hated being in there. I wanted to bop that ugly monster on its nose. I fought and I fought, but I couldn't get back up that thing's gullet. I couldn't breathe. There was smelly junk all over me, and I kept getting madder and madder. And next thing I knew, Doc, things just kind of went . . . kablooey."

Doc D. stroked his mustache. "Hmm. Let me do some cogitating on the matter."

"Yeah, Doc. And think about it, too. It was pretty spooky. It was like . . . gee, it was like . . . my *thoughts* gave that monster a bad case of gas. I know it sounds crazy, and maybe I should go see Ziggy Frood, but—"

"There could be more going on in that noggin of yours than I realized, Talbot."

"You think I've actually got a brain, Doc?"

"I didn't say that. We'll keep looking for one, though, Talbot, I promise."

A high-pitched voice spoke. "Once that's accomplished, do you think it'd be possible for you to find me a heart?"

The voice had a forlorn quality, like a whiny, depressed dog. Doc D. and Troy Talbot turned.

The robot's head, turned crankcase over gearbox, pulsed with roseate light.

"Erob. You're alive," said Troy.

"Oh, dear. Sorry. I'm not Erob." The light flickered plaintively.

Troy looked puzzled. "Then who are you?"

"Ah," said Doc D. "Let me venture a guess. You must be a new expression of your robo-computer's multiple personalities."

The robot emitted a woeful sigh.

"And a pretty depressed one, too," Doc added.

The lights in the globular head turned a purplish mauve.

"If we're not going to call you Erob—then what should we call you?" asked Troy.

The robot wheezed. "I realize I'm only an electro-mechanical individual—but this position is very uncomfortable, and I'm afraid I'm such a clunky, uncoordinated specimen that I'd hurt something if I tried to topple over myself. In fact, I don't believe I could even get up. I'd just lay on the ground and rust. Forever and ever."

Deep, profound sigh, pale gloomy light.

Troy Talbot got unsteadily to his big feet. "No problem, Erob, or whoever you are. Doc. Want to give me a hand?"

"No. But I suppose it's my destiny."

Talbot began pushing against the body. It went over very easily, but once it got to toppling, it was hard to stop. Doc lost his grip, and the thing crashed to the ground.

"Have a care," suggested the robot. "I've got maybe one thermocouple left, and it's quite close to critical failure."

"Talbot, you lummox! You want to do it right this time?"

"Gee, Doc, you sound like you're old grouchy self. Glad to have you back."

"Let's just get this bag of bolts back on its feet and forget my mood swings. We have enough moody people around here."

Together, straining, they hoisted the ponderous, bulbous body up onto its wide metal clodhoppers.

Its lights flashed a dull orange. "Well, at least my sensors aren't totally destroyed. Still, I guess it's better than becoming a gigantic kidney stone for that garbage gulper."

"Is that what that horror was?" asked Doc.

"This place needs some kind of scavenger to eat the organic waste, or the smell would be even worse. I guess it just thought we were a bit of fresh and lively dinner. Usually those things eat garbage, not living things. Just bad luck that it attacked. Then again, maybe it's my fate to associate with extreme losers."

"Hey, that's not very nice," said Troy.

"So knock me on my butt again. Maybe I'll click over to someone more satisfactory. Some pansy-assed Milquetoast. Face it, chumps. Life's a ditch, and then they bury you in it. If you're lucky." The lights flickered a painful magenta, and the sigh this time was a wind through barren mountains.

"But you're a robot," Troy protested. "That pessimistic stuff doesn't apply to you. You can't die."

"Great. Life's a ditch, and I get buried alive."

"But we dug you out."

Dr. Dimension broke in, "Don't argue with Tweedledum, here, Talbot. This particular personality emanation definitely teeters on the manic-depressive—minus the manic."

"Then he's not going to be much help to us."

"Maybe not. What do you say, Twinkle Toes? Do your laws of robotics still compel you to help us install the new space drive in our ship?"

"I'll do what I can, but I can't guarantee a thing. And by the way, the name is Tobor."

"Tobor . . . the roboid?" asked Troy.

"Just 'robot,' if you please. I'm not one to put on airs. 'Roboid,' indeed."

Dr. Dimension held out his arms. "Well, will you help carry some of the stuff inside, then look around and see if any more of this junk rings a sensor?"

The robot sighed. "I suppose I have to, or you might well cannibalize me for spare parts. As I'm also compelled to protect myself, you're well-covered on the helping question, legally speaking."

"Oh, we'd never break you down for your parts, Tobor," said Troy. "Not without your permission. I mean, Doc and me—we aren't cannibals or anything. Are we Doc?"

Dr. D., staring thoughtfully at the peevish light show, did not respond immediately. "I wonder what you've got in that tarnished shell of yours, Tobor, what technological wonders you're hiding."

The head of the robot twirled. "Spaceship drive. I feel a sudden renewed access to permanent memory. Yes. I do believe that I might be of some assistance."

"Thought you'd see it my way," Doc said, chuckling. Then he snapped his fingers. "Come, come, gentlemen. Let's not be slackers. We've got a spacetime ship to rebuild, a vivacious and beautiful woman to rescue, and a home to search for. All we need is a little music to put a hep in our step and a glide in our stride. Got any music in you, Erob? Excuse me—Tobor?"

At once, brightly upbeat music, not quite Earthlike but close to it, emanated from the robot.

Troy began to dance. "I got rhythm!"

"I got music," Tobor said.

"I got a headache," Dr. Dimension averred, laying a hand on his forehead.

"Who could ask for anything more?" said Tobor, gay butterfly wings of turquoise and yellow light dancing in his head.

"Hand me that bastard file."

"Gee, Doc, you mean a file of a certain grade of coarseness suitable for use on metal? I'll bet you want to file a bit of flange off that thermocouple in this space drive we're cobbling together from junk."

"No, you son of a bitch, give me that bastard of a file down there in the toolbox. I'm in a foul mood, I'm cursing, and if you don't hurry, Talbot, I'm going to switch into sailor's vocabulary, and it won't be pretty."

Troy Talbot found the file in the toolbox, and quickly slapped it into the doctor's hand.

"Ouch. Thank you, you clumsy oaf."

"You're welcome, Doc."

"And thank you both for this most enlightening experience," said Tobor the robot. "I assure you, it's all going into my memoirs, filed under 'Fascinating Starship Drives I Have Known.'"

There had been no way to fix the ship's original spacetime drive, the one Dr. Dimension had invented and which had been supplemented and made finally to work by alien components that had mysteriously arrived at Dr. D.'s lab door. With this mechanism it was possible, theoretically at least, to travel between any two points in the universe instantaneously, regardless of distance. However, the drive had only worked once to date, propelling the doctor and his crew into regions unknown, possibly millions of light-years away from Earth. Then the machinery had failed. Doc had done his best to fix it, with the help of a race of gangster aliens called the Pizons, but it had not been tested since then. Now it lay in ruins. Without spare parts, there was no way to fix it. And as far as anyone knew, this was the only engine in the universe of its type.

Doc and Troy concentrated their efforts on the ship's conventional drive, the one supplied by the Pizons. It, too, was almost a total wreck.

Panels and floorboards had been flung back and scattered, revealing the cavity of the engine bay. Inside it, hulked a Frankenstein's monster of a spaceship drive, cobbled together over the last few hours from the remains of no less than four junked ships. The contraption was haphazardly bolted together. Also providing adhesion were ingenuity, sweat, spit, and a few wads of chewing gum.

Wires bunched and squiggled in ganglia-like complexity. Colorful parts, almost like new, contrasted with tarnished, half-rusted components.

"Gee Doc," said Troy Talbot, smearing a smudge of lubricant along his square jawline. "This thing's really something. You think there's a chance it'll work?"

Doc D. measured one final calibration, twisted one more wing nut into place, and then regarded his handiwork with some satisfaction.

"You've got to be shitting me. This is a disaster looking for an excuse to happen."

"Heck, Doc, we have some kind of chance. I've been soldering and arc-welding like mad. The hull's all patched up tight. The batteries are charged, and all the instruments are working again."

Doc D. popped his frizzy salt-and-pepper head out of engine bay, and nodded. "That's what I said, the frigging thing's a disaster looking for an excuse to happen. Oh, hell, that's just about all we can do. Tobor, you're absolutely sure that what we've grafted into place here is a hyperspace drive?"

"Absolutely, Dr. Dimension."

"Can't decipher these alien chicken scratches, so I'm taking your word for it. If you're lying, I'm going to take that arc-welder to you."

"Robots don't have emotions," Tobor sniffed, "so your threats are useless."

"Yeah, but it makes me feel better," the lab-coated physicist said.

Doc D. accepted Troy's hand and was pulled from the bay. He patted his hands together.

"Good enough. All that remains is to try to blast off.

It just occurred to me, though, Tobor. Erob knew where the imperial planet is. What's the name again?"

"Ovaria."

"Ovaria. Interesting. Well, do you have an inkling where it is?"

"I have access to the same memory storage areas, yes. Now there's simply a different personality accessing them."

"Whatever," Dr. Dimension said, breathing a sigh. "Okay, let's give her a shot. What have we got to lose, except our lives, our fortunes, and our sacred honor?"

"That's the spirit, Doc!" Troy enthused. He slapped his boss heartily on the back. Too heartily.

Doc winced. "Talbot, if I were a headshrinker, I'd have to charge you half price."

Chapter Eight

In all her adventures thus far in the realm of outer space and its environs, Diane Derry had faced danger bravely, confident that any problem could be solved if faced squarely and dealt with using plain old common sense.

Now, though, things looked pretty hopeless. It was awful being shut up in this cell (it was pretty big for a cell—in fact, it was more like a temporary holding area for lots of prisoners, much as one would find in a municipal jail).

Things looked pretty bleak. It was hard to maintain your sense of optimism inside a cold, smelly dungeon of a nightmare fairy palace. Diane was depressed and forlorn, and she almost never felt that way. And now, on top of it, she was afraid.

The figure that was carved out of the darkness moved closer; its lineaments were those of threat and dread. Light began to limn some detail: a tall scarecrow of tattered draping rags, an oval of darkness for a face. The arms were raised and moving slowly, slowly, like ragged claws scuttling across the floors of silent seas. (For all its implied menace, it was a fetchingly poetic figure.)

"Beware" came a voice hauntingly out of that tall bundle of must and mildew.

"Holy hell," said Wussman, jumping back.

"Take care you don't wet yourself, Geoffrey," Vivian said sardonically.

"Don't ... don't be frightened, my darling," said

Wussman through chattering teeth, still backing away. With a thunk, he bumped up against the wall.

"Don't be silly. I'm not afraid."

"You're not?"

"Of course not. Whoever it is, he's in the same boat we are. Why should I fear him? You disgust me, you worm."

"Viv, this is no time for love talk. We're in deep trouble."

The ragged figure halted at the edge of the circle of light thrown by the cell's single fixture, which threw less light than a candle. A chuckle issued from the folds of threadbare cloth.

Diane Derry had always believed that the best way of dealing with one's fears was to confront them, but this seemed a little extreme. Nevertheless, as the dark figure probably would *not* be going away soon, and there seemed no way out and no way around it, displaying some defiant sense of bravery appeared to be the only weapon at her disposal. Cleft chin up, dimpled mouth firm, impressively sculpted breasts jutting forward, she took two steps toward the shambling thing and then proudly took her stand.

"Greetings," she said. "We are from the planet Earth, and we mean you no harm."

The figure was silent for a long moment. Then it spoke.

"Oh, well, that's a relief then. It's astonishing the barbaric creatures they dump in this place. Best to put a fright in them from the start. But I see that I'm in no danger."

With that, the ragged threads dropped to the concrete floor. The figure stepped into the light, and Diane's eyes widened. Before her, in silver space boots and a nifty magenta one-piece utility suit with yellow piping, stood an attractive man with a neat little goatee and a mane of jet-black hair coiffed above a noble brow. Although neither overmuscular nor giving the impression of great physical strength, he exuded virility. Diane was reminded of Errol Flynn, and as he regarded her with an ironically impish, self-assured smile, a little thrill went through her, identical to the one she had experienced seeing his handsome movie-actor counterpart swinging through the trees of Sherwood Forest in *Robin Hood*. She had loved that movie, and she had loved Errol Flynn.

Diane blushed to her neckline.

Vivian was not so daunted.

"Well, hello, handsome," she husked, sashaying forward with her hips swiveling with great calculation. "Name's Vivian, and am I ever glad to see *you*."

The gallant fellow bowed, took Vivian's hand and placed a kiss thereon.

"My pleasure." His gaze swung to Diane. "And this charming young lady who was brave enough to confront the specter I presented?" His eyes twinkled with good-humored charm, and his white teeth fairly sparkled, even in the dim flickering torchlight.

"My assistant," said Viv. "A mere child."

"Let her speak." The man politely disentangled himself from Vivian's paws.

"I'm not her assistant. My name is Diane Derry."

"A wonderful name for a wonderfully brave lady. May I kiss your hand?"

A bit startled, but not adverse to the notion, Diane allowed the debonair stranger to lift up her hand and gently touch his lips to her fingers. His lips were warm and moist, but not *too* warm, or too moist.

In fact, as lips went, they were just right.

A delightful tingle shot up Diane's arm, and she had to work to suppress a sigh.

The gentleman let go her fingers and smiled at her. His eyes were a warm hazel color, flecks of cool green in them.

"You look like Errol Flynn," she blurted.

"Eh? I don't know the man. Is he a friend of yours?"

"Huh? Oh, no. He's an actor, a motion-picture actor on our planet. On Earth. He's famous, and very good."

"Then you've complimented me greatly, and I thank

you for it. Earth, you say? Can't say I've ever heard of the place. It's not within the Ovarian empire?"

"No. It's ... well, it's millions of miles—no, millions of light-years away."

"You've come a very long distance to be shut up in a place like this. Whatever did you do to deserve it?"

"Nothing! We're innocent!"

The man nodded. "Of course. That's almost a requirement for being one of Estrogena's enemies. The woman's mad."

"She says we have something of hers, or know where it is. And we don't! We never heard of the thing."

The man nodded sadly. "Ah, I see. What a tragedy, to lock up such beauty."

Diane blushed all over again.

A polite cough came from Vivian. "Pardon me for breaking up this charming tête-à-tête," she said with enough bite to chew off a hunk of steel. "You might care to meet the third person in our party—Dr. Geoffrey Wussman."

The man turned and bowed. "An honor to meet you, Dr. Wussman."

Wussman merely nodded, looking profoundly embarrassed and befuddled, preferring to stick to the shadows.

"You have the advantage over us," said Vivian.

"Oh, I wish." The man shot her a smile that could have melted helium ice.

Vivian could not help a giggle. "No, I mean, your name."

"How impolite of me. I was so caught up in the spell of loveliness that I've neglected my manners." He bowed again, deeply. "I am Zorin."

"Zorin?" Wussman said. "You're the person that insane woman up there was talking about?"

"I see you've encountered Estrogena in her element. Many people have, and it is usually a significant moment in an individual's life. Also, usually, the last." The dapper, slender man winked. "However, fate has brought you here to me, and clearly for more than one reason."

Zorin turned his eyes on the ladies and took their measure in a manner too analytical to be a leer, then sized up Wussman. "I sense that you are worthy people, and that I can trust you. Is this true?"

"Oh yes," said Diane dreamily.

"Splendid. For I have a story to tell. I need ears to fill."

"Just what we need," Wussman groaned. "Our ears filled. And then we'll have our brains splattered on the ceiling. Delightful." The runty man giggled, on the verge of hysteria.

Vivian walloped him across the chops, converting the giggling to gurgling. Then she saw the stranger's dismay.

"Sorry, Zorin. Dr. Wussman needs an occasional whap across the mouth to keep him from going to pieces. He'll be all right."

Zorin frowned. "Instead of blows, perhaps a few comforting words would do him more good?"

"Not this cream puff. Speaking of words, what about 'M'Guh Fon'?"

The handsome man's eyebrows shot upward expressively. Doubt reformed the noble brow. "Something occurs to me. At times, though not often, Estrogena's paranoia has some basis, and my judgment is not infallible. Are you people soldiers of fortune seeking the M'Guh Fon?"

"Are you kidding? This bunch would have trouble with Mah Jong, let alone M'Guh Fon." Vivian snorted derisively.

"We learned about it from Estrogena," explained Diane. "She thinks we were looking for it on the trash planet, along with Dr. Demopoulos—he's my boss— and Troy Talbot . . . he's my boyfriend. That's why we're in the hoosegow. She's trying to get us to tell her what we know. Which is absolutely nothing. We crashed on the trash planet, and we had absolutely no intention of going there in the first place."

"What was your destination?"

"Well, we really didn't have one. We're lost in space, you see. It's a long story."

"I see," Zorin said. "You had the misfortune to blunder into this affair, and came under Estrogena's suspicion. How unfortunate for you. Although I sense that powers other than Her Imperial Bitchiness might have had a hand in this turn of events."

"What powers?" demanded Vivian, very curiously.

Zorin smiled. "All in good time. Let us merely say that our meeting may not be entirely the result of mere chance. If you allow me to tell my story, I can explain further."

"Can you include an explanation what the hell the M'Guh Fon is?" said Vivian pointedly.

"I shall be centering on that very subject. But let me forge onward before I get too caught up staring into those enchanting green eyes of yours, Vivian. Please, please. Pull up a seat. Relax. Get comfortable. I'll relate my tale, and you shall be enlightened—and perhaps even a bit entertained."

Diane found a pile of straw that looked reasonably clean and applied the well-rounded Derry derriere thereon. She stared up at this dashing gentleman, her heart going pitter-patter. Troy Talbot had always seemed an inevitable factor in the equation of her middle-American, middle-class life. She accepted him like an item of sturdy furniture.

This Mr. Zorin, though ... Whew! Furniture?

Not by a long shot!

Chapter Nine

"Troy, batten the hatches. I'll power up the engines. We'll set course once in orbit. Hop to it."

Troy hopped to it.

"I had better secure myself," said Tobor. "I will induce a molecular adhesion field on the undersides of my pedal extremities. To be safe, I will hold onto this stanchion."

Dr. Dimension said, "You do that. Strap yourself in tight! Because, my metal friend, we are about to leave this junkyard world behind in a trail of ions! That is, if I can get that engine started."

He sat at the control panel and snapped a switch.

The result was instantaneous. A whirring, a chirring. A choke, a gag. Sparks geysered up from parts of the engine.

"C'mon, baby, c'mon!" Doc D. coaxed in a soothing voice. "Work for Poppa."

Troy returned and strapped into his seat. "All set Doc. Seals are tight. What about the engine bay access doors?"

"Leave them open. We might have to perform some adjustments."

The engine heaved. Spectrographic halos began to dance around it. The thing sounded like a tubercular tugboat engine without a muffler. It wheezed and chugged asthmatically, sounding as though it would die any second.

The sides of the ship creaked and shuddered, but thus far the vessel had not moved the merest centimeter from the surface.

"Come to think of it, Talbot, I may have cross-wired the neutron distributor. Have a look, will you?"

"Sure thing, Doc." The big football player unstrapped, got up, and leaned into the cavity that held the churning, chugging engine. "Oh, jeez, yeah, Doc. You've got the negative on the positive and the positive on the neutrino filter. Here, all I got to do is to take this wire here"—BOINK!—"and move it over to this lead here and—"

Wonk!

"Yiiiiiiiiiiiiiiiiiii!" screeched Troy Talbot.

His feet lifted from the deck, suspended on a corona of blinding white energy that sizzled the air. Doc looked back, surprised but somehow pleased to see his hired hand levitating. At least something was happening. He wasn't sure what, though.

Suddenly, the ship rose and flung itself at the sky like a rock from a slingshot.

"Good job Troy!" said Dr. Dimension. "Whatever you did, it worked!"

"Yiiiiiiiiiiiiiiiiiii!" replied Troy Talbot.

"Sorry it's causing you pain, but we're moving now, boy. Hoo boy."

The Doc watched the dun-colored terrain drop away with dizzying speed.

"Hoo *boy,* are we moving. Hey, Troy? Troy. Yo, Troy."

"Uhhhhhhhhhhhhhh!"

"Look, you might want to just tweak it a little in the other direction, whatever you did, because I do think we're moving just a *tad* too fast. Jesus H. Christ. Troy?—"

Tobor the robot was holding on for dear metallic life.

"Yahhhhhhhhhhhh!" Troy averred.

The Pizon ship hurtled upward and upward.

"Wait, belay that last order! We're doing it!" Doc D. studied the instrument panel. "We're going to reach a stable orbit. We're—" The meters and verniers twirled and whirled, then flipped and flopped.

As did the ship.

"We're going down!" said Dr. D. "Troy? What the hell did you do?"

The ship dived back down toward the surface.

With one final ZAP! Troy Talbot was hurled from the engine to the ceiling, where his shoes attached themselves to the ceiling. He hung there like a human chandelier.

"Doc, what's happening?"

"I was going to ask you the same question."

"How come I'm stuck to the ceiling, Doc?"

"You've been reincarnated as a fly."

"Doc, get me down!"

"Extremely doubtful. We're falling, Troy. We're going to crash again. We're—" Doc looked up at the ceiling and watched Troy wave his arms helplessly.

"You're magnetized, Talbot."

"Huh?"

"You have steel toes in those clodhoppers of yours?"

"What? Oh. Yeah, they're steel-toed work shoes."

"Q.E.D. We haven't got ourselves a quantum drive in there—we've got some sort of electromagnetic drive. It's interacting with the strong magnetic field of this planet, and maybe with all that metal junk down there. Let me check the gauss gauge." The doctor's eyes quickly found the dial.

"Jumping rheostats! Incredibly erratic. The ship's turned itself into a giant magnet with one pole that keeps switching back and forth between north and south."

"Doc, the primary coils. Maybe if you reduce the voltage, it'll stabilize."

No sooner said than done. The correct lever was pulled, and the effect was immediate. The *Mudlark* stopped, hung in stratospheric midair for a nanosecond—

—And then re-rocketed orbitwards.

"Yowwwwwww!" howled a newly demagnetized Troy as he dropped to the floor.

Tobor the robot held on, beeping piteously.

Dr. D. adjusted the magnetic field distribution, hoping to stabilize the trajectory and prevent whatever had happened before from happening again.

A red light appeared on the board. Doc didn't know exactly what it meant, but it couldn't be good.

Again, the ship began wobbling and bouncing about like a pinball in an invisible arcade game. Up and down, down and up. Over and under, loop-the-loop, alternately tumbling and soaring. All efforts to wrest control from freakish forces were futile. Troy kept banging off the bulkheads like a hammer hitting a bell. Tobor the robot's mood-color went to a uniform gray as he conked his bubble-domed head against the stanchion. Dr. D. felt every sinew in his body independently give an anguished aching cry to be released from its bony shackles. Dr. D. told everyone to shut up, and stay put. He had to order his consciousness to do exactly the same thing.

At the top of one bounce, Doc had an idea and hit the engine cut-off switch. The patched-together mechanism whined and then died.

Then, like night changing instantaneously into day, the reverberations stopped. The shaking ceased. Peace seemed finally to have descended upon the universe. Dr. D. looked at the view screens. They showed a wealth of stars above a curving sweep of the trash planet.

Orbit.

They'd made orbit.

But how was that possible? Dr. D. was hardly a man to look a gift horse in the mouth—but his inquiring mind wanted to know (to coin a phrase).

He thumbed a vernier. Sensors detected something approaching. He punched it up on the screen and tracked the tiny image as it hovered above the curve of the horizon. In a short time the tiny image grew into a disturbingly large one: that of a huge interstellar craft, bristling with protrusions that looked uncomfortably like weapons, nasty ones fully capable of blowing whole worlds to smithereens. As regards targets such as small space cruisers, the remains would be quantum fluctuations in the ether.

Dr. Dimension took a look at the communications station. Yes, a voice call was coming in.

"Phone's ringing, Troy. Think I should answer it? Troy?"

He looked back. Troy was out cold on the deck.

"That boy's head is taking a beating. I'd worry about permanent brain damage, if he had a brain."

The Doc heaved a sigh. He hit the button marked ANSWER INCOMING CALL.

"Good morning," Dr. Dimension said in a suave voice. "Home for Wayward Women. Mr. Wayward speaking, can I help you?"

"Attention, ship of alien scum! You will prepare for immediate boarding, or die! This is your only warning! Any resistance will result in your immediate annihilation! Acknowledge!"

Dr. Dimension was rubbing his ears. He'd lunged to turn down the gain immediately but the initial blast of sound had practically deafened him. The voice was a sonic horror of rasps and wheezes, sounding barely human. But for all that, it was tinged with an accent that sounded, strangely enough, vaguely German, or perhaps Austrian.

"Jesus H. Christ, what the hell's eating you, pal?"

"Repeat—prepare for immediate boarding!"

"I don't care if you want *rooming* and boarding, keep your goddamn voice down! What the hell did you do this morning, gargle with sulfuric acid?"

"Repeat—any resistance will result—"

"Yeah, yeah, I heard you the first time, Golden Throat. Okay, okay!"

Doc took another gander at the dreadnought coming his way. It had the look of a military ship. The prickly guns and other nasty stuff were becoming more formidable with decreasing distance. The warship's vast bulk blotted out the multicolored stars as it closed.

What to do? Flee . . . or fight?

"I surrender."

"You have made a wise decision," the rasping quasi-Germanic voice told him.

"As if I had a choice," grumbled Doc. "By the way, can you stay for lunch? And if so, what are we eating?"

Chapter Ten

Diane Derry was settled and prepared for enlightenment. She took a glance around at her companions.

Vivian looked as though she'd just as soon drag this handsome stranger off into a corner and ravish him as sit and listen to his story. As for Wussman, his sotto voce mutterings were punctuated now and then by a semi-hysterical giggle. Diane didn't think he was doing so good.

"My name is Zorin, and I am a scientist and a philologist."

Pitter-patter, went Diane's heart. Not only was he good-looking, he was smart. And an academician, which she aspired to be.

Diane was prepared for enlightenment, but her hormones were flowing. She wondered if her brain could function with all those sexy fluids gushing around. Wouldn't it short-circuit?

"I am from the planet Baryon," continued Zorin, "where I attended the Cathedral of Learning, specializing in nuclear chemistry and interstitial quantum vortex analysis, with a minor in symbolic paradigm theory."

Wow, thought Diane.

"Baryon," Wussman griped. "Why are alien planets always named after science stuff?"

"Quiet, Wussman," Vivian said.

"I bet he went to grad school on Krypton."

"Shut up, you fool!" Vivian composed herself. "Please continue, Zorin."

Zorin bowed slightly. "Thank you. While a student, I studied ancient texts, delving deep into various arcane subjects. Alien scientific systems were a particular interest of mine. I founded the New Paradigm Club, which fostered the study of alien scientific texts. We pored over many an ancient alien codex and manuscript—and printout and information retrieval file, of course. It was very interesting material. Many good thing came out of this research, but the thing that interested me most were the many references to a legendary database created by an ancient race of near-godlike beings whose name has been lost in the dust of eons. But the name of their artifact survived."

"The M'Guh Fon," Diane said.

Zorin began to pace. "The M'Guh Fon. Have you any idea what those syllables mean, literally translated?"

" 'Lucky Strike means fine tobacco?' " Wussman ventured, and tittered inanely at his own incandescent wit.

Zorin ignored him. "*M'Guh Fon.* Translation: 'That which is unknowable.' The M'Guh Fon is, among other things, an information storage device containing the sum total of the scientific knowledge of this race of godlike beings. The empress Estrogena seeks it because it is reputed to be, potentially at least, the greatest source of power in the known universe.

"But allow me to leap forward to the discussion of my involvement. You see, from my studies, I learned that these ancient beings encrypted their deepest secrets in a complex code. Although the artifact was lost, samples of this code could be found in a few scraps of text dating from the galactic epoch in which the M'Guh Fon originated. Down through the years, many cryptologists have had a go at cracking that code. After years of labor, I alone succeeded. Don't think me some sort of genius. I was persistent, implacably persistent. And I had an advantage, a new technique of information processing, developed only recently and adapted by me for use in cryptanalysis. The trick worked, and I had the key to the M'Guh Fon. Of course, I didn't have the M'Guh Fon. No one did.

"I needed to do more research in myth and legend. I pored over more alien texts, searched through many a quaint and curious volume of forgotten lore . . ."

"Striking turn of phrase, that," Wussman commented.

"Thank you. But quest was in large part quite tedious. I read endless cook books, romantic potboilers, pet books, how-to books, joke and riddle compendiums . . . the worst sort of literary sweepings. But some of this material, believe it or not, had market potential, in translation, of course. In fact, some of it was published by our club, and sold like sizzling breakfast cakes. The New Paradigm Club became wealthy beyond the dreams of most scholars.

"This new financial security enabled me to retire from teaching and devote my time exclusively to my studies. Finally, after wading through an ocean of text, I stumbled on a vital clue in a pamphlet I had previously overlooked because of its unsavory title— *Getting Horizontal: A Galactic Guide to Red Light Districts.*"

"These godlike beings," Vivian asked, "were a bunch of sleazeballs?"

"Not in the least. It wasn't the text—which was in a very primitive form, incidentally—bound plastic sheets covered with ersatz cloth—it was something tucked between the leaves of the volume itself. A redemption coupon for a supposed item of value that bore a name similar to 'M'Guh Fon,' and which could only be a variant in an obscure alien tongue."

"Redemption coupon?" Vivian's plucked eyebrows went up.

"Yes," Zorin said. "A voucher given by a loan emporium that enables the bearer to redeem an article on which the loan was collateralized."

"A pawn ticket!"

"Precisely."

"You mean . . ." Vivian's beautiful eyes went wide at the implication. "Somebody *hocked* the M'Guh Fon? Who?"

"We don't know. Its last owner, presumably, which could have been anyone. Remember, the artifact itself is useless without the key to the encryption. However, I had in my hand the name of the emporium where the artifact was pawned! If this place were still extant, and if it could be found, could not the M'Guh Fon still be there?"

"Could it?" Diane asked, round-eyed.

Zorin shook his head, chuckling. "Chances were a billion to one. The voucher was made of an inviolable plastic and could have been millions of years old, for all I knew. The damnable thing resisted all dating techniques. I was temporarily stymied. However, another piece of the puzzle came to light some years later. In yet another alien text, I discovered mention of the ancient planet of a race called the Hymons."

"The Hymons?" Vivian said with arched eyebrows.

"They were an ancient race of merchants and wholesalers. Their planet was reputed once to have had in excess of ten million pawnshops. If a lost artifact would be anywhere, it would be on the planet of the Hymons. The New Paradigm Club at once mounted an expedition to this strange world, which lay in a remote region of the galaxy. It turned into one of the most extensive archaeological digs ever undertaken. The planet was deserted, the great cities all in ruins. The only clue to their fate was a sign on a front door of one shop that said, somewhat breathlessly, 'CLOSED FOREVER, GOODBYE. DON'T CALL US WE'LL CALL YOU.' We believe the Hymons evacuated the planet and never returned, for reasons we can only guess at. We found vague hints that the entire population had emigrated to a planet reputed to be the original home of the race, according to Hymon legend—but this seemed so unlikely a scenario that we completely dismissed it.

"We also found, to our chagrin, that we were not the first M'Guh Fon hunters to land on the planet. But the problem immediately presenting itself to any seeker after this alien prize was the sheer number of pawnshops. The thing could be in any one of millions of them, spread out over ten continents! We had a name, but nothing else. There was, strangely, no address on the ticket. Finding it necessitated yet more sifting through alien records, this time those of the Hymons themselves. It didn't take as long as I thought it would. Within a month, I had the location of the redemption emporium whose name the ticket bore! Unfortunately, it was in a distant geographical area, at the confluence of three mighty rivers, but that would hardly daunt our hardy band of explorers now. We set off on our final journey, and in time, and after much hardship, reached the exact location of the pawnshop, on a corner, in—"

"Pittsburgh, Pennsylvania!" Wussman screamed, then chortled like some mad thing.

"—A small provincial hamlet. And there it was— Reliable Loan and Resale."

Zorin paused. He stood with his hands behind his back, an impish smile curling one corner of his mouth, a puckish gleam in his eye, as he regarded his listeners each in turn.

After an unbearable silence, Diane blurted: "Well, gee!"

"Yeah," Vivian seconded. "Okay, I'll ask the obvious. Did you find the damn thing?"

Zorin chuckled. "Yes."

"Wow!" Diane rocked back on her pretty bottom.

Vivian's eyes narrowed. "You don't say?"

"I do say."

"Fine," Vivian said. "What's bothering me is this. If you're now the most powerful person in the universe, uh . . ."

"Why am I in prison?"

Vivian grinned smarmily. "I'm glad you said it."

"The reason is simple. I had the artifact. I had the key to decoding the information contained within the artifact. You might be led to conclude that the rest was simple. As it turned out, I had taken but the first step on a light-years-long journey of discovery."

"Oh," Vivian said with disappointment. "I see."

"Yes. What remained was the formidable task of dealing with the billions and billions of data contained within it. Simply getting an idea of the organizational principle of the database was a horrendous puzzle that I worked at for years more."

Gosh, how old *is* he? Diane asked herself. He doesn't look a day over thirty-five.

"Still more difficult was the task of understanding and familiarizing myself with the scientific paradigms that this new way of looking at the universe took for granted. Let's face it. One individual can hardly get a grip on the entire scientific literature of a race of our ilk, let alone that of an unknown alien superrace. I was lost, a babe in the woods."

Sherwood Forest, thought Diane.

"I made some progress, not a great deal. But I learned enough, after years of study, to come to one overwhelming conclusion."

"Which was?" Vivian prompted, looking at her perfectly manicured nails.

"That the M'Guh Fon must be destroyed."

Vivian looked up, her jaw gone slack.

"Interesting," Wussman said. "I think." He shrugged, then giggled again.

Vivian got to her feet. "You mean to tell me that you . . . ?"

"But it couldn't be destroyed. The artifact itself was composed of a virtually indestructible nuclear-chemical material. As events turned out, I simply disposed of it."

"I can't believe it," Vivian said. "You threw away

the most valuable object in the universe, the key to unlimited power? Good God, why?"

"Your phrasing is apropos," said Zorin. "Have you
deities?"

"We sure do," Diane said.

"Some of us do," Vivian said with her nose up-
turned. "I happen to be an atheist."

"There are many ways of answering ultimate questions. Deciding that there is no answer is but one of
them. However, if you believe that there is a higher
power in the universe, whether gods, or beings far beyond the ken of mere mortals, you might also perforce
come to believe that there are areas of knowledge that
are best demarcated as off-limits."

" 'There are some things man was not meant to
know,' " Diane said. "That's a quote from something,
I don't exactly know what."

"Precisely," Zorin said. "I came to see that M'Guh
Fon contains secrets that are better kept by the gods.
Dangerous secrets."

" 'A little learning is a dangerous thing,' " Diane
quoted. "I think that's Pope."

"Again, very apposite," said Zorin.

"I still can't believe you threw it away," Vivian said.
"You mean it's lost forever?"

"I didn't say that. By the time I began wrestling
with the problem of what to do, rumor had gone out
that I had penetrated this age-old secret, and eventually
the empress Estrogena got wind of it. I was returning
to my home world from a long vacation—call it a spir-
itual retreat, a time spent in solitude to grapple with
the ethical implications of the entire issue. When I
came out of hyperspace in my home solar system, an
imperial warship was waiting to meet me. With the
help of the M'Guh Fon, I eluded capture and made it
as far as the trash planet, where I ran out of fuel.
Cornered there, I divested myself of the M'Guh Fon.
What better place to hide it, after all, than a world
full of trash? As objects go, the M'Guh Fon is completely innocuous. Even if somebody found it, they

would not know what it is, and they could not begin to use it.

"I was eventually captured and interrogated. However, the tricks I had learned kept me from divulging my knowledge—and they dared not kill me outright, as they had most of my colleagues in the club, for the M'Guh Fon would be lost forever. Nor can Estrogena use any of her various messy mind-probing techniques, for fear that I'd be left a half-wit. So she threw me into this dungeon until she figures out what to do next."

"You said something a moment ago," Vivian said. "About tricks you'd learned. So you did get something out of the M'Guh Fon after all."

"Yes. But the situation is more complex than you might think. I have discovered since that I am in mental contact with the M'Guh Fon. Once one has the thing, one never loses it. I fear it will be with me until I die."

"Gosh," Diane said.

"The artifact, if you haven't guessed by now, is something more than an information storage mechanism. Much, much more. It is also a thinking machine, a computer, capable of granting access to itself to any individual attuned to it. And this access may be afforded across vast reaches of time and space. Though the trash planet is half a dozen light-years away, it is as if it were broadcasting from across the street. However, don't think I have mastered the M'Guh Fon. I am still very much a babe in the woods."

"Marvelous," Vivian said. "Absolutely marvelous. But . . . what good is it doing you?"

"Well, I've been working on something very special, a possible way out. But I need brave and hardy souls to help—and who should show up now but your delightful selves!"

Geoffrey Wussman's jaws were agape. "A way out? Did you say . . . a way out? You mean, I don't have to have my head cracked like an egg, all messy and gooey and yucky all over the walls and ceiling, all sticky on the rug and into the corners and—"

Vivian silenced him with a smack across the side of the head. "Geoffrey, you're not well. Shut up." She turned a beaming face toward Zorin. "My gracious. A way out. Why, that just happens to be exactly what we're after. Is there any possibility that the M'Guh Fon could help us find a way back to our home planet? There's a certain university back there sorely in need of our services."

Diane Derry could not believe her ears. The fate of the universe itself seemed to be at stake. And this woman could only think about wielding power back home at Flitheimer University. Nor did she seem at all concerned for the fate of Dr. D. or Troy Talbot.

But then, she was a bit of a bitch, wasn't she? What more could you expect.

Oh, dear, Diane thought, chastising herself. How uncharitable of me. She was sure Dr. Vernon had her good points. None came immediately to mind, though . . . Oh, bother.

"We were separated from our friends. Can you help them, too?" asked Diane.

Zorin smiled. "I'm willing to do anything to help you. However, I desperately need your assistance first."

"Exactly what is your escape plan?" said Viv, her eyes screwed up with new suspicion, only slightly mitigated by her obvious attraction for this dashing figure of a man. "By the way, Zorin . . ."

"Yes?"

"Could anyone be eavesdropping?"

"You mean, is this place equipped with surreptitious listening devices? Oh, almost certainly. But I've made allowances for that already."

"Oh. Good."

"As to my plan of escape . . ."

Zorin went over to the cell's solitary lighting fixture, an affair shaped like a torch, and extracted it from its wall mount. Beckoning with his free hand, he walked off in the direction from which he had come. "Follow me, if you please."

The torch's light illuminated an opening in the far wall. Zorin walked through it. The Earth men followed.

"As you can see, these cells down here are interconnected."

"Strange," Vivian commented.

"I did the interconnecting myself, to give myself some room."

"Uh, weak walls, or the M'Guh Fon again?"

"The latter. Please watch your step among this rubble here."

"Ouch," Dr. Wussman said as he stumbled over something. He grumbled briefly, then giggled again.

The torchlight flickered through another dank straw-filled room and through another breach in the wall. The way then led through a zigzagging corridor, its floor squeaky with rodent-like creatures, walls glistening with moisture.

"Ewwwww," Dr. Wussman said. "Rats. I hate rats."

"Those don't look like rats," Diane said.

"Don't be such a sissy, Wussman," Vivian said sharply.

Finally, the corridor debouched into another cell. Zorin halted. The torch's feeble light guttered as though disturbed by what it shed its light upon.

When she saw the strange affair in the middle of the cell, Diane stopped in her tracks. Vernon and Wussman bumped into her.

Wussman was the first to react. "What the hell is *that*?"

Diane had been about to ask the exact same question. It was nothing more than a pyramid-shaped frame about six and a half feet high at the apex, constructed out of synthetic-concrete reinforcing rods.

"It's a pyramid made out of concrete reinforcing rods," Zorin said.

"Interesting," Vivian said skeptically. "What's it do?"

Zorin hung the torch on its mount in the wall. He turned.

"That, my friends," he said, pointing, "is a teleportation device."

Chapter Eleven

"I surrender, I surrender," said Tobor the robot, floppy arms wobbling as it clanked about in a circle.

He looked about to foul his metal breeches in fear. Dr. Dimension half expected little nuts and bolts to drop from the creature's backside.

"Calm down, robot," he admonished. "We've been in worse situations. Haven't we, Talbot? . . . Oh, Talbot. Wake up, sleepyhead."

"Huh?" Talbot sat up. "Boy. How long was I out?"

"You passed out when the blond began to dance on the bar and do a striptease. It's closing time."

"I missed last call?"

"I was just telling our robot friend that we've been in scrapes half again as dicey as this one."

"We have? Oh, yeah, we have. Uh, what scrape are we in now?"

"Nothing much. Aliens are going to board and kill us."

"Oh. Is that all? Boy, things have sure been happening lately. All kinds of crashing and blowing up and stuff like that. Don't worry Tobor. Doc'll handle things."

"You don't understand," said Tobor, his voice a neurotic whine. "You don't recognize that voice. It's, it's—"

The video screen began to warble and sputter. An image began to resolve.

Dr. Dimension reached to adjust the tuning.

"Do not attempt to adjust the picture."

Doc halted his motion. "Huh?"

"I am controlling transmission. I control the horizontal, I control the vertical."

"Yeah? Well, you're doing a lousy job. You ought to get a pair of rabbit ears. In any case, good luck."

"Silence."

"Anything you say. Is this a party line, or are you just having a good time?"

"Impudent alien pond-scum!"

"Say, can you change your focus to a soft blur? I don't like you in crystal clarity."

"How do you choose to die, alien scum people? Slowly? Or *very* slowly?"

On the screen, metal gleamed in a rainbow of chromatic dance. Stainless steel meshed with flesh. It was a face from some dark technological hell, half humanoid, half machine. The creature's mouth was an experiment perpetrated by a mad prosthodontist.

"We surrender!" cried Tobor, still dancing in contraption conniptions.

"Look, our hands are up," said Troy.

Doc snorted as the ghastly half-mechanical face on the screen. "You want us to raise a white flag? Bend over and tie our shoelaces with our tongues? Do you see threatening weapons pointed your way? What, is your rube-meter broken? Does this trio of losers look likely to kick alien behind? You've got us, whoever you are. Our goose is cooked, our cat is out of the bag and skinned." He wiggled his fingers. "You see these erect appendages? In human it means 'we give up.' "

A grating grunt. "A wise decision. You will stay exactly in those positions while our grapplers deal with your pathetic vessel. Prepare your tiny brains for interrogation."

Doc D. grimaced. The voice sounded like a garbage disposal with an Austrian accent. Nor did Doc much like the looks of the hole from which it originated. The mouth was big, filled with shiny chromium teeth filed to razor-sharp points.

"You know, pal," said the Doc, "if you ever bit your tongue, you'd be in big trouble."

"Repeat that statement?"

"Just trying to be friendly. Permit me to introduce myself. I'm Dr. Demetrios Demopoulos, a.k.a. Dr. Dimension. I prefer the latter appellation. The quivering pile of useless muscle, there, is my assistant, Troy Talbot. If I was born with a name like that, I'd be president. The sniveling bucket of robotic bolts is Tobor. Now, if you have a little leisure time to spare, we wouldn't mind knowing who our captor is."

"Danger!" warbled Tobor. "That's Baron Skulkrak. You don't mess with the Baron! We're doomed. Doomed. Ahhhhhh—" The robot keeled over and crashed to the desk noisily, legs kicking and arms spasming with naked robot terror.

"Baron? We have an aristocratic in our midst? I am honored." Doc bowed.

On the screen, lights twinkled in the lenses of cyborg eyeballs mounted in a head that was a horrific assemblage of stitched-together sections of leathery flesh. A studded metallic hockey mask affair half covered the face. The guy looked like he needed a fistful of aspirin every hour just to get by.

The mouth pulled into a rictus of a smile. "I am Skulkrak. We shall be up close and personal soon. Prepare for pain."

The image on the screen moved off-camera.

"Did you hear that, Troy? Prepare for pain. How do you do that, anyway? Exercises?"

The little space cruiser began to shake as though in the clutches of some giant invisible bird of prey. Doc tumbled to the deck and rolled. Something rolled onto him. Troy.

"Ooof!" he said. "Hmmmmph! Mumphaz!"

"What was that, Doc?"

"Mumphaz rifmell."

"What? What was that?"

"Mumphaz . . . rifmell!"

"Mumphaz rifmell. Gee, I have no idea— Sorry, Doc, let me get off you, here. Now, what did you say?"

"I said, get the hell off me, you big jerk!"

"Didn't sound like what you said."

Doc D. was able to get up just in time to be hit by the concussion as the main hatch blew open. He got knocked back and down, and Troy fell atop him again. Acrid smoke filled the ship.

Soldiers dressed in exotic spiked armor stormed in, blasters at the ready. They did not look like people who were in touch with their emotions, nor did they give the appearance of ever having taken sensitivity training. They had probably never joined a consciousness-raising support group or thought about going on a strict vegan diet. They did not care whether trees or animals lived or died. They did not recycle bottles.

They cared nothing for stewardship of the land.

Tobor was positively abject, groveling before the invaders, moaning and begging for his life. Not a pretty sight. Lost on everyone was the fact he had no life to beg for.

"Well, this is it, Doc," said Troy. "We've had it. We're goners."

"Troy, don't you see?" said Doc, out of the side of his mouth. "This is the best thing that could have happened."

Troopers swarmed over the ship like army ants. Our intrepid heroes were hoisted up and roughly carted away toward the main hatch.

"The best thing that could have happened?" said Troy Talbot. "It is? Oopph!" The exclamation was due to clumsy troopers dropping the lad on his head.

"Talbot, you ninny. These must be the blokes that kidnapped Diane, right?"

"Gee, Doc— Yah!" Troy's head whanged against the side of the hatch as the eager troopers bustled to get him out. "Ouch! Darn it. Never thought of that, Doc. You're absolutely— Yow!"

Doc winced. "I wonder if brain damage is reversible in some cases." He clucked in pity.

"Gee—this is great," Troy trumpeted. "We're going to rescue Diane!"

Whang!

Troy's head nearly sheared off an overhanging instrument rack inside the alien ship.

"Doc, this is great! We're going to see Diane. Doc. This is great! We're going to see Diane. Doc, this is great, we're going to see Diane. Doc—"

Two troopers had Doc, carrying him like a sack of potatoes between them.

"Troy, shut up."

"—Is great! We're going to see Diane. Doc, this is great—"

"Troy shut the hell up!"

Pain, torture, being trapped in a room full of insurance salesmen—anything was better than listening to this human broken record, babbling.

"Somebody slap him," Dr. Dimension said.

One of the troopers did.

Whap!

Troy blinked, his face turning pink again.

"Thanks, Doc, I needed that!"

"My pleasure, Talbot."

"Where are they taking us?"

"Straight to hell."

"Gee, and me without my suntan lotion."

"Well, not hell, really. We've been invited to tea with this Baron fellow. Tea for three, and me for thee."

"Never touch the stuff, Doc. Don't drink tea or coffee. The body's a temple, you know."

"I think someone's rung your temple bell, mahatma."

Behind them came a *clunk-clunk-clunk,* Tobor's head bouncing on the corrugated floor as the troopers dragged him along.

"Oh, mercy, mercy me," moaned Tobor.

"Have a care there, fellows," said Doc. "You're liable to bash him into a different personality, and I'm fed up enough with the ones he's been through."

"Danger! Danger, Will Robinson!"

"Oh, crap," said Doc. "Bounce him a little more, huh? Hard."

* * *

Although Dr. Dimension had been in space but a short time, he was already a bit jaded about it, weary of the black reaches, the majestic vastness, the cold, star-swept emptiness of it all. And he was by now fed up with spaceships.

However, he had to admit that Baron Skulkrak's had a new spin to it. The troopers carted them into a room with a pronounced art deco feel, severe, jagged lightning-like lines abounding, absolutely electric with implied power.

The troopers dumped Troy and Doc unceremoniously onto the deck.

The robot was deposited beside them. For some reason Tobor was mercifully quiet. Doc D. stood up and brushed off his stained and tattered not-quite-white lab coat.

"Smells like the Fourth of July, Doc," said Troy, hauling himself to his feet like the brave quarterback he was. After all, he'd been in rougher games than this. He had survived worse pileups on the old gridiron.

Doc sniffed the air. "I detect the distinct odor of manure. Weird taste in incense."

"Sure smells bad."

"I believe that's the idea, Talbot. Now, the question is, where is our host? Maybe underneath that brash exterior is a shy kind of guy."

"Doc, you're a card," Troy said with a little chuckle.

Hidden speakers suddenly telescoped from the four corners of the room. An orchestra of trumpetlike instruments blared a fanfare. Flares lighted up to either side of a dais, and flashpots or their equivalent went off, billowing noxious clouds of smoke.

"P.U.," said Troy, holding his nose.

"Smellavision!" quipped the Doc.

When the smoke cleared, a gigantic creature stood before them, bearing the head that they had seen in the video screen. The body was immensely repulsive, a solid seven feet high. Here and there, flesh lived with steel and titanium. The arms were gargantuan, bulging with muscles and ... what were those things at the elbows—gears? A spiked morningstar dangled from an immense codpiece. A jet-black cape depended from barbell shoulders.

"Shudder, puny nothings. Cringe before the might of Baron Skulkrak."

The giant held up a fist studded with black metallic spikes.

A gurgling, extenuated fart rumbled from the Baron's nether parts.

"Doc!" said Troy. "Did you hear that?"

The surrounding troopers froze.

"Yes, Troy. I believe I did," said Doc. "I believe that Cleveland heard it as well."

The Baron stood rock solid. The protruding eyes seemed to dare anyone to comment on the sound that had just occurred. He glared down at the puny humans on the metal deck before him and opened his fearsome mouth again to make a proclamation.

"You will tell me in detail what you were doing on the trash planet," he demanded, his voice throbbing, his pronounced Adam's apple bobbing, his morningstar swinging menacingly.

"We crashed," said Dr. Dimension. "By the way, nice codpiece. You could hide a good-size tuna under there, let alone a cod."

The cyborg's eyes blazed. "How dare you act impertinent with me, hairy one! Now the others will observe as I crush your head."

The monster stepped down from the dais, reaching out with a sinewy mailed hand, its fingers talon-tipped.

For once, the Doc regretted his overactive mouth. He wished for a time machine to go back and kick himself in the butt. Alas, no such contraption was available, and the only instrument available to save him was what had got him into trouble in the first place.

"Won't that rather damage all the information you want?" said Doc D.

"No. We have amazing information extraction methods," said the Baron. "Yes. I think I'm going to enjoy this."

The creature approached.

There was no escape. Doc braced himself. He'd always wondered what his brains looked like. Hopefully, he'd be able to remain conscious long enough to find out.

The Baron's fearsome hand advanced.

The doctor's fearing brain retreated. However, there was this cranium in the way. Nuts.

The Baron laughed and snarled maniacally.

Another fart caught him mid-step. The Baron froze.

It started innocuously, enough. A slight murmur, no more than one from an upset tummy. But instead of dying off, it built. A murmur to a mumble. A mumble to a grumble. A small grumble to a medium grumble that grew into a roar of gastric distress.

The Baron looked down at his mid-section.

"Body plumber!"

The roar pushed and churned. Volume and expansion were too much. Flimsy and delicate metallo-flesh gave way, halfheartedly holding in place.

Brrrrrppptttt.

"Body plumber!" barked the Baron again, what little flesh in his face turning a violent greenish-red. "Body plumber, the wrench!"

Bbbbbbbbrrpppppttttt!

From a hidden recess, a gnarled dwarf of a creature trotted out, a toolbox in his hand.

"You called, Boss?"

Brrrrrrpt!

"Are you deaf, you idiot? Fix me!"

The dwarf was a creature with pointed ears, a pair of eyes like dots on a die, and a button nose. It nodded and ducked underneath the Baron's cape, which billowed in the breeze aft.

Brrrrrppppppppppt!

. . . And was summarily blown out again.

The little creature reached into a pocket, pulled out a clip, and fastened it over its nose. Then it ventured bravely back into the gale, intently, fighting inch by inch.

Brrrrrrrrrrrppppppppppttttttt!

Dr. D. was so astonished, and so grateful to still be drawing breath (no matter how increasingly foul) that he could not move, could only stand in awe at this spectacle.

Troy Talbot was similarly affected. The robot moved not a jot.

Squeaking, hammering, and wrench-turning sounds emanated from beneath the folds of the robe.

Plumbing finally completed, the dwarf emerged, bowed, and got away quickly with its life.

"Now then, where was I?" said the Baron.

One final toot. *Brrp.*

It was too much for one of the troopers. The helmeted humanoid started tittering. He clamped his gloved hands over his helmet to stop himself, but could not. He was like a man with terminal hiccups.

Baron Skulkrak's eyes, glowing with rage at the affront, swiveled their gimlet gaze to the offender. His hand went to one of three holsters on the utility belt and drew out a blaster the size of a cannon. The other troopers cleared away from the line of fire. The doomed trooper held up a pleading hand.

"My lord, I beg you—!"

Brrpp!

Oops. The trooper doubled over with laughter.

Skulkrak fired, and a long plume of flame roared from the business end of the weapon.

The trooper was blown to bits.

Total silence as the scattered remnants burned.

Those malevolent eyes tracked along the ranks again, daring anyone else to let out so much as a titter.

Dr. D. had felt mirth trembling inside of him, sure enough, but the sight of that trooper getting immolated scotched it sure and certain.

"You will be happy to know, Dr. Dimension—if that absurd name really is yours—that I have slaked my anger," said the Baron. "For now." Those sharp jaws snapped down with immense finality.

"Glad to know that," said Dr. D. "Now, perhaps you'd like to help us out. We're not looking to cause any inconvenience or trouble. We're looking for lost companions and a lost home planet. If you can put these together for us, preferably in that order, we'd be mighty obliged!"

The Baron looked down on the doctor much as a spider might look down on a fly that had politely requested release from its web. "You are not answering my questions satisfactorily. I think you are hiding something." The ends of the mouth turned upward in a parody of a grin. "Besides, I have the itch to use my interrogation equipment." He clapped his hands. "Guards. See to it."

Troopers bustled. They hauled butt, then hauled Dr. D. and Troy Talbot and the robotoid. Tables slid out from the sides of the room, and Doc D. and company were strapped into place. (It took quite a bit of effort to accomplish this with the robot, but somehow the task was done).

Baron Skulkrak pressed a button on the side of the wall. An elaborate array of machinery lowered from the ceiling, extensions extruding, probes twirling, flashing lenses rotating. From the middle of all this, three conical devises extended.

Lights glittered on this machine from hell, with the same maniacal ruthlessness that glittered in the orbs of the monstrosity called Baron Skulkrak.

"What—what is it Doc?" said Troy, sensing that this thing did not mean them well.

"Looks like an information extractor of some sort to me," said Doc D. "And doubtless an effective one. This Baron Skulkrak means business. But we're telling him the truth. What more can we do?"

"Uhm—Die horribly?"

Dr. D. thought about that.

"Actually, Talbot, I'd really rather not at the moment, thank you."

The sinister conical devices bore downward.

Chapter Twelve

"I said, it's a teleportation device."

"Pardon me, Zorry," said Vivian. "By 'teleportation,' do you mean the process of breaking down a mass into its constituent atoms, transmitting those atoms to another place, and then reassembling the original mass?"

"No," replied Zorin. "That would be matter transmission, a different proposition entirely. Teleportation is the instantaneous displacement of mass from one location to the other."

"That's utterly impossible," stated Dr. Vivian Vernon, Ph. D., speaking ex catehdra.

"Perhaps," Zorin conceded. "The physics of uncertainty says that the various properties of matter are hard to pin down, one of them being position. You might say that, as far as subatomic particles are concerned, their mass, energy, momentum, *and* position are negotiable. Teleportation merely seeks to exploit these ambiguities."

"Hmm, the new physics," Vivian said. "That's just being developed on our planet. I'm not sure the whole thing's not a Western bourgeois delusion. Besides, you're dealing with things a lot bigger than subatomic particles."

"Quite so. And, for all I know, teleportation might well be a delusion. For, you see, I have not tested this device."

"So, you need a guinea pig?" Vivian pushed Diane forward. "Take her."

"Just a darn minute," said Diane. "First of all . . . Dr.

Zorin, forgive me, but this contraption doesn't exactly look like super-science."

Zorin replied, "I realized that as contraptions go, this one's unprepossessing, but I haven't told you something. This isn't the teleportation mechanism. Think of it as an antenna."

"An antenna? What's it supposed to receive? Radio waves?"

"Nothing so mundane. The analogy only goes so far. All mass effects the curvature of the space around it. Do you understand this?"

"Sure, according to Dr. Einstein."

"I have never heard of the gentleman, but he was absolutely correct. This pyramidal shape, for some reason that is still obscure, acts as a focus for certain energies, and merely facilitates the process of teleportation. It does other things, too. Oddly enough, razor blades stored inside this device stay sharp much longer. However, as I said, this simple metal framework is not what does the trick."

"What does?"

"The M'Guh Fon."

"Wow," Diane said in wonderment. "How can that be? I thought it was back on the trash planet."

"It is. And that is where you will teleport.'"

Diane gave a little joyous jump. "Oh, goodie! I'll be able to tell Dr. Dimension what happened to us—" She broke off. "Oh, I didn't tell you about the rest of our party."

"You have companions stranded there? All the better."

"Good. Uh, will you teleport these two?"

"If they wish."

"I want nothing to do with it," Vivian said adamantly.

Zorin was immensely puzzled. "Pardon me. Am I hearing you correctly? You're saying that you'd rather stay and rot in this hellhole? Perhaps not. Perhaps you prefer the idea of facing Estrogena again?"

Vivian screwed up her face. She was stumped.

"Oh, don't worry about them," said Diane. "They're both fuddy-duddies, but they'll go along with it." She stepped forward, chin held up bravely. "I'm ready to be a guinea pig."

"You must be the loveliest specimen of whatever animal it is you refer to. But realize first why I must test with a subject other than myself. If it fails, I could try again. But if there's a mishap, there would be no way to fix it. You do understand that I'm asking you to risk your life?"

"Yes."

"Yet you are still willing?"

"I trust you implicitly, Dr. Zorin," Diane said. "Really, I do. Believe me."

He drew close to her and looked deep into her eyes. "I see you do," said Zorin. "But don't worry. I would not ask you to do it if I thought there was great risk. I'm fairly sure it will work. But I must be sure. Excellent. I knew you were a brave woman as well as a beautiful one. I just felt it in my bones."

Pitter-patter, pitter-patter . . .

"How will you know it works?" Vivian asked.

Zorin turned to her. "I will know. If we are successful, I will teleport the two of your first, then follow. There is enough raw material on the dumping planet to gimcrack together any gadget we might wish."

Zorin turned to Diane.

"Are you ready, my dear?"

"Ready as I'll ever be."

"Oh, there is one detail that might disturb you. Your clothes might not teleport with you."

Diane nodded. "Uh-huh." She swallowed. "Why?"

"The molecules of your clothing aren't connected, really, to the mass of your body, which is the primary mass being teleported. Your garments could make the journey, but they might arrive in scraps. I'm not sure about this. The subtleties of this new process are somewhat arcane. I think it would be safer if you disrobed before teleporting. Will you?"

She looked into his eyes and surrendered.

"Yes," she said, as his eyes mollified her fears and love bloomed in her heart. "Yes, I will, yes . . ."

Diane Derry shed the last article of her clothing.

Modesty dictated that she did so cloaked in the darkness of the next chamber. She'd exacted from Dr. Wussman a solemn promise to keep his eyes closed, but Wussman had held up a hand to swear while concealing the other behind his back. Fingers crossed, the rat. Doubtless. But what was a girl to do in these dire circumstances? As for Dr. Vernon, well, who cared. And she didn't mind if Zorin looked or not. He more or less had to. After all, he was a scientist, and this was his experiment.

She threw her bra and underwear out into the other room for Vivian to collect and save.

No, she didn't like being naked in front of other people . . . not like this. But what other choice did she have? There was no question that she had volunteered. Still, she had reservations. Shedding one's clothing was not exactly the sort of thing a nice girl did, and Diane could already feel the blush creeping up from her ample chest to her round cheeks . . . and down to her rounder cheeks.

However, this was science.

And this wasn't Earth.

In her heart she was still a proper lady, and what she was doing now was for a good cause. A small sacrifice, but then, who would be around to see her? If a tree falls alone in a forest, does it truly make a noise? If a woman travels to an alien planet starkers, but there's no one there to see her, is she truly—?

Whoa. Of course, Troy and Dr. D. might be there. But chances were slim that she'd teleport directly to the crash site. Zorin said it was a million to one that would happen. She would materialize near the M'Guh Fon, wherever it was, and odds were against it being anywhere near the *Mudlark*. Well, in any case, Troy was a pussycat. But she might have trouble facing Dr. D. in the nude.

Best not to worry about it. It really didn't matter that she wasn't going to be wearing a stitch even if she happened to teleport to the crash site. After all, she had spare clothing in the ship. She could slip into a jumpsuit quick.

"Are you ready, Diane?" Zorin called.

"As ready as I'll ever be. Okay, everyone, eyes shut!"

"Oh, come on out, you silly girl," Dr. Vernon said with annoyance. "No one wants to ogle you."

"I do," Wussman tittered.

Whap.

"Dr. Wussman, you promised!"

"Ouch. Okay, Diane, I'm not looking."

"Okay, here I come."

Diane peeked around the corner. Everyone, including Dr. Zorin, stood facing away from the device.

Arms around her rib cage—it was chilly down here!—Diane tiptoed to the pyramid and stood directly under the apex, as she was instructed to do.

"All right, Diane," Zorin began. "As I've told you, this teleportation technique is really mental in nature. You will be using the power of the M'Guh Fon. I will be channeling its power for you, but you will be using it. Get your mind into a receptive mood."

Diane closed her eyes and tried to make her mind a blank. Impossible, but she tried anyway.

. . .

. . .

. . . Wonder what Zorin looks like with no cl—

No good! It's impossible to think of nothing! All right. What did she want most? What would make her happy? Going home! Of course. She was homesick as she had never been before.

She tapped her bare heels together three times.

"There's no place like home," she murmured. "There's no place like home."

"Good, good," said Zorin, his back still turned. "Now, let yourself be carried off by the M'Guh Fon."

Diane opened one eye to a slit and saw that Dr.

Wussman had his head turned and indeed was ogling her. The sneak. Well, never mind him. She wanted to go home. Home. Yes, home.

Home . . .

Chapter Thirteen

"And now, in the spirit appropriate, please turn to Hymn Number Ninety-Two. 'Naked We Stand Before Thee, O Lord.' "

The wheeze of a pipe organ flowed.

There came a whoosh of displaced air.

Diane Derry blinked against the sudden daylight filtered through stained glass. She found herself standing on steps that faced a church full of worshipers in their Sunday best. Perfume and shaving lotion smells came to her. To her right was the pulpit, and sermonizing from it was a minister in black robes. To her left, in white robes, a church choir and organist.

Before her spread the crowded pews of the First Lutheran Church of Flat Butte, Nebraska. In the front row, mouths agape, were her parents, her brothers and sisters, and a high school boyfriend, left behind in her pursuit of scientific knowledge.

There was a collective gasp.

She looked down at herself.

She was still buck naked.

She screamed and covered herself.

"Diane?" she heard her father say with stunned disbelief as he half rose from his pew.

"It's Diane Derry!" she heard the congregation whisper.

"Amen!" the Reverend Beekman intoned, not having seen her immediately. He turned and saw. His jaw would have dropped to his feet had it not been attached.

"Uh . . . hi, everyone. I can explain—"

ZAP!

"POP!"

A whooshing of air, a whirligig of colors. The sounds of a crowd, the chill of exposure, the smell of anger and hate.

She was on another platform, in another place.

Flags whipped in a stirring breeze. A crowd of hands were raised in rigid salute. A foreign barking echoed through a stadium in an alien language.

"Sieg heil! Sieg heil!"

A few yards from her behind a podium was a man with oddly cropped black hair and a Charlie Chaplin mustache. His voice boomed.

He seemed to have been in the midst of a speech, but now the man was gawking silently.

Diane Derry felt tens of thousands of Nazi eyes trained upon her. And she was still naked as the day she was born, although quite a bit larger.

She covered herself again.

"Ach du lieber!" said the Führer, eyes bulging.

"Sorry to interrupt," Diane said.

She ran and tripped over a jackboot.

ZAP!

"WHOOSH!"

"Now here's a gal I know you'll enjoy. She flew in all the way from Hollywood to entertain you folks, and boy, do her arms hurt!"

Diane found herself on yet another stage, this time running pell-mell toward a man with a ski-slope nose holding a golf club. Breasts jiggling madly, she ran directly into him, knocking him over, her bosom almost smothering him to death.

"Mmmpph!" said the man.

The audience was entirely of men in U.S. military uniforms.

They cheered wildly.

"Well, hi there," said the man, struggling for breath. "What planet did you drop from?"

"You wouldn't believe me," said Diane. "But I really need to get back there."

"Stick around for the next set. Speaking of sets, you have a nice— Hey, where're you going? You can be part of the act."

She pushed herself back up to her feet. The servicemen were going wild, whistling and throwing their hats into the air.

"I need to get back to Dr. Dimension and my boyfriend Troy Talbot!"

"Aw, do you have to go so soon? I want you to meet a friend of mine. Name's Bing. You'll like him." His smile faded. "They always do, the rat."

She tapped her heels together.

ZAP!

"WHOOOSH!"

Suddenly, the whirling lights again, this time longer than before.

Abruptly, she found herself on a podium yet again. Apparently, she was destined for show business. This podium was occupied by an seven-foot-tall armored robot-man with a morningstar phallus and a surly attitude. Ranks of troopers were arrayed all over the chamber, and she immediately recognized them. At least they were much like the chaps who'd captured her on the trash planet.

Shackled to tables with all kinds of mechanical paraphernalia around them were Dr. D., Troy Talbot, and a funny-looking robot. "Doc?" she said.

"Diane?"

"Diane," Troy yelped. "Have I got X-ray vision now, or are your clothes gone?"

Doc D. simply ogled the sight with a silly grin.

Diane slapped her arms down to hide her nakedness. "Doc! Hang on. We're coming to help you. We've got the tools of the M'Guh Fon to help you."

"Seize her!" cried the fierce robot-man. The troopers struggled among themselves to be first.

Diane closed her eyes and brought her bare heels together, three times, fast.

ZAP!

"WHOOSH!"

And as quick as that, she was back in the dark cell, standing inside the pyramid. Her knees buckled, and she fell.

Zorin was first to her and helped her up.

"Are you all right?"

Diane nodded as she was led out of the pyramid. Her clothes were handed to her and, she got into them as quick as she could.

"Well, something went wrong," Vivian was saying. "Nice try, Zorin. She was barely gone a second or two."

"It was a bit longer," Zorin said. "Diane, can you talk?"

"Sure. It worked, all right. Boy, did it work. You wouldn't believe the places I bopped around to."

"I gather not the trash planet," Zorin said.

"No. But I found Dr. Dimension and Troy. There was this funny robot with them. Anyway, they were prisoners, aboard ship, and their captors were the same guys who took us, led by this huge man who looked more like a robot than a man."

"Skulkrak," Zorin said, nodding ruefully.

"Whoever he was, he was scary. Zorin, what happened? Why did I teleport there?"

"This is very interesting," Zorin said. "I will have to think on the matter awhile. Um, you said 'places.' "

"Oh, it was probably a dream or a hallucination. Some weird effect. Forget it."

But she'd never forget the hundreds of pious, moralizing eyes on her nakedness. Never!

"No doubt. This complicates things."

Vivian had seated herself on a wooden pallet. "Well, we'll never get out of this dump."

"Perhaps not," Zorin said. "But we know the technique works. The easiest thing to do is to teleport to the location of the M'Guh Fon. Using the artifact to teleport to a different location is a very difficult trick; unless, you happen to have an exact set of coordinates. Which, it just so happens, I have."

Diane asked, "Really? Can we still escape?"

"I believe so. Diane, I'll need your help. I will give you some very explicit instructions, which you must carry out to the letter to achieve the intended effect."

"Sure, Zorin. Anything you say."

"Are we all going to get naked now?" Dr. Wussman asked eagerly, his tongue slavering inside his mouth.

A thrown pebble went *pock* off the side of his head.

"Ouch! Damn you, Viv, that really hurt!"

"The intended effect," Vivian said casually.

Chapter Fourteen

Among the tangled electronic clutter in Baron Skulkrak's interrogation room was a large television screen.

When the rotating conical devices reached the foreheads of Dr. Dimension, Troy Talbot, and the robot (whatever identity it was traveling under at this moment), they stopped.

The television flickered to life with swirling vague images.

Baron Skulkrak's huge form bent over. Cyborg eyes appraised his helpless victims.

"First, extract information from the young one's cerebrum," Baron Skulrak ordered.

The conical device glowed a cherry red.

A keening sounded. The lights on the dangling device began to pulse on and off. "Ooooh," said Troy. "Doc—uhhhhhhhhh!"

"What's happening, son? Are you in unbearable agony?"

"Yeah, Doc. My brain—it itches."

"Oh, that's terri—" Doc did a take. "It itches? Unbearable agony, eh? Well, at least you know you've got one. When it stops itching, though, that might be a bad sign."

"Gee, Doc. I never thought of it that way."

"Enjoy your brain while you know you have it."

"Okay."

Skulkrak seemed volcanically disturbed. "This exercise was not created to be enjoyed."

"I'm not having the best time of my life, here, I assure you," said Doc D. "The robot seems pretty unthrilled about it as well."

Baron Skulkrak was not satisfied. "No. That will not do. I demand simperings and sobbings. I demand pleas for mercy. I demand howls of anguish. You idiots are in a hopeless situation. I am about to tap your minds much as a Entithuvian bush sloth taps the heart of a *manungi* tree."

"Charming conceit, that."

"You will quail. You will weep. You will implore!"

"Ouch," said Troy. "That bunion of mine is acting up again, Doc."

"Your feet itch now? Or is that where your brains are?"

Doc D. thought things over. On one hand, if he continued with this stiff-upper-lip act he'd have the satisfaction of satisfying his own sense of self-pride. On the other hand, if he failed to make the pitiable noises Baron Skulkrak seemed to relish, then His Horribleness might surely apply further unpleasant techniques to wraggle that out of his victims.

Hmm.

There was but one logical and practical thing to do.

Doc D. groaned. He whimpered. He groveled. "Ohhhhhh. Baron Skulkrak. Please. Have mercy. Don't suck our brains dry. I won't be able to work in my profession. The only thing left would be running for congress."

The Baron leaned closer. "Yes?"

"And whatever you do, don't throw me in that briar patch!"

Those mottled, knife-gash lips curled up horribly. "There. That's better. Music to my ears. What are we drawing from the big one?"

"Nothing yet, fearsome one," replied the goggled attendant at the controls.

"Increase power!"

"But Your Horribleness. We could liquefy his gray matter. It could leak out of his ears."

"Do it!"

"Yes, Your Mercilessness."

The attendant's clawlike fingers turned the knob.

The humming and squawking of the machine increased threefold, working up to a feverish pitch.

The static on the television set began to take on a kind of shadowy form.

"Great leader! Something is coming into view," screeched the attendant.

The Baron's eyes blazed. "The M'Guh Fon. It must be the M'Guh Fon!"

Doc D. turned to see what all the fuss was about. The image in the television screen was resolving into focus.

A jockstrap.

"What?" said the Baron.

"I'd always expected as much," said Doc D. "Of course, it's a very mechanically oriented jockstrap. Looks rather uncomfortable, though."

Secretly, he was glad, for once, that Troy was as dense as he was. Actually, there was no doubt more in his head than an athletic supporter—a pair of sweat socks at the very least—but Troy was managing to stall them.

"Bah!" said Baron Skulkrak disgustedly. "Forget this one. Try the graying old one with the big mouth and the snide attitude. I am enjoying the way he screams."

"You should hear me with a backup band," said Dr. Dimension.

What to do, what to do?

Well, nothing more or less than go with the flow, Doc D. decided. First of all, make sure that the Baron's sadistic proclivities were properly satisfied.

"No. No, please not me. Take the robot, not me."

The Baron's eyes lit up.

"Yes, Doctor. And well you should be frightened. My special ray will rob you of your very soul."

"Hell, I sold that long ago. Tell you what. Troy and I here are pretty good with mechanical stuff. Suppose you let us have a look at your colostomy bag problem, or whatever it is. If we fix it for you and if you help us find who we're looking for, and then you let us go, we'll be even."

A scraggly eyebrow rose above an electronic eye. "What problem?"

"Huh? Why, those horrendous passages of gas. The party surprises. Flatulence."

The steel-wool eyebrow wiggled.

"The farts, Baron."

" 'Farts?' I know of no farts, as you call them." The Baron swung his gaze to his men, daring them to support this claim. "Does anyone here know of . . . 'farts?' "

A chorus of denials arose from the rank and file.

"There," said the Baron with satisfaction, a parody of an ugly grin across his steel teeth. "Now then—"

Brrrp!

"—You will tell me—"

Brrrrrrrrrrp!

"—What you know of the M'Guh Fon."

Brrrrrrrrppppppppppppt!

The metal-and-flesh face was stony.

This concerto for an imposing leader and sphincter-trumpet was almost too much to bear. Doc D. felt a raucous guffaw rise up inside him.

He contained it, just barely.

He said, "Perhaps if you could tell me something more of this McGuffin, I might be able to help you a bit more."

"I have been sent by the empress, the estimable Estrogena of the Thing Dynasty, to sweep and scour the trash planet in search of an alien artifact known as the M'Guh Fon."

"How do you pronounce that again?"

"M'Guh, glottal stop, accent on the second syllable."

"M'Guh . . ."

"Fon. M'Guh Fon."

"M'Guh Fon . . . Splendid . . . Wait a moment! You are supposed to be telling me about it!"

"I'm supposed to be telling you?" Doc asked. "Nevah hoida the thing. What is it, and what's it look like?"

"It is probably very small. I do not know what it looks like or, indeed, what it is. I can only surmise that it is an article either of great value or great power. The very presence of you strangers upon the trash planet— strangers with a very poor cover story—means to me that you must be searching for the M'Guh Fon as well. You could have more knowledge than you let on. Do you?"

"Nope. None. Zilch. Nada."

"You are very probably lying. Luckily for me, I just had the extractor overhauled."

"You should have had it done at Sears; they're running a special."

A thought presented itself. Perhaps M'Guh Fon was an alien name for the Magnetic Monocle. Well, if it were, the Baron would surely be pissed off to find out that it had been inadvertently destroyed.

Uh-oh.

If this extractor truly reads minds, he'd have to somehow hide the thought, the possibility.

Dr. D. had an amazing mind, he knew.

It was time to find the "maze" in the "amazing." He began to think of what he was best at thinking of. Mathematics, physics, and other even more important things.

The conical device twirled, pulsing with a feverish red light. It aimed at Doc's ample cranium and began screeching and crackling, its power beginning to unravel the scientist's threads of thought.

The television set began to flicker.

An image grew there.

Resolved into a fuzzy focus.

Sharpened.

Pastoral music suddenly wafted from the speakers. The image showed a green vale bisected by a bubbling brook. Clouds of equations filled a cerulean sky. Mythical creatures pranced to the music of panpipes. In the foreground, a man sat on a blanket beside a picnic basket and several bottles of wine. He lay supine among three beautiful, voluptuous nymphs, all naked, who stroked his frizzy hair, fed him grapes, and massaged his bare feet.

"Bah! More power!" cried Baron Skulkrak.

The machine began to whine harder.

Sweat broke out on Doc D.'s face.

The nymphs began to get more intimate in their ministrations. The object of their attentions joined in.

A few troopers started to clap and hoot.

Inside his brain, Doc D. concentrated. He was almost enjoying himself. He could feel the device sucking on his brain waves trying to pull them up by their very roots. However, this particular fantasy was always good for getting away from things, and now it worked very well in shielding deeper levels of knowledge from the ruthless paws of Baron Skulkrak.

"Higher power. Destroy the brain if necessary. Suck out the knowledge," demanded Skulkrak.

Zap.

A whoosh of displaced air.

Doc D., amid even his concentration, detected a presence.

He opened his eyes.

Standing on the deck not far from him was none other than Diane Derry, his fabulously endowed assistant.

Without a stitch of clothing on.

"Doc?" she said.

Dr. Dimension's eyes popped out of their sockets. "Diane?" he said.

Troy seemed equally surprised. "Diane, have I got X-ray vision now—or are your clothes gone?"

"Doc," Diane said. "Hang on. We're coming to get you. We've got the tools of the M'Guh Fon to help you."

Doc stared.

Baron Skulkrak barked a command.

The troopers fought among themselves to obey it. Just as astonishment was turning to enjoyment and then to leering ecstasy, the vision vanished with all the suddenness of its coming.

The Brain Extractors, still focused on Dr. D. and Troy, were turning a fiery red. Steam and sparks coughed out.

The apparatus emitted a feeble beeping sound, and smoke rose from the works.

The burgeoning brain waves of Doc D. and Troy had been too much for the poor machine to take.

"Fix it!" demanded Baron Skulkrak of the technician.

Doc noticed the morningstar codpiece swinging like a randy pendulum.

"Pretty nice, eh?" Doc said.

"She spoke to you. She told you she has the M'Guh Fon!"

"Uh . . . uh—"

No use denying it.

"Uh, yeah. She did. That she did."

"You said you didn't know anything about it!" Skulkrak seemed almost hurt.

"Uh, well . . . I can explain. If you'll let me."

"No doubt." The Baron stewed for a moment, stroking his metallic chin thoughtfully. 'I might have to change my tactics. Obviously, whatever the M'Guh Fon is, it enables your associates to do things that seem impossible. Such as teleporting. I do believe I will defer interrogation until we get back to Ovaria, where there is better security. There, you will be subjected to procedures that will make these seem like a sunny day in the park. Prepare yourself, Dr. Dimension, for a new dimension in physical and psychic discomfort."

Once more, the terrible grin.

"Again, with the 'prepare' business. Is there going to be an orientation course?"

Doc D. sighed, his still-heated mind filled with that majestic vision of Diane in the buff.

Now, no matter what happened, no matter what god-forsaken planet he spent his final days upon, he could die a satisfied dirty old man.

Chapter Fifteen

After Zorin announced that the only hope was to try to teleport to a secret mountain hideout, where he also had his laboratory and workshop, the only task left was undressing for the job.

Wussman, suddenly bashful, retreated to the shadows.

Vivian, on the other hand, said, "To hell with it!" and simply stripped, revealing her absolutely stunning body.

Diane looked at her unabashedly, a little envious. Her own figure was pretty good, but it wasn't *that* good. She wondered how breasts could be so . . . well, perky, with absolutely no support.

Then her gaze shifted to Zorin. Diane was beyond blushing or even being embarrassed now. Their lives depended on doing this, and it simply had to be done.

But it was fun, in a way. She felt a little guilty taking in the view of Zorin's tight, slender buttocks.

Zorin turned about, and Diane looked away.

Whoa!

On second thought, better not look. Whew!

"Wussy, where the hell are you?" Vivian called.

"Here."

"Well, come out, silly boy."

"I can't."

"Since when did you get suddenly self-conscious? You haven't been that way in the past, with me."

"Viv, don't blab about our personal life."

"Would Diane get an earful if I did!"

"Viv, please, don't."

"Don't worry, Wussy, your shabby little secrets are safe with me. Come out, come out."

Wussman, hunched over and clutching a clump of straw to his crotch, edged out of the shadows.

"This is absurd. I don't believe this is necessary."

"Of course it's necessary, you fatuous fool. Now come over here and do what Zorin tells you to do."

"You first, Vivian," Zorin instructed. "Diane, as you're already a veteran, you'll be next to last, before me."

"Okay, I'm ready," Vivian said, stepping into the pyramid frame. "Stand right here?"

"Exactly. Now, I'm going to do something different than I did with Diane. I will teleport with you, simultaneously. You'd never be able to find the lab by yourself."

"This should be interesting," Vivian said.

Zorin stepped into the pyramid and put his arms around Vivian. "Press close to me. Close."

Wussman seemed disturbed. "I don't believe this is necessary either," he muttered.

"Closer," instructed Zorin.

Vivian smiled and hugged the handsome man. "I don't mind this one little bit."

"Please be silent, and concentrate. Just follow me. Clear? You will follow me."

"I will follow you," Vivian intoned.

"Don't say that, Viv," Wussman whined. "I'm getting terribly jealous."

"I will follow him," Vivian said firmly. "I love him!"

"Viv, please, you're killing me!"

"Where he goes I'll follow."

Wussman screamed in agony.

Vivian chuckled. "Just kidding, Wussy, dear. Don't fret. Hmm! Sounds like the makings of a good pop song for a girl group. A few more brilliant verses, and I'll call it 'Leader of the Knack'!"

"Oh, you're cruel. You are the cruelest—"

Wussman's rebuke was interrupted by sounds of

voices, soldierly voices coming from far off down the corridor.

"They'll be here shortly," Zorin said, stepping out of the frame and stooping to pick something up. "Diane, take this."

He handed her a length of rusty reinforcing rod.

Puzzled, Diane accepted it. "Beat 'em off with this?"

"Use the M'Guh Fon to channel energy through it. You're attuned to it now, Diane, though you probably don't know it."

"I am?"

"You are. Stand by the opening, there, and make sure no one gets through. I'll give you the signal to leave your station and teleport."

"Uh, right. Okay."

Diane took up her position, flattening herself against the cold, damp wall near the edge of the opening. She was ready for them. Of course, she hadn't the slightest idea of how she was going to stop anyone from coming through the breach. Channel energy. Right. But . . . exactly how did one go about doing that?

Use the M'Guh Fon. Okay. But how? She didn't even know what the M'Guh Fon was, hadn't the vaguest idea of what it looked like. And Zorin expected her to use it.

Using it had to be something like teleporting. How had she done that? Her heels, three times. But that was no good. She tried it, then raised the rusty, bent steel rod. Nothing. Nope. No good. Okay, think of something else. Fast.

The voices—shouting orders, calling, cursing—sounded closer.

She thought hard. What would channel energy through this rod? (Never mind what energy!) She tried to think of something on the trash planet feeding her energy, across space, all the way to this terrible hole. Energy, energy, streaming out . . .

Wait.

Hey. The M'Guh Fon wasn't on the trash planet. But how did she know that?

Voices, shouting. Thundering booted feet, ever nearer.

Okay, it wasn't on the trash planet. So where was it? Didn't matter. Concentrate! Tap that energy! Think of it as fuzzy, prickly stuff, like electricity flowing through a wire, only it wasn't coming through a wire, it was propagating through space ... through space-time! Four-dimensional spacetime, which meant it could get from there (wherever) to here almost instantaneously, not at the limiting speed of light—

The rod throbbed in her hand. She looked down. Didn't look any different. Except at the tip there. It was ... red? Red-hot? No, best not to touch it. But what should she do with a red-hot rod?

Briefly, an image of Zorin's groin flashed through her mind.

Wow! Stop thinking of that, girl! Before you know it you'll—

A castle guardsman walked into the cell, stopped, saw Vivian and Zorin standing naked inside the pyramid.

He chortled lewdly. "Well, well, what have we here?"

Without thinking, without realizing she was already doing it, Diane had come up behind the man and whacked him over the top of the head with the rod. Only it wasn't merely a rusted steel rod anymore. It had something coming out of the top of it. A nimbus of brilliant blue-white energy like the flame of an oxyacetylene torch. It sizzled through the guardsman's shiny helmet and clove it in two. The man fell over with half a smoking head.

She sensed an enemy behind her and whirled. Another palace guardsman, whom she dispatched with a sweeping crosscut. Another came through the breach to take his place, and she did away with him as well.

No more guardsmen came through, but she saw two gun barrels poking out of the darkness, aimed at her.

She fired first, sending a stream of searing blue energy into the breach. An explosion lighted up the cell. Pieces of bodies tumbled out of the hole in the wall, and flames shot out, along with smoke and dust and debris.

"Yuck."

"Diane!"

It was Zorin, and she turned. He was standing inside the pyramid, beckoning. She ran to him.

"Get as close to me as possible."

She wrapped her arms about him and squeezed, pressing her body close. It was nice!

"All right, Diane, follow me, go where I go."

"There's no place like home . . . your home!"

"Home," Zorin intoned.

ZAP!

"WHOOSH!"

Instantly, the cell and the guardsmen disappeared and were replaced by a huge chamber full of weird equipment. Zorin's laboratory, presumably.

"Zorin!" she cried. "We made it!"

"We did, Diane. We did. It was a very risky proposition, but we made it."

"I don't believe I'm alive."

"You're alive."

"I'm very alive."

His face moved in for a kiss. She found herself excepting it. His mouth was moist and delicate, yet firm, with a killer technique behind it that would have blown her socks off if she had been wearing them. He came up for a breath and then dove down for some more, which she would have gladly given him except for two little matters.

First, she was Troy Talbot's girlfriend.

Second, this was no time for hanky-panky. Besides, Drs. Vernon and Wussman were standing off to one side, watching intently. Even after her recent escapades, there were some things that Diane wouldn't do in public.

She gently pushed Zorin away.

"Sorry, Diane, I was simply overcome with emotion. Now, tell me about these other places you teleported to."

"I got bounced around, naked, all over the universe!"

"Interesting."

"It was awful. It was the most embarrassing thing that ever happened to me."

"How odd. Naturally, I'm sorry. But please relate exactly what happened."

"I don't want to even think about it."

"Of course not. Poor Diane. However, rest assured it will be in the interest of science . . . and perhaps of your friends."

Diane could not argue with that. So she told him what had happened, though in an abbreviated version.

Less abbreviated, however, than what she'd worn during the course of these jaunts. She found herself blushing, even as she spoke, particularly when she mentioned the part about shunting into Sunday-morning service at home.

"Curious. You seem to have teleported across the galaxy back to your home."

" 'Seem,' nothing. That's exactly what happened."

"And, pardon me—then you teleported directly to where your friend Dr. Dimension was being held by that monster, Baron Skulkrak?"

"You know him?"

"Alas, all too well. He is the Empress's favorite among her many henchmen, and there's not a nastier creature in the galaxy. No doubt he craves the M'Guh Fon himself, doubtless for his own nefarious purposes. Tell me—by any chance, before this occurred, were you thinking about your friends?"

"Why . . . yes, I believe I was."

"And perchance, before your jaunts to the other places—did they somehow figure into your thinking, or were they suggested to you?"

Diane considered this.

"Why, yes."

"Astonishing. That the M'Guh Fon is psi-interactive was obvious before this, but I did not know how sensitive it was. I am again amazed."

Diane said, "Well, that's all well and good . . . but we've got to find the doctor first, and save him. You promised. He looked like he was in terrible trouble."

"If he is in Skulkrak's grasp, he most certainly is. Unfortunately, it will take some time to arrange for their rescue."

"But I could just teleport back—"

"How could you teleport them here?"

Diane thought about it. "Oh. Right."

"But they can be helped. And I must see to that immediately. Meanwhile, may I suggest that you see to your other friends. There is food and refreshments in the kitchen, and you might find some clothing in the sleeping quarters. Help yourselves, while I attend to my machines. We'll be safe here for the moment, but I must fool the surveillance cameras with a few more tricks I have up my sleeve."

"Okay, but we have to help the doctor soon! You promised, Zorin!"

"I have a plan to save the doctor, but it will take some preparation. Diane, after that act of supreme bravery, how could I go back on my promise? You have won my heart." He took her hand and kissed the back of it. "Be gentle with it, please."

And then, instead of pawing her or doing something, he just left her with her heart melting.

What a gentleman!

No man had treated her with such gallantry, such chivalry before. They usually wanted to get their hands on her in some gross manner.

Except for Troy. Troy Talbot, though, wasn't a gentleman. He was just too dumb to be a flagrant jerk with women, which was part of his charm.

Zorin, though . . .

No one had ever excited her like Zorin before. When he touched her, she turned to melted Swiss cheese inside. He was brilliant, witty, charming, and articulate and . . . Oh, my!

She turned her thoughts away. This was no time for such . . . such wanton desires. She hardly knew the man. She had to remember her loyalties. There were far more important things to be concerned about.

Wussman and Vernon were hardly on the top of those priorities, but she supposed that they were the most immediate matters. So, she calmed herself down, took a deep breath, and walked over to them.

There hadn't been time before to think about it, but now the sight of Dr. Wussman's pudgy body and puny appendages was enough to make her giggle, though she suppressed it.

"Well, that was a charming little scene on the platform," Vivian said, arms crossed across her shapely breasts.

Wussman was whey-faced and a little glassy-eyed. He said, "I don't feel very well. Teleporting makes me ill."

"You think he'll live?" Diane asked.

"Don't worry about him," said Vernon.

"We're safe here for a while. Zorin says there's stuff to eat and drink in the next room. I suggest we go and get some while we can."

"I wanna go home," whined Wussman. "I wanna go home."

"We all do, Geoffrey," said Vivian. "We all do. Let's make sure we get home with our sanity and our dignity."

"I'll be happy with just my life!"

"We'll be perfectly safe here," Diane said.

"But if this is Zorin's home," Wussman said, "and he's a fugitive, isn't this the first place they'll look?"

"Geof has a point," Vivian said. "I should think this place would be under surveillance."

"Zorin's taking care of that," Diane said. "Anyway, if Zorin thinks it's safe here, it's probably safe. Let's go get cleaned up and try to find something to eat. We haven't eaten—well, I can't remember the last time."

"I can't think of food," Wussman said.

"I'm famished," Vivian said. "Let's see what Zorin has in his kitchen."

"I want some clothes!" Wussman puled.

Vivian looked down at her own nakedness, as if she'd completely forgotten. "Oh, of course."

Zorin's hideout was beautiful, a showcase of modernistic architecture combined with homey touches: a collection of exotic objets d'art, colorful throw rugs, comfortable furniture, and other amenities. And books, many, many books in various configurations from disks and reels of tape to old-fashioned bound paper, though some of these latter were strange.

They found clothes, an assortment of utilitarian worksuits that were happily of the one-size-fits-all variety. Diane chose a blue one, Vivian green, and Wussman black. They fit rather well. Shoes were another matter. Wussman found boots to suit him, but the women had to make do with stretch socks with padded soles.

With the aid of fresh running water, they had cleaned themselves up some.

"I need food," Diane declared.

"I need a drink," Wussman pleaded.

It didn't take long for Wussman to discover the bar. The only spirits available, though, was a syrupy potion in a squat decanter. Lavender, slow-moving as ketchup, nasty-looking. Its alcoholic identity, however, was unmistakable the moment Wussman removed the stopper. Diane was almost knocked over by the fumes. Vivian held her nose and made a face, and even Wussman flinched. Not to be daunted, though, he unracked a glass and commenced to decant the liqueur, glob by viscous glob.

Meantime, Diane and Viv took turns freshening themselves in the toilet facilities, which included a commode, a sink, and some odd form of alien bidet with no less than five variously shaped nozzles. Most curious, thought Diane.

When Diane emerged from her toilet, she felt much brighter and infinitely fresher. Wussman was working on a glass of liqueur, and it was obvious that he'd already sampled a large quantity of the drink.

"Tastes like licorice," he said. "But it does pack a kick. Do you want some?"

"Maybe later," said Vivian.

"Most definitely *not*," said Diane, with great emphasis, staring with horror at the sight of the vile purplish liquid leaking into the cup. Why, the man's tongue was veritably *lolling*, droplets of saliva forming at the corners of his mouth.

How disgusting. For Diane Derry, Prohibition had never ended. She came from a teetotal Midwestern town, bone-dry. As was the Derry custom in the presence of alcohol, her spine stiffened and her sphincter closed tight as a drum, and a frown turned her usually cheery face dour. It was as though a storm cloud had passed into the room.

"Loosen up, Di," said Wussman. He tilted back his beaker of the gravid goo, slurped, then smacked his lips—but only after a heartfelt shiver or three. "Whoa! Smoooooth . . ."

You could almost see steam issue from his ears. His little piggy nose glowed like a night-light.

"Ignore him, Derry," said Viv.

"I don't drink."

"We've noticed. I'm not saying I couldn't use a belt now. But not that panther juice. I love champagne myself." A little smile actually appeared on those cruelly gorgeous lips. "There are more important things to talk about."

"Such as getting back to Flitheimer so you can get your claws into our grant money?"

"Speaking of claws, dearie, retract yours a bit? I know normally we'd like to rip one another's eyes out. That's natural. We're competing females, protecting our turf."

"What a crude bestial analogy."

"I call it as I see it. Anyway, what we need to discuss, cute Miss Bunny Nose, is Mr. Z. back there."

"Who?"

"Mr. Hunk of Happiness. The alien Adonis. Our handsome host."

"Oh. I hadn't noticed he was handsome."

Viv guffawed. "Right. That's why you start quivering whenever you look at him. That's why you get all goggle-eyed when he speaks. Listen, honey. I see all the signs. So what I'm asking you is—are you going to seduce him if you get a chance?"

"I beg your pardon?" Diane said frostily.

"Are you going to have your way with him? Seduce him? You know, hide the salami?"

"That's *disgusting*."

"Shh." She took Diane by the elbow and led her a few feet away. She lowered her voice. "Chrome-Dome doesn't need to hear this. I'm asking because if you don't, then maybe I will. Fair, eh? No reason to fight any more than we normally do. And after all, he's only a man, eh?"

"But what—what about your fiancé?"

"Toy boy?" she said contemptuously. "A trifle. An intellectual amusement. When a *real* chunk of flesh and brain saunters along, I try and have my fun. So that's why I'm checking with you. Way I figure it, now, for better or worse, we're allies. We both want to get back to Earth. We need to cooperate."

"I've no problem with that."

"You've got no sights set on Zorin's britches?"

"Absolutely not. I've got a *boyfriend.* I'm faithful."

"You're *nuts,* sister. Okeydoke, just don't say I didn't ask."

Vivian seated herself on a divan, looking for all the world like a cat about to gobble a canary.

Diane felt decidedly ambivalent about the whole thing. On one hand, she had enough to worry about, what with the task of getting reunited with Dr. D. and Troy, and battling their way out of this most peculiar interstellar mess they were in.

On the other hand, she *did* rather fancy the guy.

This carnal urge, however, went against all that was Diane Derry—all she thought herself to be, all that proper society had trained her to be. She'd always prided herself on her self-control. It seemed not only prudent and wise to continue that self-control, but absolutely necessary.

And so she held her tongue, while vivid Vivian licked hers lasciviously about her chops.

Zorin walked in. Diane's heart missed a beat.

Pomade. Cologne. Whatever. He wore a snazzy ensemble of tights, jerkin and jacket, a color-coordinated suit of duds that expertly emphasized his manliness and rakish good looks.

"I see you have made yourselves comfortable," he said.

Diane could only stare with a dry mouth.

"Zorin." Vivian bounced up gaily to greet the new arrival. "I'm afraid we've not properly thanked you for delivering us from that wretched dungeon."

No doubt, thought Diane, the hussy would far prefer thanking him *im*properly.

"We could have done nothing without the bravery and courage of Diane," said the devastatingly handsome Zorin, whisking up to Diane, taking up her hand, and planting one of his incredible kisses thereupon.

Electricity that could only be measured in megawatts traveled up her arm.

Drat and darn! she told herself.

Cut *out* this nonsense!

She nodded and stepped away from Zorin.

Vivian took her place, pushing her own ample charms directly under his nose.

"Hear, hear!" said Wussman, tilting as though influenced by some phantom breeze, a cup of drink held high in toast. He tippled some of the stuff through purpled lips. A stream sped down his chin.

"Good Lord, man," said Zorin, appalled. "That's shoe polish." He stepped over and opened up another cabinet, revealing a bounty of clear bottles. "These are the drinks."

Wussman looked at the cup, then looked back at Zorin.

He shrugged.

"Oh, well. Tastes fine to me."

He lifted the glass and glugged.

Vivian Vernon shook her head sadly. "And to think, that used to be a fine mind. Now merely ruins." She smiled sweetly and demurely at Zorin. "I, on the other hand, would be happy to accept whatever you have to offer. Particularly, if it's wine and it's bubbly and if it's very expensive."

Zorin brightened.

"We have sparkling wine from Zargoth."

"Well! Bubbly seems to be a universal," said Vivian.

"Hear, hear!" Wussman raised a purple cup.

Zorin selected a bottle from a refrigerated section of the cabinet, popped the top, then brought out three long glasses. He poured, and the liquid sparkled with a rainbow of colors.

"Not just any champagne, for my cherished companions—Zargoth champagne!" He poured carefully. "Now then—Diane."

"No thank you," said Diane firmly. "I do not imbibe alcoholic beverages. Dr. Vernon, Dr. Wussman, I don't understand how you can all sit around and have a good time when Dr. Dimension and Troy are in danger."

"Diane," said Zorin, "as we speak, a device I call the wormhole machine is warming up. It will come to full power in a very short time. With it, and with a little help from . . ." Zorin scanned his guests. "Dr. Wussman, would you be willing to help?"

"Hmm? Me? Help? Oh, of course." Wussman smiled congenially. "Uh . . . how?"

"I'll explain in a moment. I think you'll do for the wormhole machine. The wormhole's diameter is limited, and, pardon me, but you're compact."

"Oh. Anything I can do to help."

"This champagne is super!" Vivian bubbled. "I'm

glad you like it," Zorin said. "The Zargoth sparkling wines are special. All manner of curious compounds from the resin of the wood used in aging." He opened a door and gestured. "I love the stuff too well and keep a hefty supply on hand."

Diane could see that the cabinet was well stocked. She was shocked and for a moment the rigidness of her Midwestern training locked down firmly upon her natural spring of cheeriness.

Zorin poured off three glasses, handed one to Vivian (who gladly accepted), and then offered one to Diane.

"Just one little celebratory snifter?"

"No, thank you."

Zorin looked at her oddly. A touch of disappointment, a hint of frost in that gaze.

"Oh," he said. "Well, then, Vivian and I shall have to drink one for you then, won't we?"

Vivian nodded emphatically. "Oh yes."

Wussman staggered forward. "I'll drink it! I'll drink it!"

He obtained an elbow in the side for his efforts. He doubled over and hobbled over to the divan, where he sat in silence with his shoe polish and a baffled, purpled grin.

"We'll share that one, Zorin. Shall we? Lips to lips?"

"How exotic. How very charming!" said Zorin. For the first time those dark eyes of his had been off Diane for more than ten seconds—

And now they seemed to notice that here, in this very same room, was another attractive woman with generous female accoutrements. Not a blond, but hey—all cats were gray in the dark, eh?

A pang of jealousy shot through Diane.

Jealousy.

Before she realized what she was doing, she stepped forward, wrested the spare glass of alien champagne from Vivian, and pulled it toward her own lips.

"When in Rome," she said, and held the glass up in toast. "Cheers."

Zorin's attention, gratifyingly, swiveled again in her direction.

"Ah. It is indeed a woman's prerogative to change her mind—particularly if she is a pretty woman. Cheers." He hoisted his glass and tippled.

Vivian drank, staring daggers at Diane.

Diane, defiantly, drank a swallow, demanding that her body ignore the fact that it was ingesting alcohol.

"Oh, my," she said in a tiny voice.

The stuff was like soda pop, only it tickled when it went down, with a dry sweet life of its own. It was as though she'd swallowed some mischievous fairy that refused to die. It fluttered to her stomach and began firing off its wand: a batch of giddy flowers, flapping through her system.

Diane blinked.

The flowers unfurled through her brain and in a brief shiny, fuzzy moment all of her taut rubber-band nerves relaxed.

She could not help a pleasant "Ah!" from escaping her lips.

"Delicious stuff, eh Diane?" said Zorin. "Glad you tried it. Imbibe all you wish." He clinked a glass against hers. It sounded like the toll of destiny's bell. In the spell of his eyes, she took another larger sip.

A waterfall of daisies and violets, a cascade of release.

Diane looked over at Vivian, who was glaring as though Diane had just run over her dog.

Dirty looks phased her not one jot. She felt emboldened, renewed. The idea that this stuff might possibly be bad, that the act of drinking it flew in the face of all the temperance tenets her parents held so dear was utterly dissolved in a wash of light tingling pleasure.

Another sip, better than the two before, and the drink was gone.

"Now, let's see about getting your friends out of the fix they are in," Zorin said.

"Oh, I wouldn't worry about them," said Vivian. "They'll muddle through somehow. What I *would* be interested in, though, would be your etchings." She moved closer, making sure to make eye contact as well as breast contact, lifting her leg and rubbing a toe along Zorin's shin.

Someone turned a light out in Diane's brain.

Fireworks crackled and spat.

She put her glass aside, stepped up, reared back a fist, and let fly a Sunday punch, coldcocking an astonished Vivian Vernon. Arms windmilling, Viv sailed directly into Wussman. A full, just-poured cup of purple shoe polish splashed all over them.

"Viv!" said Wussman.

Vivian's lights were out. She was down for the count.

"She's garbage, Zorin," said Diane, with a beatific smile. "Now let's get to work. Doc and Troy are in trouble. You save them, we'll help you get the M'Guh Fon. You send us back to Earth." She gave him a wink and then a smooch on the cheek. "And if you do a good job, maybe, just maybe, I'll chase you around your office desk."

She growled at him.

Wary, he stepped back.

She grabbed the bottle of champagne and emptied it into her glass.

"Tally ho, great scientist!" she said expansively. She took a cool delightful quaff. Picked up the bottle. Empty.

"I don't suppose you could open me another, could you?" she said.

"Well, of course, my dear. But don't you think . . . ?"

"Just do it, honey. I'll make it worth your while." She winked suggestively.

Zorin grinned. His manner became highly obsequious as he scrambled to obey her.

Diane Derry guzzled her glass of champagne. This was *great* stuff! Why *ever* had she not tried it before? Why, the nectar of the gods, all right. And a great nightlife those gods must have.

What *fools* her parents and her grandparents had

been. Teetotalism? Wasn't that what those jokers over in Europe were practicing? No, that was totalitarianism.

Oh, well.

Same difference.

She grabbed another bottle of champagne, popped the top, and hoisted it toward the stars.

"Doc!" she said. "We're coming to *rescue* you!"

Geoffrey Wussman lifted his own newly refreshed glass of purple shoe polish.

"Gurgle!" he said, and then passed out atop Vivian Vernon.

Presently, Diane passed out on top of him.

"Interesting," Zorin said, empirically observing. "Alien biochemistry is extremely unpredictable."

He hurried back to the lab to concoct an antidote.

Chapter Sixteen

"My machines may not have been effective on your puny alien brains," said Baron Skulkrak, his morningstar codpiece swinging ominously beneath his armor. "However, we have other methods of making you talk."

"Talk, shmalk," said Dr. D. "You want talk, we got talk. Small talk, big talk. Chitchat. Conversation. You name it, I got talk for you out the kazoo. But this Megaphone thing. Baron, I gotta tell you— We haven't got a clue."

Baron Skulkrak shook his head adamantly. His breath whooshed out through his ferocious fangs like a faulty oxygen tank with a bad temper. "You think me a fool? Baron Skulkrak is no fool. I smell the truth of the M'Guh Fon. It reeks from your brains like perfume amid garbage. I must have the M'Guh Fon . . ." He held up his hand and in the hand was a purple-polka-dot egg. "And I will squeeze that truth from you like I squeeze this squicky egg!"

The Baron squeezed. Dr. D. expected to see yolk and albumen squish from the egg explosively splattering all assembled.

The eggshell, however, held.

Though the Baron strained with all his might, for some reason he could not break the egg. What little flesh lay exposed among all the plastic and metal of his face turned a bright crimson. "Bah!" he said, and hurled it at Troy Talbot.

The Baron's eyes ignited with fervor and anticipation. "I will make you wander my Maze of Death!"

This didn't sound good to Dr. Dimension.

He asked casually, "And exactly what is that?"

Skulkrak's eyes flashed with fiendish delight. "You will find out soon enough. As soon as we reach my base on the moon of Ovaria."

"Oh. By the way, I like the way your eyes flash, there. Very enchanting."

"Bah! In a short while you will be not be laughing."

"Who's laughing?"

Ovaria's largest moon, yclept Progesteron, was large enough to have retained a thin but breathable atmosphere. Otherwise, most of its surface was bleak and lifeless. It had been colonized mostly by mining companies, and their domed installations dotted the terrain, surrounded by huge piles of tailings.

Skulkrak's compound lay in a remote undeveloped area in the southern hemisphere. The place was huge, a cluster of domes and cylinders nestled into the eastern foothills of a sinuous mountain range that divided the great southern desert like a twisted spine.

Skulkrak's cruiser, the *Crusher,* went into polar orbit, then dispatched its landers to the surface. In one of these was Dr. Dimension and Troy, neither of whom knew what had happened to the robot. Tobor had been carted away, presumably for further probing and torture.

After an uneventful descent, the lander did what landers do, doing it on a wide pad that was in fact an elevator platform. The platform slowly lowered itself into a capacious cavern, in a canyon that had been an excavation for a mine.

Our heroes were thrown into a holding cell with no door. Instead, cracking beams of energy made just as convincing a barrier.

Yes, Doc D. had thought. There have been a few skulls cracked in this place all right.

A half hour later, the two captives had just finished choking down a tasty repast of moldy hardtack and water when the Baron came clanking down the corridor. He stopped at the cell door and peered between the pale blue translucent bands of force.

"And now, pathetic alien near-animal creatures, it's the Maze for you both."

Doc D. picked crumbs from between his teeth. "Look, Baron baby, why don't you stop holding it all in and just tell us you don't like us much? It's better out in the open."

"Joke now," the Baron wheezed. "There will be no jokes later."

"You'll still be around. Be that as it may, why don't you limn for us, in that inimitable prose of yours, just what we're up against?"

Baron Skulkrak's eyes glittered.

"Yes. The Purple Maze of Living Alien Monster Death. A favorite playfield of mine. Filled with traps and terrors from all over the known universe. The question is, will you die first or will your minds snap?" A speck of expectant expectorant drooled from his fearsome face. "Of course, you have only to remember what you know of the M'Guh Fon, volunteer the information, and you will be instantly released." A ludicrous flicker of an attempt at a friendly smile jerked the lines of the cyborg face upward. "And perhaps we will give you a glass of beer then, too?"

Troy Talbot grimaced. He looked like he was about to crack. "Gee, a cold glass of beer sure would go down smooth about now. What kind of beer do you have, Baron? Pilsener? Lager? Root?"

"Troy, shut the hell up. Wait a minute, Baron. We've gone over this same ground over and over. Am I not enunciating properly? Are your ears working? Baron, we know nothing about any McGuffin. Nada. Zip. Zero. One minus one. Is this concept so hard to get through your titanium brain? We don't know!"

"Very well," said the Baron. "But be advised. We also have other machines. And it would be as easy to extract information from corpses as from reluctant living beings. We will be watching!"

With a swirl of cape and a flourish of codpiece, the

dreaded Baron marched off. At a doorway, he stopped dramatically, then turned that grizzled visage to an assistant.

"Drop them."

The flunky's hand fell upon a lever beside a downward pointing arrow.

"Drop them?" said Troy, brow lowered. "As from, say, a list of potential prison trustees?"

"Drop them," said Dr. Dimension. "As from, say, a high place to a much lower place, with attendant breaking of limbs and cracking of skulls."

"Oh."

"And into the Maze of Alien Purple Passion Monsters, or whatever it is."

"Oh." Troy gulped. "Uh-oh."

"I'll second that uh-oh."

Beneath them, the floor opened.

Gravity beckoned.

They fell.

They tumbled.

Not through empty air, however, but down a long, convoluted chute.

"Yiiiiiiiii!" said Troy in his usual imbecilic fashion.

"Yiiiiiiiii!" said Dr. D. with much more pith and intelligence and panache.

Troy grabbed for anything within reach.

Doc was the only thing close.

"Talbot, get your hands off my face," said Doc D.

They slid down the slick chute in total darkness, bumping into one another, willy-nilly. There was just one good thing about it, Doc D. thought as he gamboled and rolled. That damned robot wasn't along. Now *that* would be painful.

Nonetheless, even as they fell, he began to notice that sometimes they weren't exactly falling. Sometimes they seemed to be traveling a more lateral path, buoyed by some sort of artificial gravity. Sometimes they seemed to be flying upward.

All in all, the travel time amounted to a few minutes.

It became so tedious that Troy stopped yelling. He said nothing. Doc D. assumed he'd fallen asleep.

However, at long last, the trip ended. There was just one more swift plummet and then the almost welcome impact with solid ground.

"Ouch," said Troy ungratefully.

Doc D. ignored him. He got up off the hard floor, brushed himself off, and got his bearings.

Fortunately it was no longer dark. Weak light revealed a large empty room, gray and depressing.

Bearings: Impossible.

Nonetheless, a certain word had been mentioned.

"Maze," said Doc D.

"Huh, Doc?"

"The Baron said we would have to walk a maze, Talbot. Yet we find ourselves in a box. Every maze I've ever run a rat through has been a series of interconnecting corridors."

Talbot ventured nothing.

"If we are in the beginning of a maze, there must be something that would, by grace of which, admit us to it."

Talbot scratched his head. "Amazing grace?"

"Oh, my God." Doc bowed his head and shook it wearily. "What's amazing is that someone could be so unbelievably dense, so far out to lunch, that the stupidest things that come out of him are in fact sparkling witticisms. Talbot, you're so goddamn dumb, you're brilliant!"

"Gee, Doc, that's the nicest thing you ever said to me."

"Don't mench. Now, let's get back to business. What we're looking for is an entrance, a door, a gate, whatever. A stone, a leaf, an unfound door, a lost lane into heaven. Now, the question we have to ask ourselves is, do we want to go through that door? Do we really want to enter something called the Mauve Maze of Hellish Menopausal Harridans or whatever it is, or do we want to cool our heels here?"

"I vote for cooling our heels!"

"Exactissimo. However, let's look at it another way. There is probably no other way out except *through* the Mystic Maze of Doctoral Candidate Alien Monster Hell. In which case, we have no other choice but to find the entrance."

Troy looked crestfallen. "I like the heel-cooling idea better."

"So do I, but we could starve here. I don't know about you, but I could eat a horse with a rusty spoon. I'm hungry. We have to get out of here. So let's hunt up that entrance."

"Oh, okay."

"Now you take that wall and I'll take this one, and we should find something. For all the roominess, I'm getting a touch claustrophobic."

Doc D. moved to the nearest wall and felt along it. It was cold and clammy. Gently, he probed and palpated, wary of traps. What diabolical booby traps had Skulkrak installed here? Doc was alert, ready for absolutely anything, all his senses keyed up, his dynamic and magnificent mind at peak-operating condition, his keen analytical faculties notched to a spring-loaded state.

"Doc!" said Troy Talbot in his ear.

"Yah!" Doc D. jumped straight up.

If there had been a ceiling four feet above him, he would have cracked his head on it.

He landed on the balls of his feet and whirled. He halted a motion to wallop Talbot, staying his temper.

"Don't do that to me again! What is it?"

"That M'Guh Fon thing the Baron wants? Do you think it could be ... you know, back on the trash planet—that thing I—?"

Doc lunged, clamped a hand over Troy's mouth, and put a finger to his own. "Shhhh!"

"What'd I s—mmmmph?"

"Shhh! You idiot! Don't mention the Monocle!"

"I wasn't going to men—mmmmmmph!"

"Shut the hell up!"

"Mmmmmmph?"

"Yes! Quiet."

"Mmmmmph."

Doc took his hand away.

"But I wasn't going to say anything about the M—mmmmmmmph!"

"Talbot, I'm going to *kill* you if you don't shut the hell up right now!"

Talbot was silent.

Doc took his hand away and breathed out. "Now."

"It wasn't the Monocle, it was that ring I found."

Doc lunged at him, but Troy backed away neatly.

"What ring are you—?" Doc slapped a hand over his own mouth.

"Shhhh, pipe down, Doc, they might be eavesdropping."

Dr. Dimension growled through his hand.

"No shit, Dick Tracy!" Doc let out a sigh. "Okay, what's this about a ring?"

"Little ring, big clumsy thing, set with a kind of dull stone. Looked pretty, but not expensive. I'd have to chop the ring down a little to fit Diane's finger, but—"

Again the hand went up to stanch the flow of verbiage.

"Enough," Doc said. "Where is it? Whisper in my ear."

"The robot has it."

"Oh, great. That does us a lot of good, Talbot. Just shut up about it, okay?"

Well, there it was. Could this bauble Troy found be the McGuffin? Doc doubted it, but who knew? The possibility that it might be some alien talisman threw a new light on Troy's bout with the scavenging monster back on the dumping planet. Could be, could be. But what were the odds that Troy would find the very thing that perhaps the whole universe was looking for? Almost nil.

Nah, Doc thought to himself.

"Troy, just forget about it. Okay?"

"Okay."

"Go over and feel that wall over there."

"That wall, Doc?"

"That wall, ninny. Check for hidden latches, buttons. Remember, we're looking for a concealed door."

Doc turned to the opposite wall and renewed his search.

"Doc, there's no wall."

"Eh?"

"I said, there's no wall over here."

Doc didn't turn, having found a faint seam. He adjusted his glasses and tried to trace it with a finger.

"Talbot, what are you babbling about now?"

"There's no wall here anymore. Just this big area, kind of."

"Talbot, you nincompoop. Do—" Doc D. said, turning.

His admonishment stuck in his throat. He was too surprised to cough.

For what had once been a blank unfathomable wall was now a vast chamber stretching off into what seemed infinite distance, a hint of cloud-flecked blue at the vanishing point.

"Let's go, Doc."

Doc D. grabbed his assistant. "Wait, could be a trap."

"Doc, sorry, but aren't we already in a trap? What's to lose?"

Doc D. was struck by the inherent logic.

He slapped Troy on the back.

"There you go, Talbot. You're getting hot." He sniffed and rolled back on his heels. "Tell you what, though. Why don't you just go on up there and have a look-see?"

"Sure, Doc."

Without hesitation or a second thought, Troy Talbot trotted off, looking for all the world (or as the case may be, universe) like a man without a care or notion that some cosmic sixteen-ton weight might at any time crash down on him.

Doc watched, feeling a little guilty.

"Troy, be careful."

Troy walked a few yards down the corridor, stopped and turned. "Everything seems hunky-dory to me, Doc."

With this welcome news, Doc proceeded. Troy Talbot waited for him to catch up. Together they walked cautiously down the runway. Within a few feet, however, Doc D. noticed that the distance had foreshortened. There was now a rectangular opening where the lines of the immense corridor converged, and it was becoming disproportionately smaller with every step they took. Something was screwy.

"Hold it, Talbot," he said, catching hold of the man's arm. "Do you see what I see?"

"I don't know, Doc. Sounds like a loaded question to me. What do you see?"

"That portion of the horizon yonder. It's not getting any larger."

Troy turned. "Gee, that's okay. The doorway we came through is getting bigger."

"What?"

Doc D. spun around so quickly, Troy Talbot felt a breeze. " 'Swounds!" Doc ejaculated. "You're right. What the hell is wrong with the damned perspective?"

"What do we do, Doc?"

"Keep plowing on, partner. Not much else to do."

They continued onward, and after they had marched what seemed a goodly distance, the window on the daylight stubbornly refused to expand at all. Doc D. would have been distressed if another paradox had not more distressfully presented itself. They both walked into a ceiling, bumping their heads.

"Ouch," they said in unison.

Doc stopped and felt overhead. Not only was it low, it was actually tilting downward at an angle, headed off for that perplexing horizon.

"I see! It's a trick of perspective."

"Look, Doc. There are some funny-looking things up there. Like you find in caves . . . stagmites?"

Doc D. looked up. Not only were they emphatically not stalactites or stalagmites, they were moving.

Downward.

"Talbot. They're blades."

"Oh. No wonder they look metallic," said Troy.

"Hurry. Through the portal if we can."

However, although the portal now seemed imminently accessible, it was also obviously quite small, quite fake.

No sky, no exit. Things looked bad.

Dr. D. felt a pang of claustrophobia.

No, not good. Then he detected a most noisome odor. Was this Skulkrak fellow totally ruthless?

Troy was disconcertingly near.

"Whew. Sure is hot in here."

Essence of locker room.

Eau d'armpit.

"Talbot, I hate to be the one to tell you, but after all, what are friends for? You have B.O. Move away a little bit."

"I can't, Doc. No room."

Any moment those knives would descend upon them, skewering them like chunks of lamb on a shish kebab. Sacrificial lamb. Worse, Talbot was unbearably close. All Doc had to do to halt the proceedings was yell out that he knew where the M'Guh Fon was. All he had to do was to buckle to the will of Baron Skulkrak.

Or pull some fantastic escape out of his butt.

A derisive cackling came from far above.

"I do not fool around, Dimension! I get straight to the meat of the matter. Will you talk?"

"I thought this was supposed to be a maze?" said Dr. D, trying to suppress a reflex to gag.

"It is!"

"Mazes are puzzles, no?"

"Certainly."

"Where's the puzzle?"

A cranking sounded.

The knives halted their descent.

"What?"

"I mean, presumably there are supposed to be things

to solve, correct? Pardon me, but lowering knives? Closing in walls? How unimaginative."

A long silence.

"You have a better idea?"

"I'm glad you asked me that. As a matter of fact, I most certainly do."

"What?" The voice was steeped in suspicion.

"Show us a little of this great maze of yours. If I can't negotiate our way through it, I might deign to help you."

The Baron's voice boomed with triumph. "Then you admit knowing the location of the alien artifact!"

"Now, I didn't exactly say that, did I?" said Doc D. "However, with my brain as your ally, between the two of us, I'm sure we'll be able to find it together. But if, and only if, I fail to solve your supposed maze."

"I do not know why I do not crush your insolent carcasses as I would two vermin!"

"Because we'd die knowing that Baron Skulkrak is a sham, with the mind of a simpleton."

A roar of rage. "Bah! Very well, Dr. Dimension, if that insipid name is the one you insist on . . ."

"Look, no need to get personal." As an aside to Talbot: "The name change isn't going well."

"It needs work," Troy ventured.

The Baron continued, "You shall be treated to the ordeal of the Maze of . . . the Purple Maze of Malign . . . Purple Alien Monster . . . oh, hell, whatever—"

"Puce Paradox of Pungent Pudwhackers?"

". . . Maze of Living Death Alien Monsters—"

"You don't know the name of your own gadget? It's the Purple Maze of Living Manichaeans."

"—Purple Alien Monster Living Death Maze—Bah! Phooey!"

"Purple People-Eating Trash Compactor of Death?"

"Turd of a scum-eating biomass ingester! What difference does it make what the name of the thing is?"

"No need to shout, Baron."

"Pardon. Anyway, it has driven the minds of creatures greater than you quite mad."

The knives retracted. An opening gaped before them, heading away into darkness.

"Whew," said Troy. "That was a close call. I can feel the perspiration trickling down my body."

Doc gasped and moved away. "Talbot, I can smell the perspiration trickling down your body."

Troy sniffed his pits. He grimaced. "Ewww. You're right. Sorry about that. Don't know what to do."

"Just stay downwind, Talbot."

Talbot shrugged good-naturedly, wet a finger, and held it up to the supposed breeze. "Okay, Doc. Whatever you say."

"Gevalt!"

Even as Doc uttered this Yiddishism, the dark tunnel became illuminated, showing a vast panorama of terraced levels. And on each level was some sort of complex barrier.

"What's all that, Doc."

Doc blinked. "I believe that's the obstacle course we're going to have to run."

Troy rubbed his hands together. "Just like ROTC training! Oh, boy, Doc."

"Talbot, I believe that this is my forte. The trick to these things is mostly intellectual."

"Well, Doc, I used to make forts when I was a kid, too, and if I say so myself, I was pretty damned good at it."

"Well, Troy, my boy, I consider this to be the challenge of my life—but of course any contributions would be welcomed, however half-witted." He chuckled and stared ahead at the colorful array of gadgets, most of which sported blades, steel traps, and razor-topped barriers, among other attractions.

Ah, how he would show his genius this day! His self-esteem would ascend to heights undreamed of. Yes, and he would most certainly show old Skulkrak a thing or two.

And probably lose an arm and a leg to one of those turnstiles constructed of whirling machetes. Or his head.

Suddenly, however, between them and this promise of intellectual exercise, a form began to flicker.

A humanoid form, but one strangely familiar.

"Uh, Doc . . . Just a thought now, but didn't Baron Skulkrak mention something about, er, alien monsters?"

"Yes, I believe they were mentioned, Talbot," said Doc. "You know, you'd get more out of life if you paid attention."

The creature began to solidify . . .

Chapter Seventeen

The creature was suddenly there, materializing directly in front of them, an apparition from hell.

It was the most horrible thing that Doctor Dimension had ever imagined, let alone seen or experienced, except for a night in a motel in New Jersey, once. (He'd skipped out without paying the bill.)

A horrid stench permeated the room.

The creature staggered, gagged, and then vomited a purple effluvium upon the floor.

"Oh, my God," said Geoffrey Wussman. "Why ever did I let them talk me into this. I'm so very, very sick!"

Another dollop of vomit splattered sickeningly.

Doc D. could not believe his eyes. He'd never seen such projectile vomiting in his life.

"Wussman, get a grip," he demanded. "What the hell are you doing here?"

Wussman gasped and staggered. "It's not teleportation, 'cause you have to be naked. He told me what this was, but I forget. Matter transmission, or some such thing. Zorin sent me, to set up some sort of subspace bridge." Wussman caught himself from falling, then seemed to get hold of himself. "I was too drunk to say no, and Viv and Diane were too drunk to get up and do it."

"Teleportation? Matter transmission? And who the hell is Zorin?" Doc scratched his frizzy head. "Never mind, time for explanations later. I was looking forward to solving these puzzles, but I'd far rather get out of this hole."

"Me, too," said Troy.

"No, we were going to leave you here, Troy," snapped Doc D. sarcastically. He turned to Wussman. "So then get us out of here, Wuss!"

Wussman shook his head blearily. "Yes. Of course—"

A paroxysm of panic crossed Wussman's face.

He shivered, jerked, barked off another blast of purple spew—and then keeled over flat on his face.

"Gosh, *that* was smart, Wussman," said Troy. "How are you going to rescue us if you're not moving?"

"The man does have a penchant for unconsciousness, doesn't he?" said Doc D. "Oh, well, let's see what goodies he brought. Presumably Diane Derry was teleporting—"

"She didn't have any clothes on!"

"You heard Wussy say you have to be naked for that. I suppose we'll get an explanation eventually, but for right now, let me just live with the image as comfort."

Doc stepped over a pile of purple vomit and started dipping into Wussman's bulging pockets. A look of horror crossed his face, and he pulled his hand back out quickly. "Ewwww. Always remember, Troy. Put your hand in a man's pocket only if you mean serious business." He shook off his reluctance and then tried the other pocket. This time he was rewarded with an item. He pulled his hand out.

In the palm was a strange object in the shape of a dodecahedron. Its surface crawled with fine shiny wire. In fact, the object seemed to be a hollow ball made of wire.

"Well, well, well," said Doc D. "What have we here?"

"Looks like a funny golf ball, Doc."

"Yes, but not just any funny golf ball. Presumably the reason Wussman was transmitted here was to set up a stable locus for some sort of Einstein-Rosen four-dimensional bridge, so that we might escape this trap we're in. Equally presumably, he had instructions for its use."

"Wow, how do you know all that stuff, Doc?"

"What stuff?"

"Locusts and Weinstein's Four Roses bridges and like that?"

"I read the science-fiction pulps religiously."

"Gee, it's a religion?"

"In a manner of speaking. See if you can wake up old Wussy. Now, let me see. Wussman's here, and he got here by some sort of wormhole, or whatever you want to call it. My question is, why isn't the wormhole open the other way, going back? Hmmm."

Troy went over and shook Wussman. "Dr. Wuss? Doc Wussy? Yo, wake up. We need help."

Wussman merely groaned.

"Darn, he sure has been doing a lot of that lately," said Troy, shaking his head with dismay.

"No matter, Troy. Let me have a look at this. We have a geometrical puzzle here as well, and I have no doubt that I can crack it as well as anything that Skulkrak has in here."

Doc examined the ins and outs, the ups and downs of the switches, and doodads of the item. Hmm. That little stud over there looked rather like a switch.

"Doc."

"Talbot, shut up. For God's sake, I'm trying to concentrate."

"Doc!"

"Talbot! Don't you hear me. I'm working."

"Really and truly, Doc. Remember that alien monster business?"

"Yes, of course." He was staring intently inside the twisted interior of the ball.

"Uhm . . . what exactly *are* alien monsters?"

"Foreigners."

"So they'd have heads like watermelons and bones on the outside of their bodies and rows of nasty, sharp wicked metal teeth, right? Pretty scary, huh?"

"Your typical foreigner."

"And they'd, sort of, uhm, move funny?"

"Hm? Perhaps."

Hmm. There were actually a number of different possible combinations of switches. How the devil was Wussman supposed to have activated this thing in his inebriated state?

"Doc, I hate to interrupt you, but I think that we have company."

Doc D. looked up, intending to scold his assistant, but the sight that caught him stopped him short.

Three figures were coming toward them down the ill-lit hallway, straggling and shambling.

There was a sudden whiff of corruption in the air.

They were tall and powerful, with bands of gleaming muscle and bone exposed through quasi-reptilian skin.

Lidless eyes gazed inhumanly.

"Ooops," said Doc D. "Looks like those vaunted alien monsters have made their appearance. Talbot, would you delay them for a few moments while I play with this thingamajig?"

"Sure, Doc. I'll just—" Troy Talbot took a double take. "Doc, those are *monsters*. I haven't even got any weapons. What am I supposed to do?"

"Rouse Wussman there. Maybe he'll have a few ideas. I've got to crack this problem. It's a little harder than cracking a joke, believe me."

Doc turned his attention back to the interior of the odd alien assemblage in his hand.

Buttons.

Studs.

Switches.

What order should they be pushed in? That was the question. The correct sequence would open up a portal to escape. The wrong sequence could blow them up. Too much indecision and the alien monsters would be upon them.

Tough spot.

Doc D. cogitated.

Meanwhile, Troy helped Wussman up.

"C'mon, Dr. Wuss. We've got to keep the alien monsters away from the Doc while he works."

Wussman's eyes were ping-ponging about in his sockets. He staggered up and groaned.

The alien monsters slouched toward them.

Troy pointed Wussman in the proper direction, mentally calculated, and then waited for just the proper moment until the alien monsters were at just the right distance.

"Okay, Wuss. Do your stuff."

Troy punched Wussman in the solar plexus.

Wussman's eyes bugged. He gasped and choked and rumbled like a kettle just on the point of boiling.

The man let loose.

The greatest stream yet of purple vomit spewed from the professor's mouth.

The caustic purple stuff caught the lead alien monster directly in the face. With a gurgling howl, the creature went down, the remains of its face bubbling away. The creature thrashed out its death agony.

"Good job, Wuss. Keep it up."

Troy directed the stream toward another of the things, and it went down in a similar disgusting manner.

"Gee, Professor, what were you *drinking*?"

The stream died, and Wussman wilted.

"Good job. The rest is up to me."

Troy Talbot stepped up, holding his fists in classic boxer position.

"One at a time, please."

Unfortunately, the alien monsters did not listen. They swarmed toward Talbot, sharp fangs snapping, claws reaching outward.

Troy whipped out a left, a right.

His fist slammed into one of the faces, and pulpy flesh smashed and skewed off from the skull.

Crunch.

He pulled the fist back, sent it slamming harder at another of the creatures.

This time, when the fist messily connected, it kept going straight through. It erupted out of the other side of the alien monster's head, trailing slimy brains and other unsavories.

The redoubtable monster kept on scrabbling at Troy.

Troy backed away, just in time to avoid another lunge.

"How's it going, Doc?"

"Just a little while longer, Talbot."

"I don't know how long I can keep them back, Doc."

Whap. Whap. Another unleashing of fists.

"Just a stray thought, Talbot. Lift up your arms."

"Huh."

"Hold your arms up."

Troy shrugged. He'd try anything once. He held up his arms, exposing his armpits.

The effect was immediate. The alien monsters howled and snarled. A couple even tried to hold their noses. As they had none, the gesture was moot.

"Hey, Doc. Wow. You're right. I must be really ripe!"

Laughing, Troy blew a few blasts of breath under a pit, directing the smell toward the closest alien monsters.

They dropped, spasming in conniptions.

"Doc! A secret weapon."

"Just don't blow any this way."

Doc D., meantime, was struggling with the puzzle in front of him. It shouldn't be *that* difficult. What was wrong with his brain?

Then, suddenly, he saw it.

The thing was a binary code. Only one of the switches was out of sequence. Clearly, if he pressed that one, the thing would work the way it was supposed to.

He reached a forefinger to joggle, to toggle.

The polyhedron slipped from his hands.

"Damn!"

It seemed to hang in the air for a moment, like a Christmas tree bauble pendant from some invisible evergreen.

Doc D. grabbed for it, and it bounced from his fingertips, finally falling toward the ground.

He made one more grab.

Missed.

The thing dropped like a rock. When it hit the ground, it smashed apart.

Stuck with Baron Skulkrak and alien monsters, thought Doc D.

How delightful, butterfingers!

He knelt down to see if there was any retrieval to be done, and was surprised to find that, far from broken fragments, the wire dodecahedron had become unfolded. It unraveled like the inside of a golf ball into a pile of glittering thread. Then it rose up and began to shape itself. The resultant construct was a simple rectangle, higher than it was long. The rectangle became a doorway. Static charges crackled about it. Through it and beyond, Doc thought he could see people.

This was it. It was working!

That was why Wussman had been charged with the responsibility of the item.

All he had to do was drop it!

A voice erupted like thunder over all.

"What's going on down there!"

Chapter Eighteen

That particular monster's voice was the last thing that Doc needed to hear.

Nonetheless, here was the exit that was needed in this situation, yawning right before them.

All he had to do was leap through, and he was free and clear.

"My minions shall seize you!" declared Skulkrak. "Cease your efforts to escape, or I promise you agony beyond your capacity to imagine!"

"Baron, work on the prose style."

Still, it had a certain raw power. "Agony beyond your capacity to imagine" sounded like a good note to depart on.

"You know, Skulkrak. Maybe your disposition would improve if you'd do something about that personal plumbing problem Then again, maybe you should just drop dead. Troy, Wussie, let's go!"

Doc made a lunge for the wormhole, but halted when he sensed something wrong. He looked back. The last alien monster had been laid out, but Troy was out cold, too, along with Wussman.

He went back for Troy Talbot. He intended to help both the men, but after all, priorities were priorities. There were surely hundreds of sneaky, cowardly college professors in the universe. But how many handsome dumb lab assistants could tear apart a Studebaker and put it back together again inside an hour?

Meantime, Skulkrak continued his rant.

"You shall suffer as you have never suffered before!

You shall experience torment beyond endurance. You shall—"

"Yeah, yeah," said Doc D. "Bite me."

Suffering had apparently honed Doc's wit.

The Baron howled with rage.

Deep in the bowels of the place, there came a rumbling of fantastical machinery, running feet, and other sounds too horrible to contemplate.

"C'mon, Talbot. We're going to have to make a quick exit here before we get stuck with Mr. Personality again."

Doc D. pulled Talbot along. He was a heavy lug, no question—and unconscious he seemed as heavy as the anchor of a luxury liner. Doc grunted and huffed, groaned and gasped. He stopped mid-trip and slapped the guy across the chops. "C'mon, Talbot. You're going to have to help me a little bit here."

From somewhere in the subterranean depths of Troy Talbot's mind, a spark glimmered. The spark knocked his brain cells back into action. His eyes opened.

"Hi, Doc."

"Talbot, no time for pleasantries. Dive through that portal. Immediately."

"Sure thing, Doc."

Doc's wavy-haired assistant became ambulatory, wobbled a bit, but nevertheless essayed a perfect belly flop through the portal.

Doc D. turned his attention back to Wussman.

Troy Talbot had been no garland of roses to carry, what with his attendant monster-lethal B.O. However the prospect of hauling the vomitous Wussman was downright repellent.

With no time to waste being disgusted, however, Doc D. started the job. Fortunately, the diminutive Wussman was a good deal lighter than Talbot.

The man came to as Doc was carrying him.

"Oh, dear. What's happening?"

"We're getting out of here, Wussman. We're going back to Viv. You want to give us a hand?"

"Viv?" The word prompted a revival of Wussman. A flutter of eyes, a twitch of mouth.

Doc slapped him.

"Oh, *Viv!*"

Wussman reached up longingly.

"No, it's not your fiancée, you tenured moron. It's me, and you've got to get to your feet and get through that locus there because you're far too heavy, and I'm far too exhausted to pick you up."

"Locust?"

"Locus, as in wormhole, subspace bridge, or whatever it is. Remember? You came here to save our bacon, and now I'm saving yours, your little piglet, so for God's sake, *get up!*"

Wussman floundered about, finally managing to haul himself to his puke-covered feet.

"What? Where?"

Thunderous pursuit. Rattling of claws behind them.

"There!"

Doc pointed Wussman's nose in the proper direction and then gave an assisting push. The professor sailed through the air directly into and through the portal.

Doc D. paused for a moment.

"Skulkrak!" he shouted.

"Dr. Dimension! My minions will soon be upon you."

"Hold the minions, they give me heartburn."

He extended the middle finger of his right hand upward.

"The square root of minus one, Baron."

With that, Doc D. skedaddled.

He leaped, leaving behind the roaring wail of Baron Skulkrak's frustration.

He leaped and was caught within some sizzling maelstrom, flinging in a blink of an eye his corpuscular self into the arms of forever.

The doctor went around and around . . .

* * *

And he came out there.

"Oooff!"

Falling down, face first, directly onto an alien floor. And a *hard* alien floor at that.

"Quickly," said a man's voice. "I must close the aperture. Vivian, train that weapon and fire upon anything else that comes through."

"You got it, Zorin."

Doc D. looked up at a frightening sight: Dr. Vivian Vernon, a horrendous shiner emblazoned across her right eye, holding a blaster the size of a cannon. It was aimed in Doc's general direction. The barrel wobbled a bit. Viv did look the worse for whatever she'd been drinking.

He decided that it would be discreet to roll out of the way, and so executed that move.

In doing so, he not only took in the sight of the portal going through contortions, but the entirety of the room and its occupants.

The room itself seemed a marvelous hodgepodge of alien machinery, artifacts, and antiques: the otherworldly equivalent of his own shop back on Earth.

Standing at an impressive bank of controls was a slim and dapper man sporting a compelling outfit and an equally compelling profile. Doc D. was reminded of . . . John Barrymore? Douglas Fairbanks. No, someone else.

Wussman had been safely tucked away in a corner, conferring again with unconsciousness.

Sitting in a chair, head lolling, a bottle of champagne in one hand and an empty glass in another, was Diane Derry,

A clearly *drunk* Diane Derry,

Unfortunately, fully clothed.

Beyond the shifting outline of the "aperture," as the tall man had referred to it, Doc heard the scrabbling of Baron Skulkrak's monstrous hordes.

Claws and tentacles suddenly were thrust through the opening.

"Vivian! Now!"

Without comment, and with a mad gleam in her eye,

Vivian Vernon pulled the trigger, slamming energy to the tune of gigawatts into the hole.

The dapper man threw a huge guillotine switch.

The strange interdimensional gate slammed shut, snapping off the remaining claws and tentacles. They clattered to the floor not far from Doc D., where they spasmed and flopped.

"Right," said the man, and he pulled a lever.

The glittery stuff that had outlined the opening contracted back into the dodecahedron that Wussman had brought with him as he had teleported.

Doc D. stood up and brushed himself off.

"Nice job, if I say so myself." He advanced upon the man, his hand outstretched. "Dr. Dimension, at your service—and in your debt. Will you settle for a manly handshake as payment?"

The man at the controls twiddled one more dial and then turned toward Doc D. with a dashing smile. "Zorin." He held out his hand for a proper shake. "And your hand will be more than enough. It is a great pleasure to meet you."

"The pleasure's all mine, Zorin. You saved my Grecian butt."

The hands met, and a jolly good grip was given by both parties. Hail fellows well met, and all that.

"Phooey," said Vivian Vernon. She blew off a whiff of imaginary smoke from her blaster. "Don't *I* get any credit?"

"Hey, Viv," said Doc D. "Hell, you always pack a kick. By the way, where did you get that beautiful shiner?"

She growled, "I ran into an aperture."

"A delightful lady. Delightful ladies, both of them," said Zorin. "Although I fear that Diane has imbibed a little too much bubbly."

"I don't suppose you could get her to take her clothes off again, could you?" leered Doc D.

"Yeah," said Troy. "I—" Troy gave his boss a reproachful frown. "Hey, Doc, that's not very gentlemanly."

"Who's a gentleman?"

Zorin said, "We will be teleporting again, perhaps, but cautiously. It's a tricky proposition. As to the nudity, it may no longer be necessary. I have developed some personal teleportation gear."

"Well," said Doc, "if I have to do it nude, I'll grin and bare it."

"Allow me to get directly to the point," said Zorin. "You wouldn't by any chance have heard of a little item called the M'Guh Fon, would you?"

Doc D. rolled his eyes. "This line of questioning has been getting a little stale."

"Ah. Yes. Diane described the scene she encountered. I take it that Baron Skulkrak was using his subtle methods of information extraction. Not surprising. However, it is good to know that he hasn't got it."

"How are you sure?"

"The universe is not yet in his command."

"How odd. He claimed that he was looking for it for some empress."

"I am certain that Baron Skulkrak has his own agenda."

"Gosh, he seemed like such a nice guy," said Troy.

"Tell us more about his M'Guh Fon," said Doc D. "But first, why don't we celebrate our mutual escapes with a little of that elixir that seems to have snookered Miss Derry. But I'd like one little bit of information first: Where the hell are we?"

"My personal retreat, in the mountains to the north of Ovaria's capital city, Maenopahz," announced Zorin. "And quite, quite safe, I assure you, at least for the time being. Now then, first the drink and then the discussion."

Quickly, their host produced the vintage, charging everyone's glass.

"Here's to our spouses and lovers," Doc toasted. "May they never meet!" He drank deeply.

It went down smooth, and the ride got better from that moment on. For the first time since this whole wild and woolly escapade had started, he actually felt *good*.

"Magnificent."

Zorin poured him another drink.

"Now then," Doc Dimension reminded his host, "let's talk about the black bird."

"What black bird?" Vivian wanted to know.

"I suspect this is some sort of obscure cultural allusion," Zorin said. "Yes?"

"Yes, but not obscure to readers of mystery fiction—or movie buffs either, for that matter. But . . . sorry, the M'Guh Fon. What the bloody hell is it?"

Quickly, Zorin related the same story he'd given to the other about the source and the meaning of the M'Guh Fon.

Doc D.'s eyes glittered as he absorbed the information.

"What you're saying, Zorin, that this device could hold the key not only to ultimate knowledge, but to ultimate power."

"Yeah, and I bet it would be a keen football coach, too," said Troy. "Maybe with it, Flitheimer and I could actually win a game." His brow furrowed as he thought of this glorious possibility.

"But most of all, Doc," said Vivian Vernon, "it will get us back home. I think we can all agree that's something that we all would like."

"Can't dispute, can't dispute . . ." said Doc D., newly buoyant with the champagne. "And Zorin, you as a fellow physicist seem reputable enough, I must say."

Zorin gave a little bow. "I thank you."

Doc stroked his chin, and studied Zorin.

Oh, well. If you had to trust *somebody* in this universe, he might as well look like Douglas Fairbanks. Or was it . . . ?

"We think we've discovered the M'Guh Fon," he said.

Zorin's eyes lit up. "Pray, do tell."

Doc D. did tell. He told of Troy's encounter with the

cheapjack crystal ring. He told of how it had delivered them from the trash world beasties. He told how the wonders of Troy Talbot's tabula rasa had prevented Baron Skulkrak from getting his metallic fingers on the thing. He told him how Troy had planted the ring in the robot that had been carted off. He told him he had to go to the little boy's room.

"It's down the hall and to the left, past that voltage transformer," said Zorin. "Can you give me some specifics about this robot? I might be able to track him down."

"But tell me first—is that ring the M'Guh Fon?"

"Yes," said Zorin.

"Wonderful. What luck we are having. Okay, Troy, spill your guts. I'm going to see a man about watering the plants."

"Well, he was this weird metal guy who didn't know quite who he was really—" Troy began.

Doc D. went off to wee-wee.

When he returned, Zorin was already busy with his super-science gadgetry. A new machine, poking from the walls, was doing a rainbow dance. Van de Graaff generators were abuzz.

The dramatic amount of static electricity in the air caused Doc's already frizzy hair to stand on end.

"I believe I have located Tobor, your robot friend, with my subspace detector," said Zorin. "The machine is still on Progesteron. The Baron is probably unaware that the robot is of any intrinsic value. A brilliant move on your assistant's part. You are lucky to have such a smart young man here, Doctor."

Dr. Dimension was caught buttoning his fly.

For the first time in this whole trip, the doctor was genuinely stunned. "Uh . . . pardon me?"

"I said—"

"Wait a minute. You said you located the robot."

"Yes, I did."

"How?"

"The M'Guh Fon makes known to me any change in

its location," Zorin said. "Not immediately, but sooner or later. The robot has the M'Guh Fon. Therefore . . ."

"Quod erat demonstradum," concluded Dr. Dimension.

Suddenly, interrupting all this, came a squeal of delight. "Doctor, you're alive, you're alive!"

Doc D. turned and found his arms suddenly full of a bouncing, healthy blond assistant. Diane had come to. She was still quite tipsy.

She kissed him and hugged him, smothering his frizzy head between her globular breasts, and for about a nanosecond Doc felt he must have died and gone to heaven again; however, she was hugging so tight he began to have respiratory problems.

"Diane. Please . . . can't breathe."

"Doctor. Oh, Doc, I thought you were *dead.*"

"Stay tuned for further bulletins."

Finally, she let him go and lurched toward the bar. "Oh, Doctor, I've discovered the most wonderful stuff." Diane held up her bottle of alien champagne. "It's delicious, and it makes me feel—so *giddy* inside."

"Uhm, Diane, I never thought I'd be saying this but there's work to be done and—"

Again, the charge of the mammaries.

Suddenly blond hair and shapely arms and female protuberances were not items of exquisite provocation, but dangerous weapons.

"Umphh. Eak. Uggh. Diane . . . please. Talbot. Get your crazy girlfriend *off* me!"

Diane Derry was pried from her fervent embraces by Troy Talbot. She gave him a sloppy kiss on his cheek and proceeded to suck once more on her bottle, sighing happily.

"Hmmm. I'm beginning to see why the Derrys were generations of teetotalers," said Doc D. "One drink and your average Derry is on her derriere."

"She is acting a little odd, Doc," said Troy. "Should I take away her bottle?"

"Forget about weaning her for now, Talbot. There are more important things to worry about." He turned to Zorin. "So then. We must think what has to be done next," said Doc D. ruminatively.

"No thinking necessary," said Zorin. "We must get the M'Guh Fon before Skulkrak or the empress and her imperial troopers do. The very fate of the universe rests upon it."

"Urp," said Diane.

Chapter Nineteen

"That's a tall order," Dr. Dimension said. "Skulkrak's a pretty tough customer."

"And Estrogena is conceivably tougher," said Zorin, nodding, "in her own way. The operation may very well cost us our lives."

"Well, Doc, this is it," said Troy Talbot. "I just want you to know that if we don't make it out of this one—"

"Please, Talbot, spare me."

"You're a father figure to me, Doc. I figure my father never wanted much to do with me, so I found you."

A little tear formed in the big guy's eye.

"Give me a break," Doc muttered.

Talbot gave his mentor a great big bear hug.

"Ooof! I said, give me a break, don't break me! Talbot, why are you and your girlfriend trying to smother me to death with love?"

"We just love ya," Troy emoted.

"Yeah, well, if it's all the same to you, I'd rather be squeezed between Diane's hooters. I'm always up for a hooter and holler."

Troy released him. "Ah, Doc, ever with a quip." Troy wiped away a tear. "Doc, you're the top."

"Right, I'm the goddamn Tower of Pisa, to say nothing to the Mona Lisa," said Doc, rotating his eyes heavenward. Finding no sympathy, he turned back to Zorin.

"Well, I guess if we're going to do something dangerous and silly, we might as well do it now."

Zorin looked up from a complexly designed instrument console on which multicolored lights winked and blinked. "I'd go with you on the mission, Doctor, but you're the one who knows this Tobor chap. All you have to do is get to him, have Troy extract the M'Guh Fon, and bring it back."

"How are we going to do it? The wormhole machine again?"

Zorin shook his head as he scrutinized the instruments. "I'm reading a lot of subspace interference now. Unusual. Gravity wave fronts from two directions. Don't quite know what's causing it—probably momentous astronomical events light-years away. In any case, the fabric of space is fluttering like a flag in the breeze. Rules out the wormhole device. We'll have to use teleportation."

"I thought you said that was risky, too," Doc said. "And Troy and I have never teleported."

"Neither have your colleagues . . . with this." Zorin held up an article of headgear appropriate for a child of eight or nine.

Dr. Dimension's bushy eyebrows lowered in a puzzled frown. "A propeller beanie?"

It certainly looked like one: a pink-and-purple striped skullcap with a spike at the top, on which rotated a twisted bar that looked not unlike an airplane propeller, though not quite the same.

"It's a teleportation cap," Zorin said. "This rotating electromagnet extends the displacement field evenly over the entire body."

"Amazing!" said Doc. "It comes with free lessons, I hope."

"Absolutely," Zorin said with a smile. "You'll practice right here in the lab, teleporting across the room. Once you master the technique, which isn't all that difficult, you'll be attuned to the M'Guh Fon, and you'll easily teleport to its location, which is the same as the robot's."

"Wow. Okay, I'm ready for my first lesson. But first, what are the chances we can get some chow?"

"Chow?"

"Food!" Vivian said. "I'm absolutely starving."

"I think we have time. I'll have my domestics cook up a meal." "Domestics?" Doc asked, looking around.

"Automated house systems. The kitchen machinery will cook and serve an entire meal by itself."

Doc whistled. "I haven't seen the New York World's Fair, but I have seen the future. And it's a pip!"

Once fed and watered, Dr. D. and his boon companion were perched on the edge of a great and daring adventure—

With beanies perched on their heads.

Teleportation beanies, complete with their absurd propellers. "Counter-axis rotational spacetime displacement governors," Zorin had called them.

Whatever you called them, they looked damned silly. At least that's what Doc thought.

Doc adjusted the strap on his chapeau outré and sighed. The things he did in the name of super-science! He felt singularly ridiculous in this get up.

"What we have here, you see," said Zorin, tapping a bank of dials and gauges with a writing stylus, "is a neutrino beacon."

"Neutrino. Isn't that Italian food? Great. I'm still hungry," said Troy.

"Talbot, you just had four helpings of wombat-noodle casserole," said Doc D. "Listen to the man here. We're getting instructions."

"Didn't fill me up."

"Don't worry, you're full of it."

Zorin said, "I'm scanning Skulkrak's compound now to pinpoint the exact location of the M'Guh Fon. You see, the M'Guh Fon sends off a pulsed neutrino flux that is extremely hard to detect without the proper equipment. Using the artifact as a beacon . . ." The machine began uttering a low series of throbbing beeps. "Yes. Closer, closer." The beeps increased, becoming agitated and frenetic. "Indeed. There we have it. Now, all I have to do is to superimpose the coordinates onto my schematic of the Skulkrak's compound." Zorin jiggled and wiggled controls. On the television screen graphics jumped and melded. "Yes, yes, we have it and—oh my."

"Something wrong."

"The robot and the M'Guh Fon—presuming they're still attached—"

"A very hopeful presumption."

A chagrined look crossed Zorin's handsome features. "The robot appears to be in Baron Skulkrak's personal lavatory."

"I don't know much about robots," Troy said. "But do they have to go to the lavatory once in a while?"

"Not your average robot, nor any type I'm familiar with," Zorin said.

"Well, Tobor's not your average robot," Doc said. "At least I suspect he's not. Maybe he does have to take a literal leak now and then. He isn't exactly in tip-top mechanical condition."

Zorin nodded. "Then perhaps he has a legitimate function there." He shrugged. "Though I can't imagine what. Nevertheless, that is where you will have to teleport."

"My first teleport," Doc lamented, "and it's into somebody's *pissoir.*"

"Is that Latin?" asked Troy Talbot. "C'mon, Doc, we're all guys here."

"Yeah, Latin. I learned all my Latin out of Krafft-Ebing."

"Who?"

"German psychiatrist. Wrote a little book on abnormal sexuality with all the naughty parts in Latin. As an undergrad, I used to stay up nights translating." Doc's lips curled upward in a smile of fond remembrance. He sighed.

Troy looked thoughtful. "I'd like to read that book someday."

"If we ever get back home, I'll sell you my pony."

"Heck, Doc, never cared for horseback riding."

* * *

With an explosion of displaced air, Dr. Dimension and his faithful assistant Troy Talbot erupted into existence within an expansive room of marble and shadows.

"Yuck!" said Troy. "Kind of *smells* in here, Doc."

"Shhh!" Doc whispered hoarsely, "What do you expect from Skulkrak's crapper? Guy has a serious bowel problem. I believe the proper medical term for it is 'meteorism.' "

"Yeah, and he farts a lot, too."

"Talbot, shut up and start looking for that damned robot."

"Tobor! Oh, Tob —!"

Doc hit him on the arm. "Not so loud! Why don't you just step outside and scream for the imperial guards?"

"Why would I want to do that? Boy, that would be really stupid."

"Just look."

"Okay Doc . . . Uh, Doc?"

Dr. Dimension was studying the room into which they'd just teleported. It looked like the privy/vomitorium of some Roman emperor. Columns and tile and ugly murals. One side was taken up by an expansive bathtub, flanked by several linen closets. Directly opposite this was a throne-like commode connected to piping and electronic devices. It looked like the collaborative invention of Thomas Edison, Torquemada, and Rube Goldberg.

Baron Skulkrak's porcelain throne.

It gurgled ominously.

"Doc?" Troy repeated in a whisper.

"Would you be quiet? I'm looking for that damned robot. According to Zorin, he should be right here. And I don't see him. Zorin must have been mistaken."

"Doc. Tobor *is* here."

"Where?"

Troy pointed up.

Doc D. looked.

Dangling from the high ceiling were garlands of chains. Tied to several of these, hanging upside down,

was none other than Tobor the robot, looking profoundly uncomfortable.

"Tobor."

"Hello, Doctor."

"What are you doing up there?"

"I believe the phrase is 'hanging out.' "

"My God. What have they done to you?"

"Well, they appear to have straightened me right out.
I only have one personality, which fortunately incorpo-
rates all the better portions of my previous personalities." The robot now had a slight British accent. "You
may address me now as D-4PO. Alas, unfortunately it
is all for naught, as I am here to provide spare parts for
Baron Skulkrak's rather complex water closet."

"You were interrogated, er, Dee Fourpio?"

"Reamed inside and out. Upside and down. As it
happened, however, a very fortunate circumstance un-
derlay my dreadful robot torture, much as it did your
torture, gentlemen."

Troy asked, "You did spill the beans? You've still
got the ring I gave you?"

"Precisely. The fortunate circumstance that I speak
of is the fact that my interrogators were morons of the
highest degree. Incompetent boobs."

Doc rubbed his hands together.

"Excellent, excellent. All we have to do is to get you
down from there."

Doc pulled out and unfolded the spare teleportation
beanie Zorin had supplied. "Stick this on your noodle,
and we'll be on our way."

"Hey Doc, look over there. There's a pulley. That
must have been how they hauled the robot up."

"Please, I am a sentient being. I resent the term 'robot.' " said Dee Fourpio.

"Well, excuse the hell out of me. Look, resent it all
you want when you've got *time* to. Right now, robot or
not, we've got to get your metal heinie down from
there. Okay, Troy, go have a look at—"

The echoing screech of a huge metal door opening.
The rasp of inadequately oiled joints.

The plodding thump of heavy footfalls.

"Yikes! It's Skulkrak!" whispered Troy. "What do we do, Doc?"

"He might be coming in for just a quick fart," said Doc D. "Quick! We'll hide in one of those closets."

They both raced to the nearest closet and managed to secrete themselves just before the Baron burst through into the inner chamber.

Doc could see him plainly through the louvers in the closet door.

The Baron strode in, his "body plumbing" gurgling and erupting. However, it was not to his porcelain throne that the monster repaired.

He stopped still and regarded the dangling robot.

"Soon I shall be emptying my bowels into what's left of you, you sorry pile of useless junk. I only regret that robots do not experience pain."

"I wish to be referred to as a 'person of metal,' " said Dee Fourpio.

"Excellent. How admirable. A politically conscious bucket of bolts. You should be a guest on Estrogena's ridiculous show. Now, I'll be happy if you would leave me to my privacy."

The Baron lifted a finger and flipped open the front panel of Dee Fourpio.

Nestled there was a switch. Baron Skulkrak flipped it off.

The lights in the robot's transparent head-dome went out.

"Miklik, come!" thundered Baron Skulkrak. "Where is my bath attendant?"

"Oh, no," Dr. Dimension groaned.

"What's going on, Doc?"

"He's taking a bath."

"Lucky guy. I could use one of those, too."

Doc's nostrils twitched. "Tell me about it."

"So we got our beanies, Doc. Can't we teleport out?"

"Without the robot? That's why we're here, Troy,

and as long as we're here, we might as well stay until
we do what we came to do."

"What's going on out there, Doc? I can't see anything."

"You're a lucky man, Talbot. A lucky man, indeed."

What was happening was this:

A dwarfish creature, similar to the gnarled little
thing that serviced Skulkrak's cyborg plumbing, scampered out from some dark cranny carrying a huge
wrench. Huffing and heaving, he put the wrench to an
oversize faucet and opened it, letting a stream of
steaming liquid into the tub. Having a slightly greenish
tinge, it did not appear to be water.

"Ah. Nothing I need more now that a good soak in
hot benzene, Miklik. I have been having the roughest
time imaginable with those two degenerate aliens.
Truly the ugliest creatures I have seen in my entire existence. Especially the doctor."

Doc bristled.

"But that assistant of his is totally brain-dead."

"Hey!"

"Shh, Troy. He might hear you." Doc rubbed his
chin.

In truth, the roar of the spouting lubricant was nicely
covering their conversation. Skulkrak added racheting
sounds to this mix: removal of his armor. The gnome
scurried over madly to assist. An armor plate fell,
conking him on the head. Dizzily, the gnome dragged
the heavy thing over to one side, then hurried back to
collect another.

The sight of Baron Skulkrak denuding himself was
rather unsettling. For one thing, beneath the heavy,
nasty leather and armor, the monster wore pink frilly
underthings. Carefully and daintily, he removed these
and gave them to Miklik, who folded them and gently
placed them by the armor.

"Have a care, fool!" roared Skulkrak. "Precious material there. How's that bath doing?"

Fretting, the little creature leaped up to the rim of

the tub and peered in. "Almost sufficiently deep to cover the terrible buttocks, Baron."

Skulkrak grunted. "Petroleum distillates?"

Miklik scrambled to a cabinet and procured a bottle. "Yes, Baron."

"Lye-on-a-rope?"

"Yes."

"And don't forget the high-octane fuel with special detergent action."

Sweat seemed to spurt from the frantic creature's pores. "Uhm ... I forgot. Jasmine Nights or Clowntime Fun, Baron?"

"You imbecile. Clowntime, of course. I'm in a foul mood, and Clowntime always cheers me up."

Doc stared at the sight of the naked Baron. He had to cover his mouth to stifle a giggle.

What had filled out the mighty codpiece had been mere padding. Babies had more to boast about then Baron Skulkrak.

"Why does the universe create such nuisances to annoy me, Miklik?"

"To challenge your fearsomeness, my lord. To test your mettle. To prove your valor?"

"I wish they'd give it a rest. This Dr. Dimension fellow. When I had the opportunity, I should have taken that fuzzy head in my hand ..." Baron Skulkrak grabbed the lye-on-a-rope illustratively. "And just *squeezed.*"

The lye spurted messily, burning the poor bath attendant.

"Ulp," said Doc D. Suddenly he was developing a headache.

"Hey Doc. What's going on?"

"He's about to take a bubble bath," whispered Doc D. "In benzene, fercrissake."

"Gee—I like Clowntime bubble bath. It makes the biggest bubbles."

"Well, go and jump in there and you won't be disappointed, Talbot."

"Uh, uh—no way."

"Good lad."

Miklik was just emptying a clown-shaped bottle into the tub, and multicolored toxic bubbles were drifting up over the rim.

"All set, Baron."

"Good. I am getting goose bumps."

The cyborg cranked over to the edge of the tub, lifted himself over, and slipped in.

Soapy benzene and caustic bubbles splashed over the rim, washing over the hapless bathroom assistant.

"Ah!" said Baron Skulkrak.

"Gah!" said Miklik, acid burning his eyes.

"Nothing like a good soak."

Miklik stumbled around, groping for a towel.

"Miklik!" said Skulkrak, looking about with some consternation.

"Glurg," said Miklik. "Yes. Your Protuberance." The little guy found a towel and dried his face.

"Where's Mr. Quacky!" Extreme agitation.

"Pardon?"

"My rubberoid waterfowl!" screamed the Baron. A fist splashed into the liquid. "You know I can't take a bath without my Mr. Quacky!"

Miklik's eyes fairly popped out of their sockets. "The rubberoid water fowl. I'm *sorry*, Baron."

The dwarf turned and stumped toward a row of closets.

One of them was the very closet that hid Dr. Dimension and Troy Talbot.

"Talbot. Quick, look behind you. Is there a rubber duckie somewhere?"

"Yeah, Doc. And he's not actually a duckie. More like a cross between a—"

"Never mind. Hand him here."

"Gee, Doc. I'm getting kind of attached."

"Hand him over, you ninny."

"Okay, okay. You don't have to get nasty."

The little troll was heading their way.

"Talbot, this is no time to express hurt feelings. Just hand me that damned rubber duckie."

"Gee, Doc. Just when *is* a good time? I mean, I take your abuse all the time. I've got to stand up to you."

Almost there.

"Talbot, increase your self-esteem later. Hand me the goddamned rubber duckie."

"Oh. Okay, Doc."

Doc could see the nostril hairs curling from the ugly alien dwarf's nose. He could smell what the thing had eaten for lunch—last week.

Nothing was forthcoming from Troy Talbot.

"Talbot. Duck!"

"Gee, Doc, no need to curse. Here!"

A phthisic arm with a four-fingered hand reached into the closet and began to grope about.

"Ooff," said Doc.

There was no time to yell at Talbot. The little alien troll was reaching into the darkness, groping.

It grabbed Doc's nose.

Somehow, Dr. D. was able to substitute the rubber duckie for his nose.

Satisfied, Miklik grabbed it and closed the closet door.

"Gee, Doc. That was a close call, huh?"

Somehow Doc's fist lost control.

"Ouch."

"Sorry Talbot. Little spastic twitch. Remind me to get some medicine for that when we get back to Earth."

"Thath hokay, Doc. Diane thez my nothe ith too big anyway."

Doc gave it a few quick moments, and then peered out to see what was going on.

With obeisance in every gesture, every movement, the little troll-thing offered up the duck to Baron Skulkrak, who was already seated luxuriantly in the bath, bubbles crawling up his immense back.

Something funny about that duck.

Something awfully familiar.

Baron Skulkrak grabbed the duck with one hand, and gave Miklik a sharp swat with the other.

"Next time, speed it up a bit, vassal."

"Yes, my lord. I apologize." Great bowing and scurrying off to a safer perch.

"You may scrub my back—later. Right now, I shall enjoy my little friend."

The Baron proceeded to place the rubber duck in the chemical soup. It bobbed playfully and merrily.

A burlesque of a smile spread across the Baron's caricature of a face. He began to splash the benzene with his immense hands, causing the duckoid to cavort marvelously.

The Baron began to croak. It took a few moments for Doc D. to realize that the croaking was singing.

Ah me, ah my. This is the life.
Terror is my lover, murder is my wife.
Universal dominance I'll be sharin'
Nothin' better than to be a bad old Baron!

The Baron hummed out a few more bars and splashed playfully again, fluffing up frothy mounds of bubbles.

"Lah di da, lad di di. Bad bad big old me!"

It was then that Doc noticed what was odd about that rubber duckie. Perched upon its bizarre bulbous head was something that should not be there.

"Uh-oh."

Doc reached around for the extra beanie they had brought along to teleport the robot back. He couldn't find it, and there was good reason for that.

The beanie was now perched atop the rubber duckie's head.

"Doc!" said Troy. "What's wrong?"

Dr. Dimension told him.

"What are we going to do?"

"What *can* we do?"

"Gee Doc, you remember how you told me once you didn't believe in God."

"What's that got to do with anything?"

"Maybe you better rethink, that, huh?"

Doc was going to smack him again—but then, the big lug maybe had a good idea.

Prayer was about the only option.

The Baron leaned back, looking blissfully relaxed. "Ah . . . Miklik?"

"Yes, sir?"

"Miklik, my plans for control of the empire proceeds apace. I feel good about my future. I do."

"Wonderful, sir."

"Yes. Option A, of course, is marriage to the Empress. She has my proposal and is presently considering it. Option B is to simply destroy her and all loyal subjects. I have the capacity, you know. The secret project that will make it possible has almost achieved fruition."

A noisy bubbling and a green gas troubled the benzene's surface.

The baronial flatulence, acting up again. A huge bubble formed on the surface of the bath liquid, green and shimmering.

"You are the master, master."

"Bite it," the Baron ordered.

Apparently the trollish creature knew what he meant. It scurried to the tub, went on tiptoe, stretched, and opened its wide, toothy mouth. Bending toward the quivering, delicate bubble, it bit. Its crooked front teeth broke the critical surface tension.

The bubble went BINK as it vanished, and a puff of reeking gas expanded and filled the room.

"Yes. She *is* a pretty thing, no? Estrogena, I mean."

Gagging, Miklik gasped, "Lovely, sir."

"I shall, of course, have to eventually cut off her head, but I shall give her the time of her life beforehand, though."

"Yes, sir."

"In fact—hold a moment. Miklik, what is this?"

"What, your overbearance?"

"A surprise for me. How thoughtful. Some sort of crown, on top of Mr. Quacky. You anticipated my fondest desire."

"What?"

The Baron took the beanie off Mr. Quacky and put it on. It barely fit his massive head, but the chin strap secured it.

"Yes, Miklik, a very good model of the Imperial Crown of The Ever-Rotating Cosmic Nebula. Although I must say, whoever made it had far better taste."

"Yes, my lord."

"I think I shall try this particular crown on for size. What do you say, Miklik?"

"Er—" The little troll-thing cast a quick nervous glance at the closet wherein our heroes huddled. "Yes, Your Bombast, I mean, Your Bodaciousness—er." Big grin. Bow. "Why not?"

"To get the full effect, I suppose one must spin the propeller, eh Miklik?"

Panic began to rise inside Dr. Dimension.

"No," he cried. He burst out of the closet, holding up his hands. "Don't . . . !"

However the sausagelike finger had already flicked. The propeller rotated.

Baron Skulkrak's eyes bulged.

"Dimension! You dare to enter my chambers. Prepare for—"

However, Dr. D. never quite learned what he was supposed to prepare for, because the Baron flickered like a TV image with the electronic rug pulled out from under it.

The Baron went "POP" and disappeared.

Chapter Twenty

The Empress sat in her boudoir with her favorite hand-maiden, getting a perm.

"Gladys-Ar," said the Empress.

"Yes, my lady," said the handmaiden.

"Did you realize that Baron Skulkrak has made another proposal of matrimony? He has presented me with a cache of diamonds the size of goiters, and a spaceship full of rubies."

"Most impressive, ma'am. He is a man of great wealth and power, and his loyalty to you is without question."

"I hesitate even at the thought of putting him on my talk show, let alone putting him in my bed."

"A woman of your beauty and regalness must be careful in her choices."

"Yes. Nonetheless, sometimes, when I look at him, I have—thoughts."

"Thoughts, ma'am?"

"Yes, Gladys-Ar. Sometimes I wonder what the Baron is like without his armor. Sometimes I wonder what it would be like to have mad, passionate, powerful sex with a man of his, well, potency."

"Ah. Yes. This is understandable, Your Grace. I admit, from time to time I, too, have been impressed at the—well, I blush at the thought."

"Yes. The girth of his loins. Most impressive, Gladys-Ar. Can a woman help but get a little tingle at such a sight?" She sighed. "But I wonder if I can trust him."

"Your Grace?"

"Yes. I have heard the Baron has a tendency to eventually liberate lovers of their heads. Anyway, that's the rumor. Do you think he's after my empire?"

"But surely, Your Grace, with his own personal holdings and power as your Main Defender, he has enough to satisfy his cravings. Perhaps the diamonds and rubies bespeak his love."

"Yes. But my intelligence agents have heard rumors that the Baron has secretly established bases and is building up forces on a solar system, and is working on a secret project to develop the offensive might of a powerful star."

"Perhaps your intelligence agents also have overactive imaginations. I have given perms to many women in the empire, and some have whispered of dalliances with the Baron, and none of them have voiced dissatisfaction."

Of course, Gladys-Ar was also in the employ of Baron Skulkrak, so it was not at all surprising that she said such things.

Their conversation continued along other roads. However, they were interrupted just as the perm was finishing up.

From out of nowhere, a figure erupted into the Empress's private chamber.

Baron Skulkrak.

Baron Skulkrak, wearing nothing but a beanie and a few shreds of soap bubbles.

The hulking behemoth blinked, looked around, determined where he was, and then his great head swiveled around to lock eyes with the Empress.

He assumed a posture of great dignity.

"Your Imperial Majesty." He bowed.

"Baron Skulkrak!" said the Empress. "Why . . . why . . . you're tiny!"

As though trying to warp reality itself, Baron Skulkrak peered down at himself.

Yes, quite naked.

The Baron covered what little there was to cover with his hands.

"Arggghhhhhhhhhh!" said Baron Skulkrak.

Brrrrrrrrrrrpt! said Baron Skulkrak's faulty bowels and sphincter.

Plop, went the handmaiden.

Flop, went the Empress's new perm.

Red went the Baron's face.

Desperately, the powerful brain worked and came up with a solution. He moved a stumpy finger up to the beanie.

"Your Majesty, you must be having a hallucination," said the Baron.

Brrrrrrrrrrrpppppppppppppppppt!

Desperately, the Baron twirled his beanie.

Brrrrrrrrrrrrrrrrrrrrrrrrrrt!

And then he was gone, leaving a cloud of foul green gas in his wake.

The Empress of the Universe had one full moment of consciousness before that green swamp gas overwhelmed her, but it was long enough to come to a very important conclusion.

Something decidedly odd had just happened.

In The Royal Academy of Sciences on the same planet, there was a special gymnasium-size room. In that room, a clutch of scientists busily worked at their stations, performing important scientific experimentation.

This was a very special room, because the scientists had full banks of null-gravity generators in the walls, floor, and ceiling. Today, they were performing a very special experiment, determining if the Empress's special wisdom-weed plants would grow larger without the constraints of gravity, thus supplying Her Imperial Bitchiness with the enormous amount of narcotics that she enjoyed so much. These were desperate scientists, for they had been given a dictate: get more potent weed, or die.

They were working very hard, indeed.

Part of the problem was that in order for the plants to have the desired kick, they had to be grown in the purest of nitrogen/oxygen mixtures. Any introduction of foreign gases would hurt the plants.

The scientists bustled and hustled, measuring and whatnot. The plants had grown up green and luxuriant. In just hours, the plants would reach full potency and could be harvested. The Head Scientist, Carbunk, knew this, because he had personally sampled the weed just an hour before, and he was quite stoned, and quite happy.

It looked as though the scientists were going to be able to save their necks.

Whew.

This was the happy, industrious scene as it was the moment that a certain naked, dripping, blushing Baron teleported in. Zap.

Carbunk's earphone crackled.

"Sir, there appears to be a foreign body in the midst of the null-G chamber."

Carbunk did a double take. He was seeing a lot of double lately as well.

"What's it doing there, Zorka?"

"Well, actually floating sir!"

Carbunk managed to focus his TV screen on the field of green, frilly plants. Sure enough, there it was, an ugly blob of flesh and metal, hanging in the air above his precious plants.

What was it, anyway?

He upped the magnification.

"I recognize that hunk of foreign matter," said Carbunk.

"Yes, sir."

"That's Baron Skulkrak, isn't it?"

"Yes, sir."

"What's he doing there?"

"Well, actually, still floating sir."

Carbunk fumbled for the communicator.

"Hail, Baron Skulkrak. This is Head Scientist Carbunk. What are you doing in our null-G chamber?"

"Get me down from here, you idiots," thundered the Baron. Bummer, thought Carbunk. True bummer. The

Baron was probably the meanest, nastiest, ugliest son of a bitch in the galaxy, and it was not a good thing to have an upset Baron Skulkrak in one's immediate vicinity.

However, Carbunk noticed one small detail about the naked body that so astonished him that he could not keep his drug-addled speech center under control.

"Baron! You're minuscule!"

"Argggggghhh!" said the Baron, covering himself. His faulty plumbing system was apparently equally embarrassed, because it expelled considerable gaseous ballast. *Brrrrrrrrrrrrrpppppt!*

The blast, however, also served as strong rocket power, propelling its creator with great force toward the ceiling. Unfettered by gravity, the Baron went very quickly, indeed.

BOINK!

The Baron ricocheted like a wobbly billiard ball off the ceiling, and tumbled off in a different direction.

"Baron!" called Carbunk. "Redirect toward the entrance. We'll throw you a rope."

"Unnnnnngh," said the Baron, groggily trying to flap his way into the proper position.

Too late, however . . .

Brrpppppppptttt.

The Baron, whooshed along a greenish plume of high density rear expectorant, shot away, albeit heading for another course—but not a much improved course.

"Not that way, Baron!" cried the Head Scientist. "You'll slam into the—"

"Nooooooooooooooo!" cried the Baron.

Boink!

"—Wall."

The semiconscious Baron bounced back to the middle of the field. The green gas that he had farted so voluminously and loudly was already drifted down toward the forests of weed.

The weeds began to wilt.

"Get him out of there!"

Grappling rods and waldoes shot out, but somehow each time they neared, one more short burst of flatulence would send the Baron away from reach.

"He's killing the crop!" cried Carbunk.

The Baron recovered sufficiently to shoot off a suggestion. "Just turn off the null-gravs, you incredible null-brains."

"Oh, yeah," said Carbunk.

His finger shot out.

"But first—" The finger hit the cancel switch for the generators.

The generators stopped humming.

The Baron hung in the air for one nanosecond—and then dropped like a rock into the weed patch.

"—Get a net."

"Ooops. Men. Go help the Baron up. Have a care. He may be dangerous."

The Baron, however, seemed far too groggy to be dangerous. Carbunk watched as several men in gas masks raced out to attend to him.

"Hey, what's that on his head?"

"Looks like the Cosmic Crown."

"I dunno. Looks like a beanie to me. Look, there's this silly propeller."

"No!" cried the Baron. "Don't touch tha—" The propeller was touched, however, and it did spin.

With a TWIP! and an implosion, the great naked Baron Skulkrak disappeared as quickly as he had arrived, teleporting to parts unknown.

Affected now by gravity, the greater cloud of green gas settled down upon the once-thriving wisdom-weed plants.

The plants shuddered and died.

"Zorka," said Carbunk, after beating his head several times on the control panel. "Would you please contact my travel agent? I have the sudden urge for a one-way ticket to the Rhio system."

It was a feat on naked cosmic engineering.

Imagine! Harvesting the energy of a sun, utilizing

a ring around said sun, only two million units away from the fiery surface. With this powerful device focusing the energy with a powerful lens and thus using unimaginably powerful beams to destroy anything that came near the planetary system, be it a single offending ship or a whole armada.

This was the ultimate defensive devise utilized by the Secret System.

A ring around a sun called Hellwipe.

It was in the Secret System that vast numbers of ships were being built to conquer the universe, if need be.

It was in the Secret System that some of the nastiest mercenaries and pirates had been assembled to do the dastardly deeds ordered by their Master.

Their Master, and the owner of the system, was none other than Baron Skulkrak.

"Arrrrrrrr!" said the head pirate scientist, Scumdog. He took the last bite of baby flesh, munched it, and then used the bare bone to scratch his empty eye socket under his black eye patch. "Arrr, me maties!"

"Arrrrr!" said the maties.

"Arrrr! Stop mating, maties, and let's get on with the experiment!"

"Arrrrr! Arrrrr!"

Scabrous, oily men disconnected, pulled greasy trousers back on, and signaled their full attention to the pirate scientist: "Arrrrrrrrr!"

"Right. Much better. Now listen up, you pack of mangy comet hyenas. We're about to perform a test of the Death Beam. First, though, we must power it up."

"Arrrrrr! Arrrrrrr!" Plasma-cutlasses flashed approvingly.

"This is a might delicate stage of our operation, however. The Transducer Chamber must remain sterile. Did you remove all the salt-pork, Genital-Breath?"

"Got it, Cap'n."

"And the dead man's chest?"

"Right. A bit rotten and ribby, that. Hosed off the floor good."

"Excellent. The walls will be conducting a high temperature. The atmosphere is now utterly controlled. The merest speck of explosive matter might set off a chain reaction." Scumdog dug a finger up a hairy nostril, looking thoughtful. "Puke Pile?"

"Arrrrr!"

"You did remove the gunpowder we were snorting?"

"Right-o. Capital stuff, Cap'n."

"Good. We're all set. Aren't we just the most reprehensible bunch of mangy beetle-dropping pirate scientists ever to scuttle our way across the universe."

"Arrrrrr. Arrrrrr!"

An errant cutlass accidentally loped off an ear.

"Don't worry. He's got two of them. Let's get to work. Arrrrrr!"

The pirate scientists proceeded to flip switches, flip levers, and just plain flip out. Not only were these the nastiest pirates in the universe, they were the nastiest tech-pirates. Give them a crate of beer, a bottle of rum, and a skull-and-crossbones, and they could make a starship.

Mighty engines hummed.

Gigawatts of power crashed through unimaginable alloys.

The entirety of the millions of miles of circumference began to glow a bright, pretty peach.

Scumdog peered into the Tranducer Chamber. "Arrrr! Who left the banana peel in there?"

"Arrrrrr!" Fingers pointed to the guilty party.

Scumdog lifted his singleshot and put a hole right between the guilty pirate-scientist's eyes.

"Let that be a lesson to you, me hearties. When I say clean, I mean clean! We can be as scurvy as we want to be, but when it comes to important stuff, like Transducer Chambers, when it's a matter of our lives, we'd better keep it clean. Right!"

"Arrrrrr. Arrrrrr."

"And again, what's the seventeenth letter of the alphabet?" The pirate scientists looked at each other in puzzlement.

"Uhmmmmm——— T?" suggested a man with a peg leg.

Scumdog pulled out another pistol and shot him as well.

"Arrrrr! Arrrr!" said the others.

"Right! Now let's get this ring going." Scumdog rubbed his hands together with glee. "Too bad we don't have some innocent cruiser we can test her out on, eh?"

"How about a beer bottle!" suggested another. Scumdog nodded. "Arrrr. That be a fine idea. Eject. The Death Beam will pulverize it! Arrrrrr!"

Well satisfied, the pirate scientist looked back into the Transducer Chamber. The walls were glowing a cherry-red. There was no turning back now!

Yo-ho and a bottle of ru—

Suddenly, right in the middle of the chamber, an seven-foot-tall figure erupted into view.

A naked seven-foot-tall creature.

Wearing a beanie.

"Why, it be Baron Skulkrak!" yelled one of the men. "What's he doing here."

Scumdog stared, astonished.

"Asteroids!" roared the Baron. "I'm on Hellwipe. And it's hot!" A sweat broke out all over his massive body. "Let me out of here, you buzzards!"

Scumdog's eyes lowered to the Baron's midsection. He barked in astonishment.

"Baron! You're—microscopic!"

"Arrrrr. Arrrrr," said the pirate scientists.

"Gaahhhhhhhhh!" said the Baron, covering himself. The Baron's bowels had their say as well.

Brrrrrrrrrrrrrrrrrrrrrrrrrrrrrrrrrrrrrrrrrrrrppppppppppppppppp ppppppppppppptttttttttttttttttttttttt!

Baron Skulkrak thereby committed their longest and most voluminous fart yet, issuing forth a truly massive amount of highly ignitable gas at precisely the wrong moment.

Scumdog's jaw dropped when he saw the massive green gas billowing out.

"Turn on the blowers. Turn on the fans. Get that stuff out of—"

Baron Skulkrak watched helplessly as a tendril of gas touched a side of the walls.

"Dr. Dimension," he growled, unrepentant. "You shall pay for this. All of—"

The gas blew.

The chamber blew.

"Arrrrrrrrrrrrrrrr—" said the pirate scientists.

The ring blew.

Chain reactions tending to react in a chain kind of way, the next item in the sequence was the sun called Hellwipe.

And when stars blow, it tends to be in quite a spectacular fashion.

It's called a nova.

And as it happened, this one was, indeed, a sup-arrrrrrrrrrnova.*

* One of the authors of this book was in favor of excising this enormity, surely one of the most egregious puns ever perpetrated in a science-fiction novel. However, after much negotiation, it was allowed to stand in the manuscript. It doesn't matter. The whole chapter is silly and should be ignored.

Chapter Twenty-One

"Gee, Doc," said Troy Talbot, back in the Baron's lavatory. "The knot they used on this chain tying up the robot is really weird. I can't quite figure it out."

"Work on it, Talbot," said Doc D. "I'm having my own problems."

Doc's problem was the troll-thing called Miklik.

He was sitting on the guy now, trying to control the slippery little devil, and not having a great deal of luck.

The thing squeaked.

"Look, Buttlick, or whatever your name is. Shut up, or I'm going to have to wring your scrawny, pathetic neck!"

As soon as the Baron had winked out of existence, Doc D. raced out and tackled the mangy, puppety little thing. Now he was trying to tie it up with the lye-on-a-rope.

It was a slippery proposition.

"You will never win, you weak pathetic aliens. The Master will return and crush you. Your trick will not work. Help! Help!"

Dr. D. gave him a good smack, which shut him up.

"Since my family moved from Greece, I have resented the term 'alien.' We are all brothers, under the skin. Can't anyone see that?" *Smack.* "Now, be tolerant, or I'll kill you."

"Doc, I think I'm getting it."

"Yes, but Lick here isn't getting it? Goddamn rope. Goddamn creature, stay still and stop wiggling."

"Doc!"

Doc looked up. "Confound it, Talbot, what do you want?" For a moment, he lost his concentration on the job at hand.

Baron Skulkrak's little gnomish bath servant made one more incredible convulsion, squiggling like an eel beneath a boot.

He slipped free.

"Doc! Doc, I got it . . . I untied it."

Quickly, Miklik hopped up to his feet, scampering backward even as he thumbed his nose at Dr. Dimension.

"*Nyah, nyah.* You are doomed. I shall race off and call the guard. They shall tear your spines out and use them for toothpicks. *Nyah, nyah!*"

"Whoops," said Troy Talbot.

The hapless assistant had indeed untied the chain, and he had been attempting to lower the robot slowly down from where it had dangled from the ceiling.

His hands, however, had slipped.

The robot fell.

"Farewell, stupid alien. Fare—"

Crunch.

Splat.

The robot landed directly on Miklik.

Breaking its fall, and breaking Miklik as well.

Dr. D. stood and walked over to the mess, shaking his head sorrowfully.

"Ewwww," said Troy.

"Oh, well. It couldn't have happened to a more deserving Miklik."

"What about the robot?"

"Help me get him up, Talbot."

Together they heaved and hauled the big robot up, somehow getting him up to his treads.

What was left of the gnomish bath servant dripped and plopped off ingloriously.

"He's dead, Doc."

"Of course, he's dead. He got squashed."

"No. I mean Dee Fourpio."

"Of course he's not dead, you ninny. The Baron turned him off."

"Oh, yeah."

"Doctor D. opened the cabinet and turned the switch. The robot hummed to life, lighting up like an Xmas tree. "Well, is Dee Fourpio still in there. Or have we got someone different this time?" asked Doc.

"Oh, indeed, it is me. At your service."

"Just wanted to know who we were working with in there."

"What happened?"

"The Baron copped your teleporter beanie and accidentally split."

"Teleporter beanie? Never mind. What are we going to do?"

Doc brought his nifty wrist communicator near his lips. Another Zorin invention, straight out of Dick Tracy. "Zorin? Come in, please."

Nothing but static gave a reply.

"Damn. Must be the same cosmic disturbance that nixed the wormhole device. What we're going to have to do, I suppose, is have Troy here teleport back and tell Zorin to bring another beanie for you, my metallic chum."

"Who? Me. Alone."

"Yes. You. All by yourself. It's your chance to prove yourself, Troy. I won't be along to hold your hand, true, but think how proud I'll be of you when you come back."

Troy took a deep breath and nodded.

"Okay, Doc. I'll do right by my mission."

"Good boy."

"Doc?"

"Yeah?"

"Uhmm . . . What direction do I go in?"

"None, Troy. You just spin your beanie. Now, the problem with Baron Skulkrak was that he was spinning it in the wrong direction. You just spin it in a clockwise rotation."

"Uh—could you do it?"

"Sure Talbot. It'll be my pleasure."

Doc stepped forward and spun the propeller beanie.

"Bye, Doc."

"Good-bye, Talbot."

"Bring back that beanie."

"You bet."

Troy Talbot "POPPED" away.

Doc D. felt the slight breeze from the implosion.

He was a bit doubtful about sending Troy Talbot back for another beanie, but he was even more doubtful about leaving him here with Dee Fourpio. At least on the other side of his jaunt, Zorin was waiting and would know what to do.

Doc turned back to the robot.

"We'll just have to wait for a little while."

"Oh, no problem. In the meantime, perhaps I should debrief."

"Look, I just saw Baron Skulkrak naked, and that was enough."

"No. I mean about Baron Skulkrak's plans for universal domination."

"Oh, you mean Plan A and Plan B. Yes, we heard his bathtub patter. The guy seems bent on conquest, by hook or by crook."

"Actually, he has both and then some."

"I don't think Baron Skulkrak will be too much of a problem for a while. Hopefully he's even teleported himself into raw ether."

"Yes. In the meantime, perhaps we should examine this room for actual texts containing his plan so that we can be of some use to the universe in preventing this potential holocaust."

"More like Halloween, if you ask me."

"My goodness. What's that?"

"What's what?"

The robot pointed, his light blinking with consternation.

Doc looked.

In the center of the room, a twirling began, a darkness wisping together like the tentative beginnings of a hurricane. Bright lights sparkled and flared within.

"That's odd," said Doc D. "What's Troy doing back so soon?"

"Maybe he made a wrong turn. I do so hope he has my beanie. I have grown so tired of this dank and abysmal room."

The darkness solidified.

A figure all in black stood before them.

Red eyes glared from a crisped face. Shreds of smoke drifted up above the body, as though fleeing something evil. A singed and twisted beanie propeller drifted to a stop.

"Arrrrrrggggggggh," said the figure.

It was Baron Skulkrak.

"Oh, dear," said Dee Fourpio, voice trembling.

"Out for a barbecue, Baron?" said Doc D.

"Arrrrrrrrrrrrrrrghhhhhhhh!"

Powerful hands rose and slowly pulled off the beanie from the blackened head. The Baron tossed it aside, then turned and stared toward Dr. D. Heavy-duty lasers were less powerful than the raw hatred in those eyes.

The Baron lifted up his arms toward Doc D. He began to walk toward Doc D.

His intent was clear.

More than anything, Baron Skulkrak wanted to wrap those hands around Dr. Dimension's neck.

"Arrrrrrgghhhhhhhhhhhhhh!"

"Now, Baron, can't we discuss this like civilized creatures? I mean, I tried to warn you, didn't I? I gave myself away just so that I could run out and tell you to get that thing off your head, right?"

"Arrrrrrrghhhhhhhh!"

"Can we be less monosyllabic here?"

"Doctor, what are we going to do?"

"I believe turning and fleeing would be an excellent idea."

They turned and proceeded to do so. However, Baron Skulkrak, newly arrived from the demolition of his Secret System, having escaped by the skin of his fangs, started to move faster.

A big raw hand grabbed Dr. Dimension.

Oh, dear, thought Doc D. This is it. The farm is mine. However, the Baron's foot landed in the slippery pile of fluid and flesh that had once been his bath servant.

"Arrrrrrghh—Whhhoooooops!"

The great Baron floundered, then did a double-backward half gainer. He hit the deck like a sack of over-cooked potatoes, knocking his head against a support beam, bending it severely, but also finally putting out his lights, if only temporarily.

"Well, that's that," said Doc. "Sheesh, I wonder what can happen next."

WHUMP!

There, standing before them, was Zorin.

"Fancy meeting you here," Doc said casually.

"You are, of course, aware of our communicator problems. I had to come myself."

"For no good reason, I'm afraid, because Baron Skully came back, and . . ."

Zorin went to the prone figure of the Baron. He knelt and examined the beanie on Skulkrak's head.

"This unit is inoperable. And it was the only one I adapted to have a wider field locus, which would have accommodated the robot. But perhaps it's best."

"How so?" Doc wanted to find out.

"Having a robot teleport is an iffy proposition, indeed. We will have to locate the *Mudlark,* get aboard it, fix the instantaneous displacement drive, and displace the ship back to my hideout."

Doc whistled. "Wow, tall order, Zorin. And how are we going to do all that?"

Zorin rose. "First things first." He took something out of his pocket. "First, we must sneak through this compound to the graving docks. And we will do it with this."

He held up his hand. In his palm was a tiny black box.

"What's that?"

"Invisibility device."

"An invisibility device! I've always wanted to be invisible. That is, until I passed forty and became invisible to girls in their twenties."

"A fact we must all grapple with," Zorin said, smiling wryly. "Nevertheless, not being seen does have its uses."

"How does it work?"

A groan escaped the Baron's chapped lips.

"No time for explanations. You and the robot keep close to me. The effect doesn't extend from the box very far."

"This ought to be good. Let's go, Dee Fourpio."

Zorin frowned. "Dee Fourpio? I thought he was called—"

"A robot by any other name. Let's vamoose, Mr. Personality's coming to."

The carbonized hulk that was Baron Skulkrak groggily crawled across the floor, muttering.

Things had been better.

Again, he encountered the squashed form of Miklik, lying upon the floor.

He contemplated the form, and then made his pronouncement in a grainy, angry croak:

"Plan B, Miklik! . . . Miklik?"

The Baron painfully swung his head. The lavatory was devoid of intruding aliens. He must sound the alarm. He must.

He crawled toward the security alarm button, gasping for breath.

He didn't make it, passing out once again.

The invisibility device worked.

"Actually, what a person outside the field sees is a distortion of the surroundings," Zorin explained as he, Doc, and the robot made their way down a dark subterranean corridor. "If he looks very hard, and concentrates, he can see what the distortion is hiding."

"So it's not strict invisibility," Doc said. "Still, it's pretty slick. Another trick out of the M'Guh Fon's bottomless bag?"

"Of course. Try that storeroom, there."

"Here? Okay."

Doc shouldered the heavy metal door open. The room inside contained nothing but plastic packing crates, row upon row of them.

Doc closed the door gently. "Something tells me all this stuff is fireworks of some kind."

"You mean weapons? No doubt. The Baron makes his plans to dominate the galaxy. And with the secret project he has brewing—I've gotten wind of some horrendous weapon he's developed that involves an entire star system . . . But, of course, the M'Guh Fon contains the secret of the most frightful weapon of all."

"It does, eh?" The doctor's interest was piqued.

Zorin strained to sense something in the air. "No alarms yet. Curious. Perhaps the Baron is still indisposed?"

"Let's hope the jerk's deader than the Republican party. How far is this graving dock you were talking about?"

"Actually, this next air lock should lead right into it. Number five . . . yes."

The air lock's hatch was an imposingly thick circular door of solid metal, but at the moment it hung open on its mammoth hinges.

"How convenient. We're in luck. Follow me."

Still holding the black box, Zorin led the way into the air lock. It was wide enough to accommodate heavy equipment. The door at the other end was also ajar.

"Be very quiet. The device does not mask the sound of footsteps."

"How about clanking robots?"

"We have no choice."

"I'm trying to be as quiet as is robotly possible," Dee Fourpio said.

"Shhhh!"

Doc turned to the robot and put a finger to his lips.

When they came out into the open, there was a daunting amount of open space. The graving dock was a huge chamber, festooned with titanic machines capable of lifting a space cruiser. Ropes, chains, and wires hung from the ceiling like vines. Below them, insignificant by comparison, lay the tiny *Mudlark*. It looked as though some preliminary work had been done on it. The hull, although patched in places, had been smoothed out.

And standing guard at the foot of the *Mudlark*'s entry ramp were two armed troopers.

The party of invisible intruders halted.

"What do you think?" Doc whispered.

"We will take out one, then the other."

Dr. Dimension swallowed hard. "We will? Lay on, MacDuff. *Rough* MacDuff."

"Shhh. Come."

Zorin walked boldly up to one of the guards and kicked him solidly in the groin. The man bent over double, and Zorin finished him off with a quick chop to the back of the neck. The trooper went down.

The other one rushed over. "What the hell's wrong with you?" he asked his comrade. "Hey—ooophhhhh!"

He got the same treatment from Zorin.

Doc regarded the two supine guards. They were out cold. He whistled. "Nice work."

"We still need tools, but let's take a look at your craft first."

Doc led Zorin and the robot into the *Mudlark*.

"Wow, they do fast work around here," Doc marveled. The interior was not the absolute mess he'd last seen.

"The Baron has crack repair crews, mostly mechanized," Zorin said. "They can refit a cruiser in a matter of hours. Ah, the control room. This is a small craft, if you don't mind my saying so."

"You should have seen it before some aliens named the Pizons did body work on it. The original configuration was a sphere not much larger than a basketball.

The Pizons broke that out and tacked on a few more compartments, and added the snazzy fins in the back. And the chrome piping."

"A charming little ship. And you say it has the capacity for instantaneous travel to any point in the universe."

"Or any time, for that matter," said Doc.

"That goes without saying. Instantaneous displacement would imply some sort of travel in time."

"All very theoretical," Doc said. "It's worked once, that's all. It booted us off our home planet and got us lost in space. Then it broke. The Pizons did their level best to fix it, but we really didn't have the chance to test it."

Zorin gestured toward the pilot's chair. "If you don't mind . . .?"

"Help yourself."

Zorin took his seat and studied the instrument panel. Soon he began snapping switches and pushing buttons. The central screen lighted up with numbers and symbols.

"Hmmm. Very advanced instrument design."

"You probably want to know how we came by such a ship," Doc said.

"The Asperans. Or the Dharvans."

Doc raised his bushy eyebrows. "You know of them?"

"The two warring superraces of the cosmos? How could I not, being a scholar in the field? Yes, and I've long suspected that the M'Guh Fon was based on their science, though I doubt they created the artifact."

"Just how many godlike races are there, or were there, in the universe?"

"Plenty. At least six that I can verify. The Asperans and the Dharvans are still in some sense alive. The others are extinct. At least, I am fairly sure they are. But let's discuss that later. Dr. Dimension, I think your ship is completely operable."

"It is?"

"All major systems are checking out. See for yourself."

Doc bent toward the screen, which crawled with numbers.

"I've never quite learned how to read all this garbage."

"It's highly technical, of course, but straightforward. Do you realize that the ship is entirely controlled by computers?"

"Computers. Well, yes, I do realize that, though I really don't know what the heck a computer is."

"It's a machine that electronically processes data, among other functions."

"But, how come I don't hear any relays clicking?"

Zorin laughed. "Really. Is Earth's technology so primitive?"

"Possibly more so than you can imagine," Doc said. "Have you ever tried to crank over a Model T on a cold morning? Anyway, barbarian that I am, I dimly grasp the concept of an electronic brain, or data processor, or whatever you call it."

"Good, simply put, your ship is completely automatic. You simply tell it where you want to go, and it will take you there."

"How do I do that?"

"Type in coordinates on this keyboard."

"So that's what that thing is for. I thought it was a typewriter."

"It is, in a way. I will key in the coordinates for my secret hideaway ... there. Now, let's see if the computer systems are familiar with standard galactic four-dimensional mapping—"

"Hey, it worked. The lights are all green."

"It did, indeed. Now, one merely has to activate this switch, and the ship will instantaneously teleport itself to that location. There are close tolerances here. My garage is only so big ..."

A piercing alarm signal began to screech somewhere inside the installation. Another, differently located, joined it, and inside a few seconds, a beeping chorus of them commenced to sing their warning song.

"Ah," said Zorin. "We have no time to inspect the engine or double-check the displacement distance. Fortunately, I have computed the distance between my hideout and Progesteron many times, and I think my calculations are accurate to within—"

Shouting, along with the sound of heavy boots against metal, came from outside.

Doc reached for a switch. With a clank and a groan, the ship's gangway retracted, and the outer hatch sealed itself.

"We're ready to take off," Doc said. "You're the captain."

"I would not presume to take command of your vessel," Zorin said. "But in this emergency . . . Well, enough talk."

Zorin punched a button.

Once again, Dr. Dimension felt the peculiar sensations of instantaneous spacetime travel. Prismatic lines of color began to pulsate from every surface of the ship's interior. He felt a certain giddy dizziness, and his legs became wobbly. There was a feeling of a shift of gravitational center. The whole world seemed cockeyed, for an instant. Then a sudden lurch . . . a displacement . . . a wrenching from what was, to what is, from past to present, from present to future . . . and back again. His head swam.

He fell to the deck on his ass.

"Damn, should've strapped in."

"A very peculiar sensation," said the robot. "I don't much like it."

As suddenly as it had begun, it was over. Zorin, still at the controls, fiddling with a few knobs. The central screen came to life with a shot of something. It looked for all the world like the interior of the graving dock.

Doc rose, rubbing his bottom, and looked. "We didn't move a goddamn inch!"

"Look again, my friend." Zorin rose from his seat, smiling. He left the control room.

"I wouldn't go out there if I were you," Doc warned. Then he realized he wasn't hearing any alarms. Also, the sound of approaching trooper's boots was absent.

"I'll be jiggered. Come on, robot."

Zorin had already cracked open the air lock and lowered the gangway.

The ship was no longer in the graving dock on the moon Progesteron.

Diane Derry was standing at the bottom of the ramp.

"Hi, guys! We heard a big 'pop!', and rushed in here. How the heck did you do it, Dr. D?"

"Talk to the captain," said Doc D., flipping a thumb in Zorin's direction.

Chapter Twenty-Two

"To fight Estrogena, we must build the ultimate weapon. The Cataclysmatron."

Dr. Dimension swallowed a bite of wombat salad sandwich. (Every alien foodstuff was "wombat" to Doc. It was all some sort of mystery meat and all tasted pretty much the same.) "Okay, just what is this gadget you've been hinting at?"

"Believe me," said Zorin, "I suggest this course of action with the utmost reluctance. The Cataclysmatron, placed in irresponsible hands, can lead to the destruction of the universe." Zorin heaved a great sigh. "And I am not absolutely sure that my hands are responsible enough. However, I think I have discerned a way around the problem."

"You have, eh?"

"Yes. We will build a version of the Cataclysmatron that falls somewhat short of its ultimate capabilities. Call it a semi-Cataclysmatron."

"What does the semi version do?"

"It can vaporize an entire space fleet with one blast."

Doc leaned back in his chair. He and Zorin sat at a table in the workshop of the laboratory. "So, just a popgun, eh? And with it we'll ... what, engage Estrogena's space navy?"

Zorin looked troubled. "I am not at all sure what we will do with it. But a final confrontation seems inevitable. I am half tempted to build the fully capable model."

"The super-duper-weapon? And what the heck would you do with that, besides rule the cosmos?"

"That is not my ambition. I would build the Cataclysmatron for one purpose only. And that is to destroy the M'Guh Fon."

"You'd do that?"

"I would, if it would do any good."

"And would it?"

Zorin shook his head. "No. The truth is, there is not one M'Guh Fon. There are millions of copies. Perhaps billions."

Doc sat up straight. "You don't say."

Zorin nodded ruefully. "They were personal data processing devices, available to many individuals. Meant to be worn on the person. As you can see, this ring was meant for a rather thick finger—if it was a finger."

Doc regarded the artifact on the table. "A tentacle, no doubt. Godlike aliens usually have tentacles, don't they? Anyway . . . so where are these millions and billions of copies?"

"Oh, most are no doubt lost forever. But no one knows how many of them are lying about waiting to be discovered."

Doc scratched the stubble on his face. "I understand this one was hard to come by."

"Very true. But the problem is this. The discovery of another M'Guh Fon is inevitable, and the potential for universal destruction will be inherent in that discovery. Somehow, the problem must be dealt with."

"Exactly how?"

Zorin rose and walked to the far wall and stared at a map of the galaxy.

"I don't quite know. I have some ideas, though."

Doc regarded Zorin, as the alien scientist rode his train of thought to the end of the line.

At last, Zorin turned to his guest. "Dr. Dimension, may I have your permission to have my domestics load your vessel with certain pieces of scientific equipment?"

"Load away," Doc said. "What exactly do you have in mind?"

"I will be some time explaining. While my domestics are busy, we will busy ourselves with building the semi-Cataclysmatron."

"It's something you can whip up in a jiffy?"

"It is not all that difficult a proposition. It is the theory behind what took centuries—no, millennia—to work out. The technology is fairly simple. That is why the weapon is so dangerous. Besides, I have been working on the practical problems for a good while."

Doc grinned. "So this isn't a spur-of-the-moment thing."

"Not quite."

"Okay, if I can lend a hand, count me in."

There followed many sleepless hours of hard labor. Zorin's domestics did most of the heavy machining, but Zorin and the doctor supplied the skull sweat.

Two days later, Doc couldn't keep himself from yawning.

"Behold! The semi-Cataclysmatron!"

Standing in the main cabin of the *Mudlark*, Zorin proudly pointed at the device that he, Troy, and Dr. Dimension had just constructed from an extraordinary number of odd and offbeat items culled from the hardware store that was Zorin's private workshop.

It looked like a .30-caliber machine gun with ringed flanges along the barrel. The whole affair was mounted in a movable transparent ball turret built into the overhead. There was a seat for the gunner and pedals to control the turret's rotation. It reminded Doc of similar defensive armaments aboard a heavy bomber, specifically a B-17 Flying Fortress or a B-24 Liberator. In fact, Doc had suggested this configuration.

"Cataclysmatron," Vivian said. "I kind of like the name. Can I test fire this beauty?"

"Not here, my dear. One microsecond blast would take out half the mountain, and a good portion of the province along with it. Besides, have you no faith in my technological prowess?"

"Faith can move mountains, they say. Why not move this one?"

"Your marvelously tart sense of humor is refreshing, my dear Vivian," said the dashing scientist and scholar.

Hovering nearby was the other creature he had charmed, one that had totally fallen in love with him: Dee Fourpio.

They were all waiting to hear just exactly what this semi-Cataclysmatron did.

"Gee, Mister Zorin," said Troy, scratching his head and ceasing his gum chewing. "That was fun to make. But just exactly what does this Cataclysmatron do?"

"Plenty," said Dr. D.

"I'm sure we're all ears," said Vivian. "Though may I venture the suggestion that it has something to do with a cataclysm?"

"The one inside my head?" said Wussman.

"Ditto," said Diane, sleepily.

Zorin beamed. "Well, as you might have guessed, my new friends, this is a weapon."

Vivian clicked her tongue. "No kidding."

"Yes," continued Zorin. "The Cataclysmatron works by disrupting the very fabric of spacetime itself, unraveling the various dimensions one from another. Once this unraveling starts, theoretically it could go on until the entire universe is destroyed. However, in my humble opinion, that's a tad pessimistic. I believe the effect would be limited to a spherical volume of space about one hundred thousand light-years across, give or take a few thousand light-years."

"Oh," said Troy. "That's all right then."

"But the issue is academic, for this is not a fully operational Cataclysmatron."

Diane Derry rose from her seat. "Troy Talbot, you get away from that thing this instant."

Troy sheepishly backed off.

"In truth," Zorin said, "were it the complete weapon, I have some very good ideas about how to limit the effect further—say to the size of a solar system or two." Zorin surveyed the device proudly. "Be that as it may, this is a semi-Cataclysmatron."

The semi-Cataclysmatron was not overlarge. It didn't look as though it could stitch the side of a barn, much less disrupt the very stuff of the cosmos. It did, however, look like a gun, after a very loose and exotic fashion.

Vivian said, "Am I to understand that you juryrigged this gadget together based on specifications in the M'Guh Fon?"

"Yes. Precisely. It is so good to have my M'Guh Fon back. I thank you all tremendously—especially my new best friend, Fourpio here."

Gears whirred in the robot. "I live to serve, sir."

"Uh, one little question, Zorin," said Diane. "Just what are we supposed to do with this thing now that we've got it?"

"Why, use it to defeat Baron Skulkrak and the empire, of course. We must liberate the downtrodden, vindicate the innocent. Resuscitate the—"

A Klaxon sounded right in Doc's ear.

"Ouch. What's going on?"

Troy scampered over to the sensor banks. "Gee, Doc. You know those alien ship detectors you rigged? Well, they're going off, real loud."

"I didn't know that, Talbot. Check the sensors, damn it!"

Troy checked. He nodded. "Yep, that's them."

Zorin looked abashed. "I don't understand. How could they have found us?"

"No time to puzzle that one out, Zorin. We've got to get the *Mudlark* out of this hangar, or we're sitting ducks."

"Of course," said Zorin, snapping his fingers. "A simple transmitter beacon, secreted aboard the ship. But I can find it by running an impedance test on all the circuitry!"

"'You do that, while we get the hell out of here,"

Doc said. He hopped into his seat and frantically brought the ship up to blast-off status.

"All hands, battle stations!"

Within moments the *Mudlark* was shimmering and shaking with power.

"It's too late, Doc," said Diane. "They're almost on us."

"No problem, Diane. You forget that we can zip anywhere in the universe in the batting of an eyelash."

"I realize that," Diane said. "But the flight history of this crate doesn't give me any faith in—"

The plaintive whine of some suffering, dying thing came from the engine bay.

"Oh, no!"

"I knew it," Diane said glumly.

"It fizzled again!" Doc slapped his hand against the instrument panel, which now began to blossom with blinking red lights. "I'm going to write a stiff letter to the manufacturer. That is, if I'm not a stiff myself when this is over."

Zorin's eyes gleamed feverishly. "They'll not take me! I'll use the Cataclysmatron first, I swear."

"Uhm, Zorin," suggested Wussman. "Can we talk about this?"

"Any suggestions?" Doc asked of Zorin.

Zorin worked feverishly at the communications area of the control console. "I've just sent a signal to the hangar doors on the requisite frequency. They will open shortly."

"They're opening, Doc!" Troy, in the copilot's seat, pointed through the forward view plate.

Bright daylight flooded the hangar.

"Okay, stand by to blast off, space cadets," Doc said.

Wussman said, "Dr. Dimension . . . Demetrios, my friend, can we talk about this?"

However, talking was problematic, since the *Mudlark* was taking off.

It tore from the hangar like a ball from a muzzle of a cannon, shooting up toward the approaching imperial interceptors, which were so close as to be visible to the naked eye.

"Gah!" said Wussman. "There must be ten ships there!"

"And we're headed straight for them," said Vivian. They both hid their eyes.

Sizzling beams of energy laced the sky as the empire ships fired upon the *Mudlark*.

"Talbot," said Doc D. "This is going to take lightning reflexes. You have the controls. There are thirty seconds on the clock. The football's in your hand. You don't see any receivers. You've got to run for the goal. Go for it, boy. Go!"

"Right, Doc. I see an opening!"

Somehow, the gallant vessel zigzagged between sizzling blue-white bolts of destructive energy, zipping between two cruisers like a fullback between two defensive guards. Then it sprinted for the goal line: the upper reaches of Ovaria's atmosphere, and the limitless space beyond.

"Yea! Yea! Troy, you did it!" Diane cheered.

"Sis, boom, bah." Dr. Dimension commented sardonically.

"We're saved, we're saved!" cried Wussman and Vernon.

"One little problem," said Doc, staring into the viewer. "Those ships are turning around and following."

"No problem, Doc. I'll just step on the gas."

"A wise, if metaphorical, move," said Zorin.

"Can't you use the M'Guh Fon to help us?" suggested Diane. "Or how about that nasty-looking gun?"

"Yes, of course. However, I wanted to test it first. And it's not exactly in any sort of operational shape to—"

A huge explosion rocked the vessel. Troy fought to keep on course. The sky darkened as the ship climbed toward it. Diane felt her teeth rattle like the overstrained rivets in the ship's abused hull.

"Then again," said Zorin, "I suppose we can improvise."

"Right," said Doc. "Get up into that turret and start shooting. Troy, evasive maneuvers!"

"Roger, Doc!"

"Don't say 'roger' to me, young man."

"That's space pilot lingo, Doc!"

"The hell it is. Who said so?"

"Heck, in all the movies—"

"To hell with the movies. You will acknowledge all orders by saying, 'Aye-aye, Captain!' Understood?"

"Why 'aye-aye'?"

"What do you mean?"

"I mean, why would it be navy talk? That's navy talk."

"Okay, so it's navy talk. It's appropriate for a space vessel, that's all."

"Why is it appropriate for a space vessel?"

With weary condescension Doc said, "The analogies are all too obvious, Talbot. Do I have to spell it out for you? Ships sail the ocean, a great expanse of nothingness wracked by storms and fierce wind. Spaceships travel through space, a great expanse of etcetera, etcetera. Get it?"

"No. Space isn't an ocean. It's not wet."

"So what? I'm not saying there's a one-to-one correspondence. It's an analogy!"

The ship had slipped through the last wisps of the atmosphere now. Brilliant explosions lit up the starry darkness. But now the *Mudlark* was answering with brilliant displays of her own. Searing blue-white fire spewed from the semi-Cataclysmatron. The sound, conducting through the metal hull, was like rolling thunder.

"Wow!" Doc looked up at the rotating blister where Zorin sat, huddled in a ball. "Give 'em hell, Zorin!"

"I still don't see why we have to say aye-aye and all that navy stuff," Troy said as he sent the ship rocketing toward deepest space.

"Forget it, Talbot."

"I mean, you *fly* a spaceship, you don't sail a spaceship."

"I said forget it. Besides, there's no air in space. You can't fly anything, so it's more like an ocean."

Troy shook his perpetually well-groomed head. "Well, now, Doc, I just can't see it."

"Will you two please stop bickering about trivialities!" Vivian Vernon screamed.

Dr. Dimension turned a withering dark eye on her. "The proper use of terminology and the requirements of command protocol are not exactly trivialities, my dear Dr. Vernon. I, as captain, must maintain some semblance of order aboard this ship!"

"Oh, go soak your head, idiot! You couldn't command your way into a pay toilet if I gave you a nickel!"

"I suppose you could do better?"

"And why not? Or does my sex disqualify me?"

"I said nothing about your sex, Vivian. Don't go all suffragette on me."

"Typical male bias! You can't imagine a woman skippering a vessel of any kind, can you?"

"Dr. Vernon, I am as much of a freethinker as the next starry-eyed idealist fool, but there are practical considerations—"

"Stuff it, Demopoulos!"

Dr. Dimension bristled. He said coldly, "You will *not* speak to the captain of this ship in that manner."

"Oh, I will not? The hell I will not. You turd."

"Dr. Vernon, for the duration of this journey, you will consider yourself under arrest."

Vivian unbuckled and came forward. "Listen, you, I've had about all I'm going to take."

"Vivian, sit down," Doc ordered.

"I'm not going to take any more orders from you or any of your flunkies, either. I didn't ask to come on this crazy trip!"

"You stowed away!" Diane said accusingly.

"Shut up, you overstuffed blond bimbo, or I'll shut you up."

Diane unbuckled and rose. "You and who else, honey?"

"Don't push me, Derry. I owe you a black eye."

"Want another one?"

"Vivian, you will sit down this instant, or—"

Vivian began pummeling Dr. Dimension. Doc covered his head with his arms. "Hey, stop that!"

"You leave him alone!" Diane said rushing to her boss's aid.

"I was never good in fights," Doc whined. "Especially with women."

Vivian pivoted and tried to deck Diane with a haymaker. She missed a dead-center hit to the nose, but landed a glancing blow to the cheek, with enough force to knock Diane down.

Wussman was up, playing peacemaker. "Now, people, this isn't going to get us anywh—"

Vivian's Sunday punch sent him down; then she went back to pummeling Dr. Dimension.

Diane got up, and there ensued a tussle.

"Catfight!" Troy cackled, still intent at the controls.

Meanwhile, Zorin focused the beam to a wide arc and fired. Answering fire came quickly. A blast of stunning energy shook the *Mudlark*.

The impact knocked all the intraship combatants to the deck.

"What in the galaxy is going on down there?" Zorin said, looking down from his uncomfortable perch.

"Nothing," Doc called out, "just a mutiny."

"Oh," Zorin said, and kept firing.

A sputtering spray of mauve-colored cosmic energy lanced across the ether toward the pursuing ships. The shot was a little wide, missing the lead dreadnought, but it crashed full bore into the ships on its left flank, blowing them into glittering plasma.

Doc's fist smote the screen. "Nailed a couple of the bastards! We've got a chance. Hit 'em again."

"Little problem with the thing," Zorin said. "Out of ammunition."

"Ammunition?" Doc was astonished. "What are you loading it with?"

"Mu-masons in an electromagnetic flux."

"Oh. Damn Masons get into everything. I guess we can't run out to the local gun shop for more, eh?"

"Not likely."

Debris from the exploding ships bashed into the rest of the space task force, including the dreadnought, hampering their pursuit.

"We're in good shape for the moment," Doc said. "Zorin. We need to find a place to hide. Any suggestions?"

Zorin beamed again, this time with his expression.

"I know just the coordinates."

"Good." Doc turned his attention to the squirming pack of crewmates on the deck. "Is the fight over?"

"Only if she says 'uncle,' " Diane said.

She was sitting on Vivian's rib cage, both arms struggling with Vivian's. Wussman sprawled facedown across Vivian's legs.

"I'll say . . . no such . . . thing, you blond birdbrain!"

"Say it!"

"No!"

"Oh, say it, Viv," Wussman pleaded. "Let's stop this childish nonsense."

"Viv, I'm just trying to calm you down. You're over-wrought."

"You little weasel, wait till I get up! Oooof!"

"Say uncle, you redheaded witch, or I'll strangle ya!"

Dr. Dimension rose and helped Zorin down from his high station.

Zorin surveyed the tussling beauties. "Hmmm. Girls will be girls."

"Oh, 'tis true, 'tis true. Say, what if we had them put on bathing suits and then poured vegetable oil all over them?"

Zorin thought about it. "I might pay to see that," he concluded.

* * *

The "conventional" part of the *Mudlark*'s propulsion systems took over. The *Mudlark* slipped into hyperspace for something short of a minute, the popped out again into "real" space.

"Oh, shit . . . Uncle! For God's sake, uncleuncleuncle!! There, are you satisfied?"

"Sure am," Diane said as she dismounted.

Vivian rose, massaging her chest. She looked out the forward view plate. "What the hell is that?"

She was staring down at a cold, dead moon, its color a pale, gelid white, almost spectral. The place looked haunted, if moons can be haunted. The *Mudlark* hovered above it, cautiously, as would a tomb robber contemplating the risks versus the potential yield of a cursed necropolis.

"That what we're headed for, Zorin?" Doc pointed down at a large bubble like a boil on the surface. Skeletal structures hulked around it, frozen sentinels guarding something long abandoned.

"Yes, indeed. An old and forgotten mining base. This is the planet Cystus, the farthest removed of the system's satellites. I worked here once, as a research assistant in the mining lab. Much later, when things got prosperous, I bought the place and returned to make it a secret base."

"You seem to have a lot of secret bases, Zorin," Doc observed. "Multiple hiding places are prerequisite for renegades, Doctor. Now then—if you'll just head down that chute there. That's the landing pad. Just add air and water, and we have a livable environment."

"You heard the man, Troy, take her down."

"I think I could use some of that air and water, too, Doc."

"Yeah, and check the battery. I think we all could use a pit stop, after the tribulations we've been through. And a good stiff drink wouldn't be a bad idea either."

"Someone punched me in the gut," Wussman said, holding his stomach.

"Hard to miss, Wuss," Doc said. "I mean, could you

blame a person for hitting your gut, it being the most salient aspect of your portly person?"

"Oh, stuff it, Demetrios."

"That's 'Oh, stuff it, Captain,' if you don't mind."

Chez Zorin.

Composite fibermetal and synthocrete under glass.

Grim and forbidding. Shadows within darkness. Bleak and stark. Not exactly the place to cheer up, but for a hiding place it would have to do.

Even when the lights went on, the place looked like a prison block.

"It's as cold as a robot's tit in here!" said Doc.

Tobor the robot was resting his resistors back on the *Mudlark*.

"Robots don't have . . ." Diane blushed. "Oh, Doctor, sometimes—" She giggled. "Besides, how would you know?"

"I'm sure the Doc's catalog of sexual experience has already expanded during this journey," observed Vivian.

Doc grinned. "Viv, my dear, I'd still have to get a New York City's phone book's worth of experience to equal yours."

"Maybe that's my problem," mused Wussman. "I've got an unlisted number. Viv, darling, can we talk?"

"Shut up, Geoffrey. We're up to more important things than sex now."

"Ye gods, what could be more important than sex?" Doc wanted to know.

Zorin looked up from his work. "Yes, indeed. We're interfacing."

"I prefer it doggie style myself," said Doc.

Diane said, "What do you mean, Doctor?"

Viv rolled her eyes. "Oh, why don't you grow up, Miss Goody Two Shoes?"

"Huh?"

"He's talking about intercourse. Screwing, doggie style. You know?" Viv executed a series of suggestive gestures.

Diane turned beet-red, and Vivian laughed.

"Viv's right," said Doc. "Shall we demonstrate for Diane, Viv? Show and Tell?"

"The only thing I'm going to show you is this fist, Mister."

"I'm not into the kinky stuff."

"I'll give you kinky stuff, you miserable—"

"People? Doctor, please . . . if I might have your attention?"

The renegade scientist had inserted the ring known as the M'Guh Fon into a slot in a block-long bank of computers.

"Sorry, Zorin. Just a little method for relief of stress. I truly have a scientific thought or two occasionally."

"Yes, I'm sure . . . and I have a sexual thought from time to time," he winked at Diane. "However, this is not the time or place. May I point out that I have placed the M'Guh Fon into this slot to properly tap its potentialities."

"Yes," said Doc. "And these are pretty impressive adding machines you have here. I've long thought that one day we'd see them on Earth, that one day, the common man would own his own electronic calculating machine. Crazy, I know, but I get these wild ideas."

"That's because he's absolutely nuts," Vivian explained.

"You think personal computers are crazy? Get this. I've got this notion that one day the Coca-Cola company will come out with a new flavor of Coke . . . and it'll fall on its face! How do you like them apples, eh, Viv?"

"Oh, cram those apples up your ass."

"What a mouth on this woman. Viv, Diane's ears are going to fall off if they get an redder."

"Who cares."

"Computers," Zorin said. "Very good. It is my theory, Doctor, that the M'Guh Fon itself is a computer. A computer on a submicron scale of operation and of a level of complexity to stagger the mere human mind."

"Yes," said Viv. "And because we've all been using it, we're all tuned in to it."

"Except for Geoffrey," Doc said, "who is cartooned."

Geoffrey Wussman shook his head. "What an idiosyncratic mind."

"I've voted straight idiosyncratic ever since Roosevelt was elected."

"Right," said Zorin, replying to Viv's statement. "Now, if you'll observe, I am going to tap into the information matrix at a deeper level than I have ever tried before. Ladies and gentlemen, we will delve into the secrets of the M'Guh Fon. What treasures await us, what secrets?"

"Uhm—actually I'm so curious myself, I'm not even going to fire off a quip. Carry on, Zorin."

Zorin threw a switch.

All of the lights of the computers started blinking frantically, then ... suddenly, something happened. There came a flash of light.

A puff of smoke curled up from M'Guh Fon.

Where there was no one before, there now stood a robed figure, amid a fine mist of smoke.

"It's some guardian of the M'Guh Fon," said Zorin.

"It's a genie!" said Troy.

"Like something from the Arabian Nights!" said Diane.

The figure snorted. "Have you got the wrong literary allusion!" The figure lifted to his double chin what looked for all the universe like a violin.

"Look. I'll play you a nice tune, and if you're a good crowd, I'll tell some jokes. If you applaud, I'll tell some funny ones, maybe."

Chapter Twenty-Three

"Krillman!" said Doc D.

"Krillman of the Triple-A!" Diane Derry shouted.

"Krillman, you bastard, I'm going to kill you!" screamed Vivian. "You were supposed to send us back to Earth! Instead, you sent us to crash on some godforsaken alien planet!"

"What, the food wasn't so good?"

Vivian lunged to wreak her vengeance, but Troy caught her before she could scratch the alien's eyes out.

"Let me at him. *Let me at him!*"

"Rough crowd," Krillman said, tugging at his collar. "Rough crowd. Hey, folks. Reminds me of a joke. Listen to this one. Did you hear the one about the idiot who returned the necktie he bought? It was too tight."

"Who is this buffoon?" asked Zorin, appalled.

"Name's 'Krillman,' but that's an alias," Doc told him. "First he passed himself off as some kind of agent for the Triple-A, the 'Anti-Anomaly Association.' Sort of good Samaritans, only nasty. He saved our butts, only to teleport us into the bowels of some huge alien ship run by crazy aliens . . . hell, it's a long story. Suffice it to say that we finally found out that he's really working for the Asperans, or the Dharvans. Or maybe both, we don't really know. He's a sneaky, rotten, lying, incompetent low-life trash compactor, but otherwise he's a decent sort of chap."

"Have anything to say in your defense, Krillman?" Zorin asked.

"I kind of resent the 'low-life' part of it. I have a

class act, here. Actually, though, it reminds me of a joke—"

"You are a joke," said Vivian holding up a threatening fist.

Krillman sneered. "Go ahead, I got nothing to live for. Take my life . . . please! But seriously, folks—"

Zorin rubbed his heroic chin. "Fascinating. This talk of Asperans and Dharvans all falls in line with my own studies and theories," said Zorin. "But which race developed the technology that made possible the M'Guh Fon?"

"What difference does it make?" Krillman said with a shrug. "There are millions of copies of that bauble all over the universe. This one is the closest to Ovaria, though, which is why I'm using it."

"Millions?" said Diane. 'Why did they make so many of them?"

"They're fingertops."

"Huh?"

"Fingertop computers. You heard of laptops, palmtops. Well, this is a . . . actually, it's a *tentacletop* . . . oh, I forgot. You come from a Stone Age culture."

"The heck we do!" Diane retorted. "We have airplanes and telephones, and radios, and—"

"Tinkertoys. I'm talking technology, honey. I'm talking highly miniaturized data processing and storage machines, with just oodles of other stuff inside. Nifty little gadgets, let me tell you."

"The only thing I want to know is, how do they get the vacuum tubes that small?" asked Troy, scratching his head.

"Troy, you dolt, this is super-science," Doc scolded. "Highly advanced races can shrink anything."

Krillman slapped his forehead. "Vacuum tubes, yet. I don't believe it. You people kill me."

"That can be arranged," Viv growled.

Doc's jaw dropped, and his eyes grew wide. "No vacuum tubes? Wait till General Sarnoff hears about this."

"There is no end to the wonders of the universe," Zorin said.

"Never a dull eon," said Krillman. "But let's sit our butts on brass tacks now, folks. I didn't come here just to annoy you."

"Oh, you're doing a great job of that," said Vivian.

"Really, I don't think you should irritate a possible secret master of the universe," whined Wussman.

Vivian sniffed defiantly, but shut her mouth.

"Thank you for controlling your natural womanly instincts," said Krillman. He took them here in a stern, uncharacteristically serious gaze. "You gotta understand something. There are powers beyond your understanding at work here. Cosmic forces clashing and vying. I am but a small part of the great swimming pool of destiny. And you, my friends, have just jumped into the deep end."

"What an interesting figure of speech," Wussman observed.

"I still don't believe the thing about no vacuum tubes," Doc said. "I mean, we installed all this crazy electronic stuff in the *Mudlark,* and there wasn't a tube in the whole mess, but it's very hard to get used to. You see, I assumed—"

"There are analogs to vacuum tubes in solid-state circuitry."

"Analog. Hmmm. What a great name for a magazine. You could run nuts-and-bolts stories about square-shouldered engineers who always defeat the aliens—"

"Will you forget the furshugginer vacuum tubes already?" Krillman sighed. "Let's get down to business. I'm here because you, Zorin, put together the Cataclysmatron!"

"Well, the semi-Cataclysmatron, actually," said Zorin. "I only intend to threaten the empire with its power, so they will liberate the oppressed peoples they have enslaved."

"Not 'semi' with this little addition!" Krillman pulled out from his trousers a squiggly doodad that looked like a mechanical sea urchin. "With this attached, your device becomes the Cataclysmatron. I want you to complete the project, Zorin. And then"—he paused for dramatic effect—"I want you to blow up Ovaria."

"Blow up Ovaria!" said Diane Derry.

"Isn't that a little extreme?" said Zorin.

"How about if we just take a picture and blow that up," Doc suggested. "It'd look great on your mantelpiece."

"No," Krillman said. "The forces I work for are concerned about the balance of power in this segment of the universe. And Ovaria is getting a little too big for its britches. It must be taken out of the picture altogether."

"Why don't you do it?" said Diane.

Krillman shrugged. "Hey. Why is there air? That's what cosmic pawns are for. Why do you think you got all that equipment shipped to you, Dr. Dimension?"

"Because I sent in coupons?"

"Because you were chosen. And now the secret masters of the universe have given you a task."

Doc waved him off. "Look, I don't do windows and I don't blow up worlds. I'm sorry, but a pawn has got to draw the line somewhere. Besides, mass murder's out of my line. I like the clean quiet, one-person jobs."

Zorin protested, "Evil as the empire might be, there are innocents on that planet. I will not be a party to its total destruction."

Krillman threw up his hands. "They're going to have my butt on a platter. We should have sent the stuff to that Mussolini fellow, like I wanted to. Look, tell you what. I figure you all have been on the go. Have a rest, a sleep. Think it over. This is for Good, believe it or not, and you are needed. So think about it, and let me know. I'm going to split now. If anyone one of youse want me, all you have to do is call, and I'll come."

"You're not quite real, are you?" Doc asked.

"Not really. I am an artifact."

"What do you do when you're not needed. Where do you go?"

"I just sort of hang out, contemplating my navel lint. But for the moment I need a nap. Catch you later."

Krillman disappeared in a puff of smoke.

"He's right," said Troy.

"What, that we should destroy a planet and billions of people."

"No. I'm pooped, Doc. I need a dog nap."

"That's a cat nap, Troy."

"Nope. Not the way I take them."

Krillman suddenly reappeared, minus smoke.

"Sheesh," he said "sometimes I wonder about my bosses. What a combination. Idiots with moral scruples. Like I say, sleep on it awhile. I'm not going anywhere."

Then he was gone again.

"Killers! We're pawns of a superrace of galactic mass killers? I don't like it," said Diane. "Zorin?"

The scientist shook his head dolefully. "I wish to deter the empire, but certainly not in such a Draconian fashion."

"Mussolini?" said Doc. "He was going to give the advanced science to Mussolini? What would he do with it, invent a new kind of high-tech pasta?"

"Well," said Diane, "This is all too much for my sleepy head. I could use a snooze. We could all use a rest. We're going to have to deal with this in some way, but we shouldn't do anything, feeling like we do. I say we take an hour or so and rest."

"Zzzzzzzz," said Troy, already unconscious, curled up in a corner.

"Don't get in Talbot's way to dreamland," said Doc. "I must admit, though, there is some validity. In fact, that corner of the room does look rather comfortable. I fact, I think I'll just pull up a piece of floor like so and . . . Zzzzzzzzzzzz."

The duet of snores was an odd coupling.

"I confess, I am a bit fatigued myself," said Zorin.

"That sounds like a good idea to me," said Diane.

"Actually, I believe there is are beds over yonder that would be a good deal more appropriate." In a purely gentlemanly fashion, Zorin guided Diane away.

At length, Vivian Vernon and Geoffrey Wussman were the only conscious people in the chamber.

"Come to think of it, I could use a little more rest myself," said Wussman, lying down on the hard synthocrete floor and placing his hands on his chest in an attitude of repose.

Vivian kicked him.

"Darling. Now you want romance?"

"No, you academic moron. I want something a great deal more valuable." A gleam in her eyes, she trotted over to where the *Mudlark* was parked in its berth. "And we've got an hour to do it. Now get off that soft rear end and help me."

She pulled him and the couple went about their nefarious plans. Wussman hadn't a clue as to what those were, but he went along anyway, as he always did.

He loved Vivian completely, utterly, hopelessly. He also bought whole-life insurance policies on a regular basis.

"Zzzzzzzzzz," said Troy Talbot.

"Zzzzzzzzzz," quipped Dr. Dimension.

"Zzzzzzzzzz," Troy retorted.

"Zzzzzzzzzz," riposted Doc with a crookedly impish smile.

"Zzzzzzzzzzz," Zorin interjected.

Diane, who had racked out in a side room, observed, "Zzzzzzzzzzzzzzzzzzzzz!"

Together, this concert of snores was so loud that a person in the area would barely be able to hear the sound of troop landers roaring in for a landing. In fact, several troop landers landed, with troops inside. Some had just a few troops, but others had troops of troops. (Obviously there is some confusion in the language about this troop business. See the footnote below. If there is no footnote, look up the words in the dictionary and write a letter to the publisher correcting the authors' usage.)

Within moments, the clanking of armor and the padding of boots filled the hallways.

A few moments more, and imperial guards (not troopers, but they were indeed troops) stormed into the chamber. Within just a scant few moments, the unconscious trio were surrounded by guards, blasters trained upon them and ready to render them into smoking smears of grease on the floor.

Into the room strode none other than the empress Estrogena herself, looking positively butch in a clinging black leather outfit and startlingly shiny silver helmet under which drooped long, limp unpermed hair.

In her hands, she carried her gold-plated plasma-sword, not as yet activated. She nodded at her men.

One poked Troy Talbot in the rear with the nozzle of his blaster.

"Zzzzzzzzzzz," said Troy Talbot.

This attempt at waking failed, another poked Dr. D.

"Talbot, you idiot. Get your nose out of my rear," said Doc. Then: "Zzzzzzzzz."

The third and final of the trio was nudged.

Zorin woke up.

"Well," said Zorin. He leaned over and tapped Troy Talbot on the shoulder. "Wake up, lad. We have company."

"Put me in, coach! Put me in!"

"Perhaps you should wake up," suggested Zorin.

Troy Talbot's eyes fluttered open. He looked up at the surrounding guards, the surrounding blasters.

"Doc! Dooooooooooooooooooccccc!" he said, and reached over for Dr. Dimension, patting him hard on the face.

"Talbot, you incredible boob. Can't I have one nanosecond of respite from your imbecilic—" Doc's eyes fluttered open. The first image that struck his retinas was that of Estrogena, looking imperious and intimidating in her warrior duds.

"What's this? Was there a Perversion Day sale at Bloomindale's?"

"We meet again, Estrogena," said Zorin.

"Yes, Zorin, you traitor, I've caught you and your cohorts red-handed," said Estrogena in a decidedly dominatrix kind of way. "Now, where is the M'Guh Fon? I know you have it here. Hand it over, immediately, or I'll just kill you and look for it myself."

"That won't be necessary, Estrogena." Zorin got up and brushed himself off. "Please don't hurt my friends."

"Who are these fools?" barked the woman sneeringly.

"You should be so foolish," said Zorin. "For these are brave souls of sterling character."

"We steal silverware," Doc said.

"Thanks, Zorin," said Troy.

Doc said, "Say, remind me to use you for a reference, Zorin."

"Tie them up!" demanded the Empress.

The guards took out cords and bound their captives.

"Fine. Now, prepare the torture and make sure— What?" Estrogena's attention was distracted by a trooper who was waving his hand wildly. "What is it?"

The trooper hobbled to the empress, leaned over, and whispered something in her ear.

Estrogena scowled. "Oh, God. Why didn't you go on Ovaria? I've told all of you a million times, when you're on Dr. Prissykins' Massive Water Intake Diet, you gotta go before you leave on a mission!"

All of the guards waved wildly, holding their groin areas.

"What little boys," said the Empress disgustedly. She turned to Zorin. "Have you got a men's toilet?"

"Yes. It's right down the hall. Hang a left. Right by the water fountain." Zorin pointed.

"Thank you." She turned to the guards. "Well, go ahead, all of you. I've got them now. Just don't fall in."

The guards scurried away to answer the call of the universe.

"Now, where were we?" said the Empress. She swaggered over to her captives, hands on hips. I—"

"Hold it right there, Estrogena," called a voice from the other side of the room.

The Empress swiveled around, a look of surprise on her face.

Standing in the doorway, looking positively Amazonic, brandishing a length of synthocrete reinforcing rod, was Diane Derry. She had heard the troop-bearing troop landers landing. Rooting around in a pile of junk, she had come up with the only weapon she knew how to use.

"Leave my friends alone," she said.

Estrogena sneered at her. "What? They belong to you?"

"No. But they don't belong to you."

"Sister, how can you be such a patsy? Don't you see how men have dominated and raped the universe? It is time for females of all species to break free and take our destiny in our own hands. Drop that weapon and join me in my valiant quest for the rights that these male thugs have denied us for millennia!"

"Don't do it, Diane!" said Troy.

"Shut up, Troy. She's right. But dressing up in black leather and wearing a helmet isn't going to advance the women's suffrage movement, Estrogena. Now untie them, or face the consequences." She swung the rod back and forth a few times until a brilliant plume of purple iridescent energy flamed from the end of it.

"Ho, ho! A little magic from the M'Guh Fon, eh, little witch girl? Well, we'll see whose mythos is the more powerful."

Estrogena lifted her sword, thumbing a stud. The plasma blade flashed into buzzing, flaming life.

"Very well," said Diane, advancing. "A duel."

"I just hope those guards are doing Number Two," said Doc.

The women advanced on each other.

Estrogena struck first. Diane held her own flaming sword up and deflected the blow.

Sparks scattered. The fight continued, neither combatant gaining the upper hand.

"Wow," said Troy. "Another catfight."

"Talbot, stop watching and try and untie me."

"Good idea, Doc." Troy wriggled over and proceeded to exercise his mechanical skills on Doc's bonds.

Meantime, the women were having at it, swords bouncing with abandon, shedding enough sparks and fire to serve as a superior Fourth of July celebration.

"Bitch!" screamed Estrogena.

"Whore!" screeched Diane.

"Pig!"

Bam. Blam. Slam. Clash.

"There you go, Doc. Now you do me," said Troy.

"Thank you, Troy. You're really not my type. But I will untie you." Doc set to work.

"Guards!" cried the empress. "Where are you, guards? Yo! Uh, guards?"

Diane swung mightily. Her flaming blade caught the empress at the top of tight leather pants, slashing them off, revealing her underwear:

A jockstrap.

"Well, nobody's perfect," said Estrogena.

"You—you're a man," said Diane wonderingly.

"Yes, and I'm your father, Diane."

"Huhhhh? My father's back on Earth."

Geoffrey Wussman prayed fervently, "Our father, who art in heaven . . ."

Estrogena shrugged. "It was worth a shot. Thought it might set you back a bit."

Diane's nostrils flared. She took a wicked swipe at the empress, and her fiery rod caught the female impersonator on the helmet, knocking it off.

With it went the wig.

Empress Estrogena was left standing with a stubbly, mostly bald head.

"Aeeeeiiiiii!" Estrogena warbled. "Guards, guards!"

Dr. Dimension finished untying Troy. Troy proceeded to untie Zorin.

Doc leapt up to help Diane.

A dozen guards, pulling up the zippers in their armor, came out to help the Empress.

"Got you, you jerks," said Estrogena (Estrogeno?).

Blasters leveled.

Doc raised his hands. "Well, so much for the miracle escape."

"I wonder what you look like without your hair," said Estrogena. "In fact, I wonder what you look like without your head. Most likely an improvement."

"The plasma-sword flared.

A blaster fired, knocking Diane's magic rod from her hands.

"Uh-oh," said Diane.

The Empress/Emperor stepped forward, grinning maliciously.

"So, dearie, things have come to a head between us, like the pimples on your sweet little butt—"

A thundering roar suddenly shuddered the building.

Estrogena/geno looked up with alarm. "What in all of space and time is that?"

The settling descent of rockets.

The crunch of landing gear on lunar regolith.

Then, the stomp of feet.

Finally, troopers, who also came in troop ships, stormed through the door. (Being storm troopers, this was not a cause for puzzlement.) They wore special new uniforms for the occasion, of the deepest black. The Baron had wanted his minions dressed stylishly for the long-awaited coup d'etat.

And, following them, was the immense form of Baron Skulkrak, bandages showing through his own black armor.

His arm was in a black sling.

Notice how all these one-line paragraphs pad the book out.

And inflate the cover price and make the authors more money.

For less work.

"Now, then," boomed his magnificently growly and nasty voice, "all of you, prepare for agony!"

"I've been doing my sit-ups faithfully, every day," said Doc.

Chapter Twenty-Four

"I bet you all are wondering why I'm in such a good mood," said Baron Skulkrak.

He looks strange, thought Doc.

Something was decidedly different about the Baron, no question about it.

"Baron, I have the situation well in hand," said the Empress/Emperor Estrogena/geno.

"That's all right. I'll take over from here, Your Imperial Bitchiness."

The Baron signaled to his black-armored men. They raised their blasters and, before their targets could take any defensive moves, shot the Empress's palace guards.

Only smoking boots remained.

"Skulkrak. That wasn't very nice," said Estrogena.

"Not a bit," said the Baron. "Now be advised that this is the first step in my total takeover of your empire. Prostrate yourself before me!"

"Me?" Estrogena/geno asked innocently. "Prostrate myself?"

"Check!" growled the Baron.

"I'll bet," Doc ventured, "he hasn't had his prostrate checked in a while."

"What about them?" Estrogena/geno pointed to the others. "They don't have to?"

"Why should they bother? They will be dead very, very soon. After I make sure they endure pain unimaginable."

"Doc—he keeps on saying that."

"The power of positive thinking?" Doc essayed.

"And Doc. He looks funny. Different. And I don't mean hah-hah funny either."

"Or hoo-hah funny, for that matter." Doc had indeed noticed. Baron Skulkrak did look different. Nor was it just the surgical wrappings nor the sling nor the other signs of trauma and lack of caring and compassion.

He looked—a little puffy.

A little bloated.

Even as Doc stood there observing the giant, there issued from the Baron's turbulent innards an ominous rumble.

Ah, here comes another mighty baronial fart, thought Doc bracing himself.

However, the preliminary sound diminished, faded, its significance not venturing beyond the confines of the Baron's huge body.

Hmmm.

"Dr. Dimension, I presume," said Baron Skulkrak. He walked up to the friz-headed professor, hovering over him threateningly. Suddenly, a thick arm reached down, grabbed Doc D. by the front of his shirt, and pulled him up. "We really should have a talk, Doctor."

"Hey. You put the Doc down!" said Troy.

"Troy, no," said Zorin.

However, it was too late. Troy leaped, going in for the tackle. He hit the Baron at the kneecaps—and managed to knock himself unconscious.

Baron Skulkrak seemed to regard the whole incident as he might some fly alighting upon him. He hoisted Doc up to glower at him eyeball to eyeball. "Tell me, shall I merely bite your head off now? Or should I start eating at the other end while I enjoy your piteous screams?"

"Do I get a third choice?"

"No."

"How about a question?"

"You have some courage, Doctor. Shall we see how much?"

"Look, this is a personal question I'm going to ask you, but don't take offense. You had your problem

fixed? You're not . . . how shall I put this delicately?
. . . cutting cheese anymore."

A smug grin curled the grim features.

"That problem has been dealt with."

"Congratulations. Union plumber? They charge an
arm and a leg, but they're damn good."

Another grumble, without the expected Bronx cheer
follow-up.

Up close, Doc realized what it was about the Baron
that was different. He seemed to be blowing up, like a
slowly inflating balloon.

Doc realized what the remedy was. He'd cut off his
bowels completely, and the gas his system created was
backing up.

Effective, but rather unsightly.

"Thank you, Doctor. Now let's get your nose a little
closer." The steel trap jaws gnashed menacingly.
"We'll start by biting off your face."

"Are you sure? Many have said it wasn't to their
taste."

The jaws snapped.

"Darling. What do you expect? I'm no weapons expert, nor am I a mechanic."

"Nor have you the faintest hope of being a fulfilled
husband, let alone a husband at all, unless you utilize
that book-stuffed noggin to insert that thing into that
hole properly."

Geoffrey Wussman peered down at the semi-
Cataclysmatron which he was trying to turn into
the Cataclysmatron. The special bulb that had just been
given to them by Krillman dangled below it uncer-
tainly like a testicle. He had managed to unscrew the
weapon from its mountings in the ball turret, but in-
stalling this component was proving a challenge.

Wussman appealed to Krillman.

"Would you care to give me a clue?"

"Look, if I could have done it, I wouldn't need you
guys."

Vivian Vernon sniffed. "Just make sure you make

good your promise. We get back to Earth. Doc and company don't. And have a little more care this time about the trip."

"Hey, lady. No problem. You help me destroy Ovaria, I'll keep you in breakfast cereal for life."

It had been an easy deal. Krillman was eager to strike a bargain with anybody, but no more eager than Vivian.

Create the most awesome planet smasher in history? No problem.

Destroy a whole civilization?

Where do we point the gun?

"I've got just one question, Krillman," said Viv.

"Shoot."

Smiling, Viv pointed the nozzle of the gun toward the alien.

"No, no, not me!"

"Krillman, you're the one who wants Ovaria destroyed. Why do you ask others to do it?"

"Look, you have to understand something about godlike alien superraces. They're kind of detached. Olympian. Know what I mean. They don't like to get their hands dirty. It's not becoming. Besides, you can get killed that way."

"Got it," Viv said. "And you don't like to get your hands dirty either, I suppose."

"Mrs. Krillman didn't program any dumb computer simulations."

"Hey. The only folks I like to kill are audiences. I just follow orders. Now then, Wolfman . . ."

"That's Wussman."

"Whatever. I think you've got the general idea, but try inverting it. Yeah, upside down."

Wussman did, the bulb slipped in easily.

Indicator lights played along the superweapon. Strange tonalities hummed and throbbed through the awesome, fully operational, unimaginably destructive, super-duper-this-is-for-real-Cataclysmatron.

"You got it!" said Krillman. "Now all you've got to do is aim it at Ovaria."

"Piece of cake!"

Vivian Vernon grabbed the weapon and hoisted it up. Her eyes fairly glowed with power lust.

Krillman said, "If you destroy Ovaria, you'll go down in history."

Viv's eyes flared. "Time, gentleman, for a little hysterectomy!"

"Just a little trim will do, Skulkrak," said the dangling Doc, hoisted up before the snapping jaws of the evil Baron.

"When I rule the universe, I shall create a law," boomed the giant. "No more wisecracks!"

"You leave him alone, you big bully." Diane Derry ran up to the Baron, fists flying.

She was easily deflected.

"I wonder if you Earthians are truly brave, or really truly stupid. Now come, Doctor, and receive your due!"

Horrible laughter issued from the Baron.

He drew the doctor close.

"Zorin, Zorin, isn't there anything you can do?" demanded Diane.

"Baron," called Zorin. "Spare Dr. Dimension, and I will help you in your new position as emperor."

The Baron's jaws were closing around Doc's face. They stopped. The cyborg Baron grinned evilly and dropped the doctor to the hard floor.

"Oooof! Hey, watch it!"

"Deal!"

"Boy, that was a close one," said Doc, crawling back to Troy. "You've got some pretty fierce dental work there, Baron, but I do rather think you should see a periodontist."

The Baron ignored him. "Now then, Zorin. Perhaps you will give me the M'Guh Fon."

"Very well," said Zorin. "You're in luck, Skulkrak. It's right over there."

He pointed.

As it happened, Vivian Vernon and Geoffrey

Wussman were just emerging from the *Mudlark,* carrying the newly completed Cataclysmatron. As a hand weapon, it was a heavy, bulky thing.

"Uh-oh," said Wussman. "Company."

"Seize them!" cried the Baron.

"Stand right where you are," said Vivian. She smiled slyly. Her eyebrows arched. She looked every inch a woman in control, and clearly was enjoying every delicious minute of it.

Zorin gasped in horror. "Vivian! Don't tell me you've completed the Cataclysmatron!"

Viv shrugged. "All right, I won't tell you."

"Do you realize the power, the awesome puissance in your grasp?"

Vivian winked. "You bet, buster. And don't you ever forget it!"

"Here, puissy-puissy," Doc called. "Well, Viv, you've gone and done it now, haven't you. Selling out seems to be your forte. And to Krillman, yet. I should have seen it coming. You caught me sleeping on the job. Oh, well. I guess the universe can kiss its starry butt good-bye."

"I have no desire to destroy or even control the universe," said Viv. "I, however, have every desire to control—or destroy—the physics department of Flitheimer University. And now, with the wealth of information at my fingertips, I shall achieve academic status throughout the world far beyond that achieved previously by a woman. I can see it now." Her beautiful green eyes glittered with vision. "I'll start up an entirely new area of academic inquiry. Women's Studies! I'll create a whole new system of values: Political Correctness. I'll strike such a blow for womankind in the universe, that it's effect shall be felt forever." She puffed her ample chest out proudly. "And my first declaration shall be—no more puke-green wallpaper in classrooms!"

"Really?" said Diane. "Can I be administrator of academic interior decorating?" She put a hand to her forehead. "What am I saying?"

Vivian scowled. "Wait, what am I saying? I can't permit myself to think small. I have the ultimate weapon in my hand, right here. I could declare a world socialist state. Political correctness? Hah! Every last proletarian on Earth would be Politically Perfect or I'd incinerate 'em!"

"That's inhumane, Viv," Doc said.

"Hell, you can't make an omelet without breaking a few eggs."

"Well, you could at least throw them in hard labor camps. That's pretty cruel, but it's not as cruel as burning them to a crisp."

"Prison camps! Hell, I'd have prison planets! I'd need 'em to hold the likes of you, Dr. Demopoulos, a.k.a. Dr. Dimwit, a.k.a. Dr. Dunce, a.k.a—"

"We get the point, Viv. You are one hard woman."

"I'm just trying to make the universe a better place to live. And if I have to destroy it to do so—well, so be it."

Baron Skulkrak stomped over to her. "You are a fool. Give me that thing. Now."

"Stand back," said Viv, "or I'll let you have it, I swear I will."

Zorin leaped forward. "Vivian, no! The consequences would be dire!"

"What do I give a shit at this point," Vivian said. "Here I am, lost in some godforsaken part of the universe with all this crazy shit going on. I'm hungry all the time, and cold, and people yelling, and chasing us, and . . ." Vivian's lower lip began to quiver. "I . . . just . . . want to go . . . home!"

The Baron advanced, a strange gentleness in his voice.

"Now, now, then, let's have the weapon. Do not be afraid . . ."

Again, Viv raised the bulky Cataclysmatron. "Don't try it, you overgrown pile of scrap, or I swear I'll blast!"

The Baron halted.

"What, and destroy yourself in the process? You are

no fool! Hand me that weapon, which you have neither the experience nor the wisdom to use properly, and I shall honor you by taking you as my concubine."

"I said stand back, buster! Concubine, my foot. With this thing, I'll have ten hundred male slaves!"

Suddenly, Baron Skulkrak lunged at her.

Startled, Viv stepped back, and tripped over Wussman's foot. The Cataclysmatron flew over her head, banged into the synthocrete wall, and clattered to the floor.

"Oops," said Dr. Dimension, late of the planet Earth.

Strange things began to happen.

Chapter Twenty-Five

The ensuing explosion was surprisingly gentle. It did not produce smoke or fire; however its force was enough to knock everyone in the chamber for a loop.

Dr. Dimension somehow clung to consciousness. He also clung to Diane Derry, who was a great deal more pleasant.

"Zorin," Doc said, "what's happening?"

"I don't know."

"Whatever it is, I wish I had a movie camera. This would make a terrific special effect."

Zorin got to his feet, wobbly but ambulatory. "It's happening, just as I predicted it would," he said in a disbelieving voice. "The fabric of spacetime is unraveling like an old sweater—and the unraveling is starting right here. The reaction isn't what I expected, though."

"Sure isn't an explosion, per se," Doc said. "It's just . . . strange."

Indeed, in the place where the Cataclysmatron had struck the wall and expended its initial charge of energy, the very fabric of matter had come undone into wispy strands that gamboled and cavorted, looking like living filaments of iridescent steel wool.

At the center of this phenomenon was a growing patch of . . . nothingness. Absolute, mind-boggling nothingness. The absence of anything at all. No-thing.

"The universe is turning into a model of my hair," said Dr. Dimension, reaching up to touch his unruly mop. "The horror, the horror of it."

"No time for jokes, Doctor. The anomaly will spread

slowly at first, but will increase geometrically. In a few hours, its speed will exceed that of light."

"Believe me, the universe becoming like my hair is no joke," insisted Doc.

Doc looked around. He saw the unconscious bodies of troopers, Estrogena, and the Baron, all draped about the room.

He saw the unconscious bodies of his companions. He saw the unconscious body of Diane Derry, lying in a provocative position.

Never mind that, for now.

"How come we're okay and everyone else is out?"

"I summoned the M'Guh Fon to shield us. Unfortunately, I could not make the shield cover very much."

"Pretty slick," Doc said admiringly. "But what do we do now?"

Zorin said, "I have been studying the design of your engine. It is a quasi-matter quantum flux displacement interociter."

"It is? Thanks for letting me know."

"The upshot is that you can not only jump around in space, but in time as well."

"That's correct. Unfortunately, the jumping around doodads are busted."

"Yes, I noticed." He pulled out a thing that looked like a paper clip. "I have replaced a vital element in the interstitial quark reactor."

"Oh, good. I didn't know we had an interstitial quark reactor replacement part kit."

"Doctor, it's just a paper clip. Now then. This entire room and all of its occupants will shortly be destroyed. We only have time to haul our friends into the *Mudlark*."

"Good. Does this mean we can leave Viv and Wussman?"

"Power corrupts. Basically, they are good academicians. Tenure will doubtless heal all."

"I wish I'd find that out personally. Okay, let's get 'em, and get out of here." He started carrying Diane in a very tactile-rewarding fashion. "Say, Zorin."

"Yes, Doctor," replied the brilliant alien scientist as he hauled Troy Talbot along by the feet to the *Mudlark*. Talbot's head thudded as he went up some steps.

"If the universe is going to be destroyed—just where exactly are we going? Or when?"

"We will go where we can help the universe repair itself," replied Zorin. "To a time very shortly before the universe came into existence."

"Oh."

Troy's eyes popped open. "Gee—is that kinda like daylight savings time?"

The *Mudlark* flung itself at the stars.

Leaving a thin wake of ions to wash against the shores of the dark sea of space, it sped onward and outward, into the cold nebulous vastness, the black reaches, the glittering nothingness. It had men and women in its metal cells, and mad swirling atoms in its belly.

There were only beans in the mess, though.

"Damn Talbot anyway," Doc muttered. He was hungry again.

Powerful engines pulsing with energy, the ship left the galaxy, veering on a hyperbolic orbit, heading out into a greater vastness, a darker darkness. In a few hours there was nothing to relieve the eternal night but the dim glow emitted by the ship's instrument panels. The *Mudlark*'s course and heading were problematical, for there were no maps, no geodetic surveys, no charts, no atlases of the universe to consult. The *Mudlark* and its crew had booked one-way passage on a steamship named *Infinity*.

"Let me see," said Zorin, staring at the controls on which his hands rested. "Was that fall back or spring forward?"

"Would you like to flip a coin?" said Doc. He nervously looked out a window. Primal chaos nervously stared back at him.

"Submitted for your approval," Doc intoned, "case in point, lesson to be learned, filed under B for 'Boondocks' . . ."

"Whatever are you babbling about?" Vivian wanted to know.

"Oh, just getting a strange feeling."

"You're not the only one. I wish Zorin would get a move on. This stuff is looking pretty spooky."

"I told you it was a mistake to talk to that lousy comedian," whined Wussman.

"Doctor, maybe we should get rid of some ballast," said Viv nastily.

Doc glared back. "I was thinking the same thing about you, but Zorin saved your beautiful rear end. For himself, perhaps. Whatever got into you, Viv? Or whoever?"

"Everyone gets into her but me," Wussman said bitterly.

"You two give stowaways a bad name," said Diane.

"Yeah, you people are always causing trouble," said Troy.

"May I see your tickets, please?" Doc asked, holding out a hand.

"Go to hell," Vivian said coldly.

"That might be our final destination," Doc said. "You'll be right at home, Viv."

"It might be better than running around the universe like a madman," Viv said.

"What universe? It's gone. Take a look out this window. See that fuzzy splotch over there? That's the Cataclysmatron's effect, spreading out at several million times the speed of light. Even at that it'll take a while to unravel the whole shebang, but it's only a matter of time."

Vivian stepped back from the view plate. She shrugged. "So what. It wasn't such a great universe anyway."

"Yeah, Viv, but it was the only one we had."

* * *

The ship sped on, but as it did, the concept of speed ceased to have any significance. There was nothing by which to gauge velocity or direction.

Outside the view plate, raw chaos roiled. The fabric of spacetime was having conniption fits, generally going completely spastic, and doing it on a simply incredibly wide and insane chromatic scale, with a definite taste for modern art, the works of Jackson Pollack in particular (who didn't come along until later in Dr. Dimension's time line, but as he was outside time and space now, who's keeping track of these things?).

"If the universe has a Maker," said Zorin solemnly, "I think we will be meeting him . . . or her . . . or it."

"Or them," said Doc. "It could be a committee. In fact, judging from the way it's designed, I'd lay odds on it."

"Amazing grace, how sweet the sound," sang Diane.

"That saved a wretch like me," warbled Wussman, off pitch.

"I first was lost, but then was found," continued Troy.

"But I gotta take a peeeeeeee!" finished Doc D.

Diane said, "Doctor! That's . . . why, that's blasphemy!"

"The hell it is."

"Anyway, that's not the way the hymn goes. How do you expect God to listen to our prayers if you don't get the words right?"

"Diane, how do you know I'm not an agnostic?"

"I guess I never asked. Okay, are you an agnostic?"

"I don't know."

"Oh, groan."

"Gee, Doc," said Troy. "You must know twice as much as me. I guess that makes me a diagnostic."

"Troy, that was brilliant," said Doc.

"It was?" I was just—"

"Troy, shut up and kiss me," said Diane.

"Mmmmmph!" Troy said.

"That's so romantic," said Wussman. "In the face of

doom, the lovers have one last bout of passion. Darling Viv, shall we?"

"One last bout? Sure."

"Mmmmmmmmmph!"

"You lost the bout. Now don't throw up on your shoes." Viv turned to Doc brandishing the fist she's just planted in Wussman's abdomen. "How about you, Doctor? Another round before closing time?"

Doc demurred.

"I presume that you are all performing some peculiar last rites of your culture," said Zorin, looking up from his intense machinations over the controls. "However, you need not be so concerned."

"Why?" said Viv. "You mean, we may not die horribly?"

Suddenly, chaos abated, and there was a bit of light coming from somewhere.

There came a sensation of stopping. The long journey was over, somehow, and the crew of the *Mudlark* knew it. A gentle thump, and they had arrived.

"Precisely," returned Zorin. He stabbed one final button, and the *Mudlark* gave out one final shudder, one final clanking sound, and then was completely still. "Because we're here."

"Here?" said Viv. "Where's here?"

"Well, it's really neither here nor there," returned Zorin. He turned and began to fiddle with the M'Guh Fon, which he wore on his right index finger (with some heavy tape wrapping to make it fit).

Doc wandered over to the forward view plate.

It was a total blank.

"Okay," said Doc, "let me put it this way. When are we?"

"We have arrived approximately five hours and five minutes before the birth of the universe."

"*Before* the birth of the universe?" Doc said.

"Five hours and five minutes before. We needed some time to build a new scientific device. I trust I can request your help in the process, Doctor. You too, Troy.

By the way, you may not realize it but Diagnostics are a sacred and wonderful scientific religious group on the planet of my birth and are highly regarded."

"You hear that Doc?" said Troy. "Gee, isn't that just peachy keen."

"Wait a minute," Doc said. "Let me get this straight. We're back before the universe began."

"Correct."

"Before space existed."

"Correct."

"Before time began."

"Absolutely."

"But we're at a point five hours before time began."

"Approximately."

"How the hell can that be? If time hasn't begun yet, how can we be back five hours before the very word 'hour' has any meaning?"

"It is somewhat of a paradox, I admit. But it's very simple to resolve," Zorin said. "The entirety of time and space is contained within this vessel. We are a universe unto ourselves now. A complete frame of reference. Time does have meaning for us, inside the ship. Outside, it is problematical. However, our metrical spacetime frame of reference will begin to leak outside the boundary formed by the hull of the ship. In time . . . yes, I know . . . in time, a very strange sort of time, the universe will come into existence. For it has to. We are a paradox here, an anachronism. The universe will begin. We must be there when it does."

Dr. Dimension regarded the alien scientist with considerable skepticism.

Zorin asked, "Does that answer your question?"

Doc shrugged. "What was the question?"

Zorin smiled bleakly. "That is the best I can do."

"Then it will have to do. Look, what's the plan?"

"There are four basic forces in the universe, Doctor. Electromagnetism, gravity, and the two subatomic forces, weak and strong."

"You're forgetting the force that makes a slice of bread always hit floor butter-side down."

"I'd quite forgotten. There has been postulated another force, made up of the first four, which can act like a glue to hold the entire mechanism of spacetime together. This 'superglue force,' if applied at the right spot, can knit the universe back together. We must introduce this force into the cosmic cataclysm at the very beginning of space and time. Which is why it is so convenient to have a spacetime machine at our disposal. Which is why I have made use of it in the way that I have."

"Oh," said Troy. "That explains everything."

"You understood that?" Doc said incredulously.

"No, I don't understand any of that high-toned science stuff. I'm a practical man, Doc, you know that."

"You're practically a man, yes, I know. Listen, Zorin. I think you mentioned that you had some materials from your lab stowed away? For this purpose?"

"Yes. I anticipated it, though I did not think it would be necessary. I had hoped, anyway."

"What can I say? In space, shit happens. As usual, I'll help in any way," said Doc.

"Well, then, let's roll up our sleeves and have a go at it," replied Zorin. "We will build the Superglue Applicator."

Wussman was staring mournfully out at the nothingness, holding his abdomen. "It looks like the center of my soul, Vivian."

Viv said nothing.

She just sat down and sulked.

"Five hours, gentlemen," said Zorin. "That's the sum total of all the time that we have left to save the universe from becoming what you see out the view plates."

"I don't know, said Viv, finally. "It's not so bad. It looks rather like Pittsburgh."

They worked.

Troy hauled out Zorin's equipment, plus some leftover materials obtained from the trash planet. Troy found an old, flattened piece of bubble gum in the back hip pocket of his jeans, and it also turned out to have use as an adhesive.

"Why do you think I chew it?" explained Troy. "More engines than I can count got fixed with a sticky wad of Bazooka Bubble Gum."

"Troy, remind me of this the next time I complain about your gum chewing. That is, if I get a next time."

"I believe you will, Diane," said Zorin. "Only the supreme sacrifice here would not be too difficult to make, I think. After all, the universe is at stake."

"Speak for yourself, buddy," said Viv. "I want to live."

"And I want to love, Viv," said Wussman.

"And I want to toss lunch, if I had one to toss," said Doc.

"Please. Not on the gluon generator," said Zorin.

"I only speak metaphorically." He blinked. "Gluon? What's that?"

"The quantum interpretation of the superglue force, Doctor, posits a new kind of subatomic particle. I call it the gluon."

"Why not zorons?" said Diane.

"Actually, I rather like nickelodeons, myself," said Dr. D.

"Gluons. Trust me," said Zorin, applying one last wad of chewing gum. "There. I believe we have what we need here." He patted the device. "Right. Time to trundle outside."

Doc looked at him. "But there is no outside."

"Actually, there is. Just look out the window."

Doc D. went with Diane, and together they looked out a side view plate.

Sure enough, there was a mist-covered ground, upon which the *Mudlark* gently rested.

"How did that get there?" said Doc D.

"I don't quite know. Hurry, let's get this down the ramp."

Doc, Troy, and Zorin rolled the hastily built Superglue Applicator toward the main hatchway.

"What about atmosphere?"

"Look, if there wasn't atmosphere, there wouldn't be mist on the ground out there, now would there?"

"Oh. Good enough for me," said Troy. He cycled open the air lock and extended the ramp. Outside, the air smelled pleasant, and the temperature was balmy.

"Give me a hand, folks. We don't want this thing rolling off into nowhere," said Zorin at the lip of the ramp.

"Looks like a lot of that out there," said Doc.

"Absolutely."

Together, they allowed the device to roll down on its makeshift wheels, castors nipped from some old crate.

"You're sure we're in the right place?" asked Diane.

"Oh yes," said Zorin.

"Since there's no other place around the place," Doc quipped, "this must be the place. What about time?"

"About fifteen minutes."

"The universe is going to self-start here, right here, in fifteen minutes? How do you know that?"

Zorin pointed. "Because coming over that hill right there, is none other than the Great Self-Starter Himself."

"I'll bet He does well at job interviews."

Chapter Twenty-Six

A towering figure appeared on the "horizon." It grew bigger, but no less indistinct. It appeared to be an elderly man—however, there was some room for negotiation. Whoever it was, he or she was slightly out of focus, as if caught in a great cosmic lens with a less-than-cosmic flaw.

God, if that was who it was, was driving a golf cart. He pulled up, parked, and stepped out. He wore red-checkered knickers, blue stockings, white buck golf shoes, a pumpkin-colored pullover shirt with a white collar, and a green cloth cap.

"Hello over there," he called to the space travelers. "Have you seen my ball?"

The golfer grinned at them—then he squinted, and the grin faded a bit.

"No, I'm sorry, sir, we haven't seen your ball," Zorin said.

"Oy. Well." The golfer stared down into the roiling mists. "You hit that ball, it flies a mile. If I told you how dense the material was in that ball, you'd think I was meshuga."

Zorin turned to Dr. D. "Are you thinking what I'm thinking?"

Dr. Dimension couldn't believe his eyes. Not only did God exist—but he looked like a retired Brooklyn ice-cream and candy-store owner.

The Golfer had a broad homely face and ridiculously long and bushy sideburns. He wore thick horn-rimmed glasses that hung loosely on his generous nose. Around his neck was a Southwestern-style string tie with a turquoise catch. The tie draped over his paunch.

"Fantastic!" said Doc D. "One theory of the universe postulates that all matter was condensed into a round ball of unimaginable density—just about the size of a golf ball."

"Exactly," said Zorin. "It would seem that minutes from now, someone is going to hit that golf ball too hard."

Troy piped up. "Gee—I caddy once a month. I'll look for your golf ball, Mr. God."

"Good boy," said the old man. He turned his attention back to the others as he leaned on his nine iron. "So listen. Pardon my asking, I don't want you to feel unwelcome—but what the hell are you people doing here? I didn't even create you yet."

"We've come back to save the universe you will create," explained Diane. "And then you'll create us. Oh, and by the way—hallelujah!"

"Gesundheit. So listen. What are you talking, crazy? What do you mean, I will create you? You're telling me what I'm going to do? You I need to tell me a thing? Listen, you I need like a second hole in my tush."

"Uh-oh," said Wussman. "We're getting him mad."

"I'll straighten this bozo out." Vivian Vernon walked up to the Golfer and planted her feet firmly, chin jutting up defiantly. "Listen, chum. Just what is this menstruation stunt? Think maybe you can go back to the drawing board on that?"

The Golfer grinned. "What, I did such a bad job on you?"

This mollified Vivian some. "Well, I didn't say that. I—"

"You look like a nice girl. Nice figure. How old are you?"

"No, I—you see—"

"Are you married?"

"What does that have to do—" Vivian threw her

hands in the air. "Oh, I don't believe in you anyway!" She stalked away.

The Golfer shrugged. "Now I think I know what menstruation is."

Doc broke in, "Listen, mister . . . uh . . . sir. The universe is just great the way it is. No complaints. Only, we kind of had a little accident—"

"An accident? You have insurance? Listen, get a good lawyer, don't play around."

"Well, uh, yeah. As I said, there was a little . . . you know, goof-up, and to fix it we just want to introduce a new subatomic particle called the . . . uh—"

"Gluon," Zorin prompted.

"Right. The gluon."

"That is correct," said Zorin. "And this is the device that will do it. All we ask is that we irradiate your golf ball before you hit it again."

The Golfer regarded them affably.

"Look, no problem, I'm not hard to get along with. But I tell you, this ball, it's a bitch to find in all this rough. I've lost 'em before. You find it, you do what you want with it. Me, I'm giving up this fekokte game. Strictly for goyim. I think I'll create a nice interesting world, and sit on my tushie and write about science all day. And maybe have a science-fiction magazine named after me. That would be nice. So, good luck to you."

The Golfer got back into his electric golf cart.

"But Lord . . . whatever you call yourself—you can't go!" said a devastated Diane. "You can't go! You haven't created the universe yet!"

The Golfer shrugged. He reached into his golf bag, drew out a driver, and tossed it to her. "So you create the universe, sweet cheeks. Me, I've got a science column to write. Hmm. I remember the time I was contemplating the electrical charge of a photon while chasing a cute little archangel named Chloe—hey, that would make a good opening anecdote . . . hmmm. Yeah. Well, don't take any wooden gluons. Bye!"

The Golfer trundled away in his golf cart, disappearing into the mists.

"Found it!" said Troy, leaping out of the weeds. He held up a regulation-size white golf ball.

"Gadzooks, Talbot. That should be heavy," said Doc. "Infinitely heavy, in fact."

"Gravity doesn't work quite the same way here, remember Doctor."

"How could I have forgotten? So, okay. Let's throw this superglue at the universe and see if it sticks. Time, such as it is, flies."

"Yes. My thought precisely." With that, Zorin bent over the applicator and wrapped a cord around the flange at the end of the camshaft. He tugged, once. It didn't start. He wrapped and tugged again; again, no luck. On the third try, the motor coughed to life and commenced chugging merrily away. Lights shimmered and glowed. An electrode at the other end began to glow, at first feebly and then vibrantly: a glaring cherry-red.

"Troy, place the golf ball on the target bench, right there, in front of the extenuator," Zorin directed.

"Gotcha."

Troy gingerly positioned the ball where Zorin had told him to.

"Right." Zorin hit the trigger.

"I just pray this works," said Diane.

"I think you missed the boat on that one by about a minute." said Doc.

An amber beam about the width of a pencil shot from the end of the rod, striking the golf ball directly.

The golf ball glowed eerily.

"Good job, Troy. That does it." Zorin punched off the engine, and the device coughed and wheezed its way to inertness once more. "So, the question that remains now is, who gets the honors?"

He took the driver from Diane and held it up.

"Uhmm . . . can't we just set a bomb or something, and then get the hell out of here," suggested Wussman.

"I'm afraid that just won't work," said Zorin. "We

seem to have interrupted the process of creation by a golf club, and so we have to do it ourselves."

"Tell you what, Zorry," said Viv. "We'll just scoot along, and you can be the hero."

"You can't be sure it's going to work. We'll have to try other alternatives. Besides, I promise you, my dear, you'll get quite a bang out of—oh dear."

"Something wrong?" said Diane.

"Don't look now, but I do believe we brought along an unwanted visitor."

They all turned and looked.

A bloated shape had attached itself to the top of the *Mudlark*. Now it moved, sliding off and settling on one of the rear fins, which bent under its weight.

"The Baron!" Diane cried. "But . . . how in the world did he get up there?"

"He must have climbed up there when we took off, and somehow attached himself," Zorin said.

"But . . . that's impossible!" said Vivian. "There's no air. He would have suffocated!" She turned to Zorin. "Wouldn't he?"

Zorin shrugged. "He is a cybernetic organism. No doubt he has an emergency oxygen supply. As for clinging to the ship, he has various accoutrements in and about his armor suit. It's not so difficult to believe."

"But he's so bloated," Diane said.

For all that, the Baron looked not a tad less fearsome than he normally did.

"Baron," said Doc. "Haven't had enough punishment? Thought you'd come along and get whipped some more?" said Doc D. "And getting into the cream puffs a little too much lately, eh?"

Indeed, Baron Skulkrak, as he waddled down the ramp, looked as though he were imitating a blimp. His face was even more grotesque, and his eyes—bloodshot and bulbous—looked like giant mad marbles.

"What happened to him?" said Troy.

"He tightened the cinch too much on his plumbing I believe, and his gases are expanding exponentially."

So much so, in fact, that balloons of mottled skin were blowing up between the cracks of his armor.

"Destroy!" said the Baron, clearly now totally deranged. "Destroy!'"

"Ah, well, I had hoped for a sea change," said Doc D. "Baron, you've come to the wrong place. There's nothing to destroy."

"You are here!" Skulkrak gnashed out. "And then—I shall have the universe truly in the palm of my hand."

"This guy never quits. Unbelievable. Skully, what do you say, give it a rest? Okay?"

With one fluid motion, Zorin knocked the golf ball from Troy's hand, and then with a perfect fluid swing, worthy of any country-club pro, drove it. It traveled a short distance, whacking into Baron Skulkrak's midsection with terrific force.

"Ummmmph!" Skulkrak keeled over backward.

From the small hole that Zorin had just created, a dreadful green gas began to escape.

"Oh, my God," said Viv, holding her nose. "The smell!"

"However distasteful, my dear, I see it only as a godsend. Now, in fact, I believe I understand the purpose of my life."

Zorin's smile was serenely philosophical. "People, please—get aboard the ship. I have preset the course. You need but push the button, and you will be propelled away from here—into a kinder, gentler, and it is hoped, a more peaceful universe."

"Right, bye," said Viv, turning sharply and heading for the ship.

"It's been a pleasure," said Wussman.

They tore up the ramp.

"Troy, make sure they don't leave us here," said Doc.

"Right, Doc." Troy hustled after them.

"Oh, Zorin," said Diane Derry, embracing the dash-

ing, older man. "You are so brave ... so ... good."
She bawled unashamedly.

"Thank you. Take this."

He took the M'Guh Fon from his finger and slipped
it around hers. "And use it wisely."

"I promise," she kissed him, and tearfully went up
the ramp.

Dr. Dimension nodded. He extended his hand to
Zorin, and shook it. "I won't waste time with a speech,
Zorin. It's been an honor to know you, sir."

"And I would say the same. Get aboard the ship,
Doctor. Immediately."

The doctor turned and galloped.

The hatch slammed, and the *Mudlark* blasted off almost immediately, quickly disappearing from view.

The alien scientist known as Zorin watched it; then,
when it was gone, he shifted his gaze and noted that
the cloud of green gas, although growing ever larger,
had confined itself to a single mass, still hanging about
the prone hulk of the bulbous and distended Baron
Skulkrak.

Who, groaning, was trying to get to his feet.

He looked down, saw the hole in his stomach, and
the gas escaping from it. He snarled at Zorin.

"You shall die, scum academician."

The Baron struggled to his feet and wobbled forward, clawed hands extended.

Zorin easily sidestepped him.

He held out his finger. Still attuned to the M'Guh
Fon, he summoned its power.

"It is a far, far better thing I do than I have ever
done ... Happy Birthday to you, dear universe!"

A spark leaped from his finger into the ghastly green
cloud.

The universe was born.

Epilogue

"Stars," said Diane Derry. "Stars! Aren't they wonderful, Dr. D.?"

"My favorites are Hedy Lamar and Ginger Rogers," said Troy Talbot. "I sure could use a double feature. And popcorn!"

Dr. Dimension said nothing.

He simply lay back against the bole of a tree that looked for all the world like a live oak. He looked up at the beautiful, cloud-hung, Earth-blue sky. It was an early summer evening, and the first few stars were coming out. An impish zephyr gently played through the branches above, and a brook babbled pleasantly in the valley below. The heady smell of jasmine floating came to his nostrils, and the glow of warmth and relaxation settled over him.

Yes, it was nice, after saving the universe, to have a good solid rest.

"No quips, Doctor? No stinging remarks, abuse, double entendres?" asked Vivian Vernon, pacing nearby, obviously not enjoying the scenery.

"Come, come, Vivian," said Wussman, lying nearby regarding the heavens. "We've found paradise. Come and be my love, and we shall all the pleasures prove. Ooooof!"

There was a sharp intake of breath.

"Really, Vivian. Could we give that kind of thing a rest for once? I'm getting bruises on my bruises."

Dr. Dimension finally spoke. "Yes, Viv. May I suggest a truce?"

"Truce, Doctor?" Vivian remonstrated. "We're still

not back on Earth. I'm still not in my rightful place—Chairman of the Physics Department of Flitheimer University."

"But Vivian," Dr. Wussman protested. "I'm the chairman."

"Shut up, you weasel."

"I think what you need, Dr. Vernon, is some time in the philosophy department," suggested Diane. "Perhaps you'll get philosophical about things."

"Oh, Viv's philosophical. But then so is Hitler. Ever hear of Nietzsche?"

Nearby sat the *Mudlark*, resting as well from its incredible journey, its backdrop a deepening blue sky flecked with stars, stars that beckoned ... Within it, Tobor, the robot, was washing clothes and doing the dishes.

Zorin (that brave, noble alien scientist) had indeed left navigational data in the ship's computers, along with a recorded message:

Yet another hideaway, my friends. This one, I think definitely to your taste. It is a little pocket universe, which I calculate will be one of the interesting results of the installation of gluons into the fabric of the universe. It is about one light-year across, with a wealth of beautiful suns and planets to choose from. I am sorry to be unable to send you back to your native planet, but you see, by my lights, beings who have been bestowed with such a gift of a spacetime machine must also have the responsibility of serving the causes of goodness and right. Naturally one day perhaps you will find your native Earth. But by then, I trust that the wisdom of the universe will by yours, and you will transform your home planet into a more peaceful and salubrious place. Meanwhile, the spacetime engine of your ship will take you anywhere you wish to go, in all of space and time, at your discretion. You have the M'Guh Fon at your disposal. Through it and with it, you will learn much about the universe. I envy you.

You are Masters of Spacetime (second only to the Asperans and Dharvans, of course).

Rest, good people. Rest, and sip of the waters of life. Eat the bread of sleep, and drink the wine of health. And then get out there and boot some villainous behinds! Good-bye, my friends. This is your friend and colleague, Zorin . . .

Diane Derry sighed. "This is such a nice place. I'm sure that M'Guh Fon will help us build a shelter."

"Hey, me, too!" said Troy.

"Yes, of course, Troy. That was a lovely doghouse you built for me last year."

"May I suggest that we all get some sleep?" said Dr. Dimension. "We've been through some damned tough times, and my fevered brow, for one, could use some rest."

"Okay, Doctor."

There was a moment of silence, and Doc D. let himself drift off into slumber land.

Ah. Peace.

"Doctor?"

"Confound it, Diane. What?"

"Doctor, I was just thinking about Zorin."

"Wonderful. So share."

"Doctor . . . it occurs to me that if Zorin was at the Big Bang or Big Bung—"

"Or Big Kablooey!" said Troy.

"Whatever—if he was there and was . . . blown up . . ."

"I think it's pretty obvious he was, Diane."

"Yes. Well—then—there's a little of Zorin in the whole universe. In me, and you . . . and all the stars that twinkle down so purely above us—uniting us all in a never-ending search for truth, justice, and the American way."

Doc sighed. "Super, Diane. But you must remember. Baron Skulkrak was there as well, and most certainly met the same fate. Which also means"—he reached over and placed his hand on its favorite portion of Di-

ane Derry's anatomy—"that there's a bit of Skulkrak
in each and every one us, too."

"Brrrrrrrrrrrrrrrpt," said Troy Talbot. "Ooooops,
sorry."

"Really," Vivian said.

"Now is everyone through yapping?" Dr. Dimension
asked. "If so, I'd like to get some shut-eye."

No one had a thing to say.

"Good."

Doc settled back. Ah . . .

Doc opened one eye. He sat up.

Diane sat up, too. "What is it, Doctor?"

"Did the ground just shake?"

"A little. I felt it."

"Me, too," said Wussman.

A sound like thunder came to them, and the ground
commenced to shake in earnest.

"Earthquake!" Vivian screamed.

"Yep," Doc agreed. "Oh, well, nothing to worry
about."

"What do you mean, nothing to worry about. You
fool, it's an earthquake!"

"So what? Do you see any buildings about to col-
lapse on us? Don't worry about it. This is a young
planet, still geologically unstable. It'll subside in a
minute."

It didn't. The shaking got worse, and the thunder
grew deafening. The quasi-oak tree wobbled. A branch
snapped and fell, nearly crowning Troy.

Doc had enough. "Let's get back in the ship and get
the hell off this planet!"

But they couldn't make it. The ground heaved and
tossed, and they could barely keep on their feet.

The ground opened up, a jagged chasm forming
across the hillside.

Diane screamed. Vivian swore. Wussman cried.

They hugged the rim of the chasm, hanging on to
tufts of grass as the ground tilted, as if intent on rolling
them off into the abyss. The other side of the hill fell

away completely, forming the dizzyingly sheer face of a towering cliff.

Diane began to slide, and Dr. Dimension caught her. "Hang on, Diane!"

She grabbed onto his tattered white lab coat. But Doc's hands were slipping.

"Uh-oh," he said.

"Oh, no," Troy wailed as he clung to a shifting wedge of exposed rock. "Doc when you say 'uh-oh' that means we're in deep trouble! Are we in deep trouble?"

"Is the pope Catholic?"

"Hell, Doc, you know I'm Jewish."

"Oh, that's right. I keep forgetting that about you."

Diane screamed again as she felt Doc's coat tearing at the seams.

"Doctor, help me!"

"Hang on, Diane!"

"Dimension, I'm going to kill you!"

"Huh? What did you say, Viv?"

Vivian Vernon's beautiful legs dangled attractively over the abyss. "You creep! This is yet another fine mess you've gotten us into!"

"I do have a knack," conceded Dr. Dimension. "Yup, here we are, hanging from the edge of a cliff. Yup. Sure seems that way."

Red-faced, Vivian screamed with frustration. "You . . . you . . ."

"What, Viv? Go on, say it. Get it all out of your system."

"You wild-haired maniac! You're making jokes, and there you are in mortal danger—"

"Annnnnnd . . . *loving* it!" Dr. Dimension said with panache.

He meant it, too.

To be continued?
That, dear reader, is up to you!